War on Drugs

**A
Fake News
Mystery**

By Gary Engler

Cover by Frank Myrskog

RED Publishing

203 32nd Street West, Saskatoon, Saskatchewan, S7L-0S3

1.

    Waylon Choy had intended to follow the advice of the most successful freelancer he had ever met. "Maintain a routine," Adam Wainwright had told him the night before he died. "Go to work, even if you don't actually go to work." But, it had been impossible to follow a regular routine for the first six months after he left his job as a reporter at the *Vancouver Sun*, not so much because of his new (lack of) employment circumstances but because he also put his house up for sale at the same time. The parade of potential buyers, then negotiations, then planning for a move, then looking for a new place to live, then his father's offer to sell his last remaining property to him for one dollar as a step towards dealing with his long-time gambling addiction — simply attending the counselling sessions for two straight months was emotionally and intellectually exhausting. Then there was more disruption resulting from the move into an 130-year-old house with his father, plus his two kids for half of each month, getting used to a new place, especially one that needed so many renovations, getting reacquainted with living under the same roof as his old man, whose addiction could flare up at any time, then all the hassle from Ben and Samantha who complained constantly about their new Downtown Eastside neighbourhood the hipsters had labelled Railtown, but which Choy had always understood to be the old residential part of Japantown.

    Despite the disruptions, Choy did not regret any of it, especially quitting his job and selling his house as Vancouver's real estate market hit crazy new heights. The $1,500,000 net proceeds and the $150,000 buyout from his former employer provided the security he needed to start his new career as a journalist/novelist. (Not that he couldn't decide which one he wanted to be — he was determined to be both, not pigeon-holed.) But the sale, the new house, renovations, attending Gamblers' Anonymous had all been distractions that kept him from both journalism and fiction.

Or maybe he was simply making excuses for his lack of discipline.

Regardless, over the past two weeks, after the unusually heavy Vancouver snowfall had finally melted, he had settled into a pleasing and productive routine. Breakfast and a quick glance at a few of his favourite news websites, followed by a half-hour run from his new, but very old, house on Alexander Street to a few loops of Strathcona Park and back, then four hours of writing, with the rest of the day available for research or leisure or whatever he felt like doing.

It was during his fourteenth run, as he was thinking about how good it felt to finally get into a productive routine, that he found the body.

***

Choy didn't know her name but had said hello at least a dozen times. She hung out on Cordova Street, about a half block east of Oppenheimer Park, near the chicken processing plant, probably looking for customers. Although he had never actually seen her soliciting, based on her clothing, or lack thereof, Choy was pretty sure she was a prostitute, a hooker — although he really shouldn't dismiss her that way. He was even more certain she was a drug addict — the 80 pounds or so on a five-foot-eight frame and rotting teeth the giveaway — who might have been 30 years old even though many of her features suggested 65.

But she was obviously an educated hooker and drug addict. Two days earlier a look suggested she knew what he thought about her. She glared back at him and then launched into what seemed a strangely appropriate soliloquy from some classical play.

"'Nay, never play the brave man, else when you go back home, your own mother won't know you. But, dear friends and allies, first let us lay our burdens down; then, citizens all, hear what I have to say. I have useful counsel to give our city, which deserves it well at my hands for the brilliant distinctions it has lavished on my girlhood. At seven years of age, I was bearer of the sacred vessels; at ten, I pounded barley for the altar of Athené; next, clad in a robe of yellow silk, I was little bear to Artemis at the Brauronia; presently, grown a tall, handsome maiden, they put a necklace of dried figs about my neck, and I was Basket-Bearer. So surely I am bound to give my best advice to Athens. What matters that I was born a woman, if I can cure your misfortunes? I pay my share of tolls and taxes, by giving men to the State. But you, you miserable greybeards, you contribute nothing to the public charges; on the contrary, you have wasted the treasure of our forefathers, as it was called, the treasure amassed in the days of the Persian Wars. You pay nothing at all in return; and into the bargain you endanger our lives and liberties by your mistakes. Have you one word to say for yourselves?'"

At first he thought she was simply another crazy street person talking to herself, but it quickly became clear she was performing so he circled back and kept running in a tight circle in front of her to listen. He only learned that it was from a chorus section of Aristophanes' Lysistrata when she responded to his clapping by telling him. Later that day he Googled the play and found the passage she had performed. Near as he could tell she had gotten the English translation from the ancient Greek almost word for word the same as what he found online.

As Choy jogged down the sidewalk on the south side of the street about 6:30 a.m. two days later she was sitting on stairs to one of the oldest buildings in the city of Vancouver, a run-down wood frame flophouse with very narrow wood channel siding that indicated construction sometime in the early 1890s or late 1880s. She looked up from tapping her left arm, smiled and said the same words as every morning when he ran by: "Go with the wings of Mercury."

The reference to the Roman god of swiftness and successful commerce surprised and comforted him each time he heard it. "Beautiful morning," he responded.

"Going to get even better," came the answer.

Seeing her fidgeting and checking her veins, Choy knew she was getting ready to shoot up.

What would it be like to have a life centred on a fix? Would it be that different from one centred on fashion or food or writing?

He needed to focus, be disciplined, think about his book. His morning run was contemplative, creative time, necessary to start the day's work off right. Still, it was hard to get the image of this walking-dead, daughter-to-someone committing slow motion suicide out of his consciousness. It was a struggle to think about his work.

How was it coming? So far mostly pages of notes, the grand outline of a novel based on someone much like his great-grandfather, a man with a Chinese name, but who mostly looked European, living in 1920s Vancouver who gets caught up in the city's most infamous murder case. A maid, Janet Smith, working for a rich, well connected family is found dead in their mansion and after an initial police investigation determines it was suicide, a media storm ensues that forces authorities to reopen the case. In a milieu where anti-Asian racism is commonplace — the Ku Klux Klan is a growing force, especially in the exclusive Shaughnessy neighbourhood where Smith worked and died— the media focuses on a 27-year-old Chinese "houseboy" Wong Foon Sing, and despite absolutely no evidence against him, he is tried for murder.

His great-grandfather, or a character very much like him, has successfully "passed" into whiteness thanks to three generations of non-Asian grandmothers, but needs to be careful, especially because of his name, to maintain his acceptance as a proper English Canadian. Unfortunately for him, he comes into possession of information that would reveal the real killer and prove Wong's innocence. Because he worries that his neighbours will question his whiteness if he tells authorities what he knows, his great-grandfather never reveals the secret of who really killed Janet Smith.

Choy thought it was a good foundation on which to build a novel and a perfect idea for someone who had spent 25 years as a newspaper reporter — a story at the boundary between creative-non-fiction and literature for which he could use his skills as a journalist and historian to write a work of fiction. He'd long been praised, sometimes condemned, for his creativity as a journalist; now he had an opportunity to truly "make it all up" and yet tell some truths about the past, ethnic identity, family and racism that were almost impossible to reveal through straight journalism or history.

This morning he had two problems to solve while he was out running. How and what does the main character find out about the real killer? What does his great-grandfather do for a living?

What did he do? I know he started buying properties. I've got to ask Dad.

"Go with the wings of Mercury."

She has a southern American accent. How does a white kid from down there end up here, on Vancouver's skid row, a hooker and a drug addict?

What if his great-grandfather, in the novel, owned an opium den? Or owned the Chinatown building that housed an opium den? That's how he learns the truth about Janet Smith's employer.

Am I happy or nervous that Joy is moving here?

Since he had learned his long distance girlfriend for the

past six months had given two-months notice that she was leaving the Las Vegas Police Department and was coming to Vancouver to work at the RCMP forensics laboratory, this question often intruded into his consciousness.

What will she think of my father? Living with him, in a construction zone?

After 80 years as a rooming house the necessary renovations would take at least another six months. Still, it was a very big house. Which meant that if Joy and his father didn't hit it off, at least they could avoid each other.

Focus on the book.

It will be strange living with a woman again. The kids like her, Ben especially. Samantha is a little leery about a new mother in her life.

The book. Control what you think about. The book.

There was evidence that Janet Smith's boss had, in fact, been involved in the opium trade, at least before it became illegal. What if Smith found out he was still importing the drug and tried to blackmail her boss? And that's what his grandfather found out.

Someone, a guest, living with us every day? But Joy won't be a guest.

I've gotten used to being alone. But we get along so well, why would it be a problem?

Back across Hastings Street again. Traffic is heavy this morning. Pick up the pace.

He always tried to sprint the last few blocks.

It's great Joy will soon be here.

Compatible. That's the best word to describe us. We could even work together, something I never would have dreamed of doing with Helena.

The hooker?

As Choy turned the corner onto Cordova he saw the woman doubled up, her head laying on her knees, both arms splayed like a rag doll with hands open up to the sky. Motionless.

A needle dangling from her left arm. Something wrong.

Choy stopped running and bent down to catch his breath.

"Are you okay?" He barely got the words out and thought perhaps she didn't hear him. "Are you okay?"

He walked towards her. No movement.

"Hi."

Is she breathing?

He took out his cell phone from a pouch on his sweatshirt.

"Hi," he repeated and then carefully touched her arm, trying not to catch anything. There was no response.

He had watched many TV news reports about the hundreds of overdose deaths in the past few months.

Fentanyl.

He touched her again, this time forcing himself to hold his fingers against her skin for a few seconds. She was cool. And not in the Beatnik or Hippy sense.

He dialled 911.

***

"It might have been carfentanil," Joy said. "It's another ten thousand times more powerful than fentanyl and it's definitely in Vancouver."

"I knew one of the ambulance attendants who showed up from a big feature I did a few years back, Life and Death on the Downtown Eastside. I spent a week of night shifts with her for the story so Carol let me ride to the hospital with the body and told me it was the third time she personally had given this woman naloxone. But this time nobody was with her when she shot up. She must have been lying there, with the needle in her arm, the whole time I was running. She was getting ready to shoot up when I passed her the first time. 'Go with the wings of Mercury.'"

"What's that?"

"'Go with the wings of Mercury,' that's what she said to me as I passed by," he said, wishing Joy was physically present. "Said it every morning."

"What was her name?

"I don't know, we were never introduced. Carol called her 'Reb', short for rebel, like in Confederate Army rebel, which apparently was what everyone on skid row called her."

"You found this woman dead and road in the ambulance to the morgue and you don't even know her real name," said Joy. "That's sad."

"It is," Choy said, an idea exploding inside him as spectacular as the French entry in last summer's fireworks competition. "I should discover her name. And maybe a lot more."

This could be a good story, the kind Adam, who had died for journalism, would appreciate.

"You're thinking of doing a story about her death, aren't you?" Over the six months they had known each other, Joy had developed an uncanny ability to read his mind.

"'The Life and Death of a Disposable Person' or something like that," said Choy as the electrical and chemical circuits in his brain buzzed with thoughts about the directions such an investigation could go. "Who was she and how did she become who she was, what killed her, who killed her and why, these are the questions I can come up with off the top of my head."

"Is this a magazine article or a book?" asked Joy.

"I don't know, maybe both and more. Why does someone who can recite a section of Aristophanes' Lysistrata become a drug addict? Why does someone keep using a drug that has almost killed her? Why does someone sell a drug they know will kill?"

"You could look into the manufacture and distribution of fentanyl and carfentanil — I could help with that. I did a paper for the chief here, two months ago, so the information is quite up-to-date."

"Perfect," he said as enthusiastically as he could manage, but the truth was he felt a rush of nervousness when confronted with the soon-to-be-reality of living and working with Joy. He wanted everything between them to be just right but knew, based on past experience that was extremely unlikely. If not contempt, familiarity did at least breed annoyance with his bad habits.

"Is something wrong?" she said, again reading his mind.

"No, just thinking this could be important, a great series of articles, or, like you say, a book. Subject, of course to what I find, or we find."

Choy guessed his girlfriend's silence meant she was thinking about something serious. Sure enough.

"Are you worried about me moving to Vancouver?"

"I'm excited and can hardly wait for you to be here," he said quickly.

"Are you sure?"

"Yes. Of course. I love you."

"You can love me but still be nervous about our living together," she said.

Don't say anything.

"I'm nervous about moving to Vancouver and living with you," she said. "Other than six months with that guy I told you about, I've lived alone for ten years."

This seemed as good an opportunity to raise a subject that had been on his mind ever since Ben asked him about the possibility of a stepbrother or stepsister. "Do you want to have a child?" He said the words too quickly, then immediately had second thoughts about their appropriateness.

"Is that what's bothering you?"

"It's not bothering me, I just want to know," said Choy. "Ben brought it up a couple of weeks ago and you're at that age when women …"

"Yes, I'd like a child," she said. "I've always wanted to have one or two. But I understand you already have two and they're great …"

"But their mine, not ours, and you want the experience of having a baby," he said, then felt guilty, not at having spoken the particular words, but at having brought up the subject at all. "I understand."

The silence between them lasted long enough to push Choy out of the living room and into his office, where he started straightening up his desk.

"What do you think about us having a baby?" Joy finally said.

"If we had a baby a year from now I'd be past 60 before she or he became a teenager."

"And?"

"I'm not opposed to it."

"What does that mean?"

"I'm not against it."

"Does your absence of disagreement imply a possibly positive position at some later date?"

"Perhaps," said Choy, surprising himself with the answer. The truth was the thought of having a baby with Joy was a pleasant one and he smiled.

"Are you smiling?" she asked.

"Yes."

"I love you," said Joy.

"I wish you were here," he said.

"Me too."

"Are you ready for the rain?" asked Choy and immediately wondered where the thought had come from, but then realized he was staring out the bay window where a leaking gutter produced a steady stream flowing down the other side of the glass. "I mean, after the desert."

"I'm ready to be with you, to sleep in the same bed with you every night."

"Sorry for bringing up the kid thing out of the blue like that," he said. "Seeing that woman dead with a needle hanging from her arm, the fragility of life and the ambulance attendants talking like it's an everyday occurrence. I feel ... all over the place, but not quite here, like I've been hit on the head by a baseball."

"It's a form of shock that can lead to PTSD," said Joy. "I've seen it in cops. You can never tell what might trigger it."

"Post-traumatic stress disorder?"

"I'm serious."

"I'm not getting PTSD, no way. If I were at risk for that it would have happened last year in Nevada," said Choy, who still regularly dreamed about his near-death experience in an old Virginia City mine.

"That's not how it works. The research on PTSD shows it's not necessarily the most traumatic event that triggers it. It can be an accumulation with a seemingly insignificant stressor that ultimately sets it off."

"I'm not getting PTSD. I'm a little disoriented, that's all."

"I hope you're right."

"But if I did get it would you look after me?"

"A senior citizen and a baby?"

This is why I love her: An off-the-wall sense of humour that fits perfectly with mine. Helena and I were exact opposites. Worse, she had absolutely no sense of humour.

"I better get back to work," said Joy. "I'll call when I get home."

***

"Which comes first? Living on skid row or being a drug addict and a prostitute?" Samantha asked her father as they sat on the burgundy couch across the room from a turned-off, wall-mounted 60-inch TV.

"Not everyone on skid row is a drug addict or a prostitute," answered her brother Ben as he entered the room from the kitchen.

"I never said they were."

"Have you finished your homework?" Choy asked his son, who nodded.

"I mean, does the environment, not having a home and no money, make you more likely to turn to drugs and prostitution?" Samantha continued. "Or does being a drug addict make you more likely to end up selling your body and becoming homeless on skid row?"

"Both are probably true," answered Choy.

"Lots of people who use drugs hold down steady jobs," said Ben, who was likely the only 13-year old in Vancouver who still read printed newspapers, a-trying-to-act-older-than-he-was affectation that pleased his father.

"My guess is there's probably as many reasons for ending up a drug addict or a prostitute or homeless as there are people living on skid row," said Choy.

***

The short conversation with Sam and Ben stuck in his brain until the next morning when Choy walked the four blocks to the Ovaltine Café on Hastings Street to have breakfast with the only drug dealer he knew. Over and over he considered different answers to the question: Does the environment create people or do people create the environment?

"We create the environment; we are part of the environment; the environment creates us. That's what I think," said Little Andy, who Choy talked with every few months after having interviewed him five years earlier for a feature about the people of the Downtown Eastside. "We are the forest and the trees, individuals and the collective, actors and the stage."

"Did you know her?" interrupted Choy. "Apparently everyone called her Reb."

Andy, who was about six-foot-six with a slight German accent, a remnant of immigrating to Canada with his parents when he was 14, considered himself a poet philosopher and if unchecked would dispense his particular brand of situationist wisdom for hours.

"Reb? A sex-trade worker?"

"I think so."

"Very loud, a strong voice. Called me a sexist pig at a meeting one time, then made fun of my accent and gave me a Heil Hitler salute. Flying at 35,000 feet without an airplane, if you know what I mean. Saw her around a few times."

"You ever sell her anything?"

He shook his head. "You know me, my client list is small and limited to the doctors, lawyers, cops and business executives who only want the best, unadulterated shit in significant enough quantities that I don't need to sell too often. That's why I'm still here."

While Little Andy's stories could easily be taken for tall tales, most times Choy checked out something he said, it turned out to be true. And the Ovaltine was a long-time hangout for exactly the crowd Andy claimed to serve.

"We're averaging about two overdose deaths a day in the city right now," said Andy. "What's your interest in this particular one? You know her?"

"Not really," said Choy. "Said hi a few times on my runs in the morning and then found her dead, a needle still stuck in her arm."

"Feeling guilty?"

"Maybe."

Andy broke open one of two egg yolks on his plate with a piece of toast. "For?"

"Not paying attention, I guess."

"To drug overdose deaths?"

"To the people, their environment, the legal, social and economic factors that have produced the situation we find ourselves in," Choy said and realized it was true. "Homelessness, addictions, all of it."

"Why now? Capitalism has been going on a long time."

"I told you we moved into my father's place over on Alexander, just off Gore?"

"The Yuppies are getting closer and closer!"

Choy smiled. Despite Little Andy's philosophical pretensions, his observations and analyses were usually spot on.

"And your kids are asking questions? Why do all the crazy people live down here Daddy? Why do they stick needles in their arms?" Why did that skinny woman get into that fat man's car?"

Choy nodded. "I'm thinking about writing something. Figure out who she was, how she ended up here, who sold her the stuff that killed her, everything. Personalize the problem. It could be an important piece, you know."

"So that's why you show up here this morning for breakfast? You want my help."

"I do. I want to interview some people in the drug business."

"You've asked in the past and I've always answered."

"Higher up. I want to interview someone who brings in hundreds of pounds of heroin, a wholesaler."

"Someone the cops always say they are after but never seem to actually catch," said Andy, smiling.

"Exactly. I want to ask them about their business, in generalities of course. Where the stuff comes from, who gets paid off, why the cops can never seem to make a dent in the supply, what's up with Fentanyl, their thoughts on legalization, everything. I'd like to get your thoughts on all this too, but …"

"It would be more interesting if it came from Mr. Big."

"You know how the media works."

"Like the rest of the shitty economic system, money means power and power makes you attractive."

"Is there any way you could hook me up with someone? I know it's probably a long shot. I mean, why would anyone like that want to talk to a journalist? There's nothing in it for them except exposure and that's probably the last thing they want."

Andy wiped the remaining bright orange yolk off his plate with his last bit of whole-wheat toast. He cleaned his face with the paper napkin that had been lying on the table beside the ivory coloured plate.

"If you had come to me last week or last month, I'd be laughing at you right now. A big-time drug dealer who wants to spout off to a journalist and be interviewed for a book? Give me a break! But this week … I'm not promising anything, but I heard about someone a few days ago, talked to his assistant yesterday, who just might be exactly the Mr. Big Mouth you're looking for."

***

Turns out Andy had heard rumours going back a few months that a new supplier with connections to the Russian mob was entering the Canadian market and product would soon be available in Vancouver. While talk on the street about mysterious new sources of supply was not unusual, this time the gossip was backed up by an actual person who had begun contacting mid-level distributors seemingly unworried by the certainty that such a public presence would quickly be noticed by the police and existing wholesalers who often jealously and violently guarded their sales networks. Svetlana Borovsky claimed to be a representative of an organization she called the Better Business Bureau and this BBB was not only capable of supplying whatever product was desired, it was not afraid of the police or of rival suppliers. She was very businesslike, Andy said, and not someone who struck him as an imposter or a brain-addled junkie trying to pull off a dangerous scam. While he had told Borovsky that he was not currently in the market for anything, but would think about her offer, perhaps a favour for his favourite reporter was possible. Perhaps he could call to see if she or the person who ran her organization was interested in speaking to a journalist who was discrete and kept his word. It seemed like the Better Business Bureau was not afraid of publicity, but instead sought it out in order to attract new clients, so perhaps Choy's crazy idea would prove realizable.

The reason Choy had maintained contact with Little Andy over the years, aside from him being one of the best sources of rumours about important people that often proved to have some basis in reality, was the intellectual stimulation a conversation with the guy provided. He had a way of describing events or situations and telling stories that challenged conventional acumen and made you understand the world a little better. This time was no different.

In response to Choy's use of a term often used in the media, Andy had responded: "There's a war against certain drug users and there's a war against reason, but there's no war on drugs. We love drugs and they're one of the biggest sources of profit in our economic system."

As he walked back to his house down Hastings and then up Main Street, past the most infamous corner in the city where broken people the system spit out as useless to profit margins congregated, in front of the old police station that was being turned into a centre for "high-tech innovation", whatever the hell that meant, and past the Provincial Court House in which well over half the crimes dealt with involved drugs or mental illness, often both, Choy alternated between thinking about Andy's words and the feel of Reb's cold, lifeless arm.

Uncovering the truth about this woman's life and death, who she was, how she came to be on skid row, why she died the way she did, this is a story I've got to write.

He'd had this feeling many times before. It was certainty, commitment and focus all wrapped up together.

It feels good.

2.

Choy began his search for information about the dead woman at a place familiar to every reporter in the city, the Carnegie Centre, site of the original Vancouver Public Library that opened in 1903, closed in 1957 and was repurposed into the Downtown Eastside community centre in the 1980s. It was often referred to as 'the living room of skid row' and primarily served the most destitute of Vancouver's poorest neighbourhood. Main and Hastings, the intersection at which the centre was located had long been a hypodermic needle that pumped various sorts of painkillers into the bodies of people used up and spit out by an economy that for one reason or another no longer needed them. When Choy was a child there had been dozens of giant beer parlours on the surrounding streets, but most were now shuttered as the tentacles of gentrification reached ever closer. The hipsters, with their coffee shops, restaurants and condos had the place surrounded, engaged in pincer movements that probed from more heavily yuppified old Chinatown to the south, Gastown to the northwest and Strathcona to the east. But the few square blocks around the Carnegie Centre were mostly holding off the invasion by pumping former residents of shuttered rundown single room occupancy — SROs — hotels onto sidewalks and back alleys, creating a homeless human horde that frightened yuppies much like crosses or garlic were supposed to terrify vampires.

Since her use of "Go with the wings of Mercury" and speech from Lysistrata suggested a literary background, Choy first started asking around in the library reading room.

"Hi, my name is Waylon and I'm a writer. I'm trying to find the real name of someone I found dead of a drug overdose three days ago. The ambulance attendants called her Reb. Did you know her? I'd like to contact her parents and write a story about her."

He had always found that strangers react best to a reporter's enquiries when you tell them as much as you can up front. Be polite, concise and respectful. In his experience doing stories that involved talking to people in the Downtown Eastside, the last was critical. Talking down or negative assumptions about intelligence almost guaranteed hostility rather than cooperation. A decade earlier he had come to the Carnegie with a *Sun* photographer who was notorious for his indiscretion and willingness to shoot anyone, anywhere, doing anything. He lasted less than five minutes before a posse of elderly ex-loggers escorted him out of the building.

It took 45 minutes inside and another 25 on the streets outside before he found two women standing along the wrought iron fence in front of the Main Street bus stop who knew Reb.

"Reb, sure I know her. Where did she OD?" said the taller of the two who was extremely skinny, First Nations and, Choy guessed, both a drug addict and streetwalker like Reb.

"Over on Cordoba Street, near the chicken processing plant. I was out jogging and found her. Called 911 but they couldn't revive her."

"Jeez," said the shorter, stubbier friend who looked much healthier than her companion. "I saw her like a week ago. She bought me a beer. She sure as hell liked telling stories."

"What kind of stories?" asked Choy.

"Adventure stories," said the taller one.

At first he didn't understand and his blank stare made that plain. The shorter woman reached up to take her friend's arm, as if to guide her away from an embarrassing situation. But Choy saved the interview by realizing what 'adventure stories' must mean.

"You mean like bad tricks?" he said.

The shorter woman looked him in the eye. He tried to convey reassurance that he was not judging and that he understood sex work was just a job. The taller woman nodded slightly.

"How long had she been working the streets?"

The taller woman shook her head.

"The women over at PACE may know," said the shorter woman who was again pulling on her friend's arm. "She talked about them a lot."

Choy didn't know what PACE was but didn't think it was wise to ask. Instead he said: "Do either of you know her real name?"

"Everyone called her Reb," said the shorter woman.

"Never heard anyone call her anything else," said her friend.

After the two women walked away, Choy googled PACE on his cellphone. It was a society dedicated to helping sex workers and had an office four blocks west, just before Victory Square. As he walked along Hastings, Choy enjoyed the light winter rain that for some reason always made him think of the Hastings Elementary School playground and his childhood best friend Michael George. The two of them were emperors of that playground; both arrived a half-hour before school started and stayed an hour after it ended. While both of Michael's parents were alcoholics so he had good reason to spend as much time as possible away from home, for Choy it was simply the sheer joy of playing with a friend who was always happy. Walking past the impromptu flea market where junkies sold stolen goods and just plain poor folk tried to raise a few extra bucks offering up their meagre possessions, he thought of Michael's descent into addiction beginning in Grade 7. The last time he had seen his former best friend was 20 some years earlier on this very block. He was 25 years old, but looked 50, a mouth without teeth, a symptom, he learned later, of methamphetamine addiction. He wondered if Michael was still alive. Most likely not. That happy 10-year old was certainly long gone.

"Ya, we heard about Reb," said the woman at the front counter. "You were the one who found her?"

Choy nodded. The image of a needle in her arm would be an unshakeable memory for life.

"You plan to write a story about her?"

"If I can find out more about her. Don't even have her real name yet."

"I only knew her as Reb," said the woman who looked as if she had had a life as hard as anyone on the Downtown Eastside. "People said she was from the American south, but I don't know. She could do all sorts of accents. New Orleans, Arkansas, Brooklyn, Newfie, Cockney, Boston, French, Australian, South African, even Cree from northern Alberta — she could have been from anywhere, but people said she was from one of the Confederate states. She liked to tell stories, make people laugh."

"She volunteered here a lot?"

The woman shook her head. "Not really. She'd come to meetings maybe once a month. But I'm told she was good at getting the word out, about bad tricks and such. She had a real easy time talking to other working women. Did her best to help out. I've been coming here for three years and I'd guess she first showed up maybe 18-20 months ago. That's longer than a lot of women down here last nowadays."

"Because of Fentanyl?"

"That and a lot of other shit," she said. "Reb was a good person, you know. Her heart was in the right place, even if she was kind of messed up. Everyone down here has their reasons."

"I understand and that's what I want to write about. I'd like to make her a person, not just a statistic."

The woman stared at him as if she doubted his intentions.

"Can you think of anything else who might help me find someone who actually knew her name?"

"Have you checked with the Coroner's Office? They try to

identify bodies. We've had investigators from there looking for help a few times."

"I called first thing this morning. She didn't have any ID and they don't even know where she lived. They've sent out her description all across North America, but so far no luck."

She looked annoyed.

"But hey, it was a great idea, if I hadn't known about the coroner," he said and then added. "I was a reporter for 25 years at the *Sun*."

"Used to read that paper every day, but it's gotten kind of thin. Not much local news."

"That's because there are hardly any reporters left," said Choy. "When I started there were almost 500 people working in the *Sun* and *Province* newsrooms. Now they're down to about 80 in a combined newsroom. And the company just announced more layoffs."

It was probably more information than interested her, but he couldn't help himself. People should be concerned about the disappearance of local news.

"Have you checked at VANDU?" the woman said. "I think she was quite active there."

Choy shook his head. He was familiar with the Vancouver Area Network of Drug Users. Their office was only a couple blocks away from his father's, and now his, house.

"I bet someone there knows where she lived, maybe even her real name."

"Thanks, I appreciate your help."

"Every woman who dies down here deserves to have her story told," she said, as if having saved up the words, her sad eyes telling a tale of an enduring pain.

"Yes," he said, suddenly feeling guilty.

The truth is everyone deserves to have his or her story told. That's what funerals are for.

But Reb was unlikely to ever have a funeral unless somewhere there was someone who cared. And the first step toward finding such a person was discovering her real name. Only then might he be able to contact someone who cared.

***

Choy was not exactly sure what he expected Svetlana Borovsky to look like, but it was nothing at all like the tall, athletic, blond businesswoman wearing a tailored grey woollen suit and carrying a lawyerly black leather case who entered the Smile Diner from the Pender Street sidewalk. Little Andy stood up and as she made her way to the corner table everyone in the large, utilitarian room glanced at what they likely assumed was a corporate executive, an unfamiliar movie starlet or, more creatively, a very high priced hooker.

"Svetlana, this is Waylon Choy, the writer I told you about," said Andy, keeping his voice low.

"Mr. Choy, you look nothing at all like I expected," said Borovsky with a heavy Russian accent, holding out her hand assertively.

"I was thinking the exact same thing about you," Choy responded, shaking her hand, then sitting back down.

"You want me … maybe …" mumbled Andy as he looked at the exit.

Her glance was enough for him to nod and walk briskly out of the quarter full restaurant in the middle of what once was Vancouver's used and antique bookstore district, back in a time when people still bought long-lasting, printed-on-paper reading material.

"You don't look like a Choy," she said, still standing.

"And you don't look like a drug dealer," he responded quickly. "But then what does a drug dealer in multicultural Canada look like?"

She nodded to acknowledge his point, then sat down and looked at him. Her smile was disarmingly charming.

The waitress brought the two coffees that had already been ordered.

"Do you want something else?" asked Choy.

"A coffee is fine," said Borovsky. "I am rather busy."

"I understand," answered Choy.

"The person I represent, Billy-Bob Baker, may be interested in speaking with you …"

"Billy-Bob Baker, BBB, the Better Business Bureau, I like that," said Choy, finally returning her smile.

"He has an interest right now in a certain kind of publicity," she said. "Can I ask what sort of timeline we might be looking at? And what sort of publication would you be submitting your story or stories to?"

"I'm not sure yet of the timeline or what sort of publication might be interested. I was a reporter at the *Vancouver Sun* for 25 years, so I have many connections there, but right now, I'm leaning towards a book. Probably a small B.C. publisher, but maybe a bigger Toronto-based company would be interested. It all depends on my investigation, what I find, how good the story is."

"Sometimes publishers are more interested in a book from an author who has made a name for himself from a series of newspaper or magazine articles, correct?"

Choy nodded.

"So perhaps if it suited our interest to have a few stories come out rather quickly, this might complement your interest in finding a book publisher?"

"Sure," said Choy, "but you do know what the primary focus of my book would be?"

"It has been explained that you are interested in recent

death, likely an overdose, of woman you found with needle in her arm while jogging."

"Yes."

"Most unsettling."

"Yes," repeated Choy as he tried to work through all the possible reasons why a drug wholesaler might want media attention.

"But who this woman was and why she died will be way to write about current drug business, that is correct?"

"Yes again."

"We might share certain interests in common then, but I am afraid I must leave you now," said Borovsky, standing. "I will get back to you after we have discussed this."

"You and the Better Business Bureau?"

She nodded slightly, as Choy also stood.

"Can you tell me why a person like him would want publicity?" he asked.

"No."

"Because you don't know or because it's none of my business?"

"I will be in touch if we decide to go ahead."

Choy sat back down. He was hungry and felt like an oyster burger. The Smile made a decent one and it was a favourite fuel of his to power the pondering process.

***

As Choy turned onto Cordoba for the seven-block walk to VANDU's office, he realized Reb's death had already changed his perception even though he knew almost nothing about her yet, except the very most important detail: She was a fellow human being. He'd never understood that before while sharing sidewalks with the homeless, junkies, streetwalkers and other broken people who inhabited this part of the city. Mostly he had ignored them; a few hours into his search that no longer seemed possible. Who were these people and why did they look and act the way they did? Little Andy had told him to read a book called *Chasing the Scream*, all about the so-called war on drugs. He needed to get a copy of that and anything else about addiction and related issues.

Reading about the forest was necessary to understand a tree.

***

Choy spoke to four people at the VANDU office before being introduced to Theresa, who was described as the member who knew Reb best.

"I can tell you the same thing I told the coroner person who came in yesterday," said the petit, dark-haired woman who was still beautiful, despite a prominent scar that ran from the outer edge of her eye socket down a pale right cheek to her square chin. "I don't know her real name, but I do know she called herself Belle Antebellum when she worked in the porn business in southern California."

"She was an actor?"

"She got fucked on camera," said Theresa, sharply. "What else she did, I don't know, although I doubt she was a money bags producer."

"You saw a video?"

She nodded and ran a finger along her scar. "My wonderful former boyfriend, before he did this, introduced me to Belle Antebellum and played a few minutes from a video with her taking one guy's cock in her mouth and another up her ass as part of some make-believe Roman orgy. He wanted the two of us to work in a video he claimed to be planning."

"How long ago was that?"

"Three years ago or so."

"And did she? Make the video?"

"No, said she didn't do porn anymore, but that wasn't the real reason she refused. Told me later she knew I didn't want to do it and that he would have beaten me up if she said yes and I refused. She was a good friend and always looked out for me ... except ..."

"Except?" asked Choy.

"She saved my life after that asshole cut me. Phoned the bastard and pretended to be the sister of the top UN Gang enforcer. Did this perfect impression, you know, of like this India Indian accent. Scared the chicken shit coward into believing I was her best friend and her brother would kill him if he ever even looked at me again. She could do impressions and accents better than anyone on TV. Better than those Saturday Night Live comedians."

"You were saying she looked out for you except?"

"She was a good friend but ... It's not right to speak ill of the dead."

Choy thought it best to say nothing.

After a few second Theresa continued: "She had it bad."

His face illustrated his cluelessness.

"People think all drug users are the same. We'll do anything to get our fix, lie, steal, cheat, but the truth is the need can be very different."

"The level of addiction?"

"No, not the level, the depth. When Reb needed, she really, really, really needed. When she was like that, nothing else existed, just her need. People who aren't users have a hard time understanding. It's not like you're a bad person, but your need is everything, everything."

"I think I understand."

"What did you say your name was?"

"Waylon Choy. I used to be a reporter at the *Vancouver Sun*, but now I write books and I'd like my next one to be about Reb, if

I can find out enough about her. What did she talk about when she wasn't needing?"

"Acting. Said she went to some sort of acting school. Maybe in Los Angeles."

"Is that where she grew up?"

"Don't think so, but maybe. She talked about movies. The ones she'd seen and the ones she made up. She'd have been a good writer. Always telling stories, pretending to be somebody else. It was hard to tell when she was talking about herself or making stuff up. Maybe she didn't know anymore. One day she told me she was English, the daughter of a lord, and had grown up in a house just like on Downton Abbey and for the next two weeks talked with an upper class English accent. Had me believing it was true and then just like that, she changed and said she really was a southern belle. Talked like that for the next month."

"Did she ever discuss her family?"

Theresa shook her head.

"Do you know where she lived?"

"Coroner woman asked me that too."

"And?"

"At the Regent, but got kicked out four or five months ago."

The Regent was the worst SRO in the city. If you got kicked out of there, the street was the next place to sleep.

"I know what you're thinking but it wasn't Reb's fault," said Theresa. "The guy running the cage wanted a free blow job and she refused."

"So she ended up on the street?"

A shrug. "She asked to stay with me, but ..."

"Her need?"

She nodded. "I was trying to taper down, you know? Reb was not the person to have around. And she wasn't actually living on the street. More like couch hopping, spending the night with guys who picked her up."

"Where did she keep her stuff?" Five years earlier Choy had written a feature about the boom in storage buildings and one of the strange facts he had uncovered was that homeless people often rented space. Some even tried to sleep in the tiny unventilated rooms and preventing that was an ongoing issue in the business.

"A few boxes in my apartment — I got one of the new places over on Alexander across from the old Canadian Can building — but I already looked through everything, it's just clothes, dishes and a coffee maker."

"No storage locker?"

"Talked about having a space down in LA where she kept her notebooks with ideas about movies, but never mentioned any storage here."

Seems like Los Angeles holds the key to Reb's identity.

"Anything else you can think of that might help me find her real name and where she came from?"

She shook her head.

"Anyone else I should talk to?"

"Not that I know of, except maybe this guy Ken down in Los Angeles, she mentioned him quite a few times."

"Ken? No last name?"

"Fenn, Benn, Senn something or other 'son' maybe. He worked on the porn video, maybe the director, anyway she said he was the only guy who knew anything about film and was going to be a great director someday."

"She say anything else about him?"

"They dropped acid together and that's why she came to Vancouver."

"She had a vision or something?"

"No, she fell in love with the guy and he was coming here for a job, working on some movie. She told a story about getting in a car in Los Angeles and driving all the way up here. They were both high the whole trip and she hid in the trunk to cross the border because she didn't have a passport or any other ID. Said she dropped acid then climbed into the trunk in Bellingham and didn't get out until a motel over by those studios on Boundary Road. Said it was the most intense trip she ever took."

"When did they split up?"

"He was gone before I met her."

Maybe she loved Vancouver's cheap heroin more than she loved Ken. Or maybe with no ID she was scared to try crossing the border back home.

"If you think of Ken's last name can you call me?" said Choy, offering her a business card. "Or anything else that might help."

"If you discover her real name can you let me know?" she said, taking his card. "I'd like to speak to her parents, or someone, you know, to tell them Reb was a good person, helping others right to the end. Just cause you're a drug user doesn't mean you're worthless."

Did she say that last bit for Reb or for herself?

"You can leave a message for me here."

"I'll drop by if I find anything," said Choy, trying to be friendly, but not seem to be hitting on her. "I only live a few blocks away."

She started to smile but was clearly self-conscious about how that made her scar more prominent.

The problem with getting to know people on skid row was that the stories they told were inevitably depressing. One was left with the feeling that life was too full of cruelty, whether inflicted by society or on oneself.

***

"Hello."

Who is calling?

He'd picked up the phone on the first ring, but said nothing, still thinking and writing notes about what Theresa had told him about Reb and Ken.

"Hello?"

A man. Don't recognize the voice. An upper class English accent.

"Is this Mr. Choy?"

He'd been getting a lot of wrong numbers since getting the new office number.

Why do people raise their voice when they think the person listening might not speak English?

"Mr. Choy?"

Until a few years ago he had found the assumptions people made because of his name annoying, but now mostly tried to have fun with it.

"Nǐ yào bú yào gēn wǒ tiàowǔ," he said, using one of the few Chinese phrases he knew, asking the man if he would like to dance.

"Have I got the right W. Choy? Waylon Choy? The writer?"

"Yes," said Choy, switching to serious mode as he realized the guy might be a customer.

"Why did you just ask me to dance," said the man.

"I am sorry," said Choy. "I thought ... Who is this?"

"My name is Emerson Lee. I am looking for Waylon Choy, the writer. The person who runs the website TheTruthAboutThat. net."

"This is him. I thought you were someone else."

He had assumed the guy was an upper class English twit and now it turns out he might be Chinese.

"Someone who you would like to dance with?"

"No," said Choy, embarrassed. "You speak Mandarin?"

"And Cantonese," said Lee.

"I don't speak either," said Choy. "What can I do for you Mr. Lee?"

"I called because I saw your website, www.TheTruthAbout-That.net and I would like to discuss some work," said Lee.

My first job.

"May I make an appointment?"

"Sure, of course, when and where would you like to meet?"

"Later today at your office?"

"My office? Today? Okay. That would work. It's a home office. 412 Alexander Street, near the waterfront, a block and half east of Main Street," said Choy.

"And the time?"

"Yes, of course," said Choy still flustered by his unprofessional conduct on the phone. "Does 3 p.m. work for you?"

"Yes, I will see you then," said Lee. "Good-bye Mr. Choy."

***

Emerson Lee, a sixtyish small man dressed in what looked like a very expensive bespoke dark woollen suit, knocked on Choy's door at precisely 3 p.m. He was definitely Chinese.

"Mr. Lee," said Choy.

"Mr. Choy," answered Lee, staring at the man on the other side of the threshold, as if uncomfortable about something.

"Is there something wrong?" Choy recognized the look. It was one he had encountered hundreds of times before. "You're startled by the juxtaposition between my name and what you see? You're surprised I don't look Chinese?"

"Somewhat."

At least the guy is honest.

"Are you taken aback so much that you no longer wish to discuss the business you called about?"

"Of course not."

"Then come in and please excuse the mess in here. We are renovating the house for the first time in over 50 years."

"Yes," said Lee as he looked around.

"My office?" said Choy, pointing to the doorway to the left.

"A very interesting building," said Lee as he stepped into the living room instead of the office. "Built in 1887, one of the oldest residential properties remaining in the city of Vancouver. I have seen pictures from the early part of the last century. Very beautiful, Queen Anne style. A shame that façade has been destroyed. Are you planning to recreate the original look?"

"Eventually, yes," said Choy, shocked at his guest's familiarity with the house.

"Converted to a rooming house in the early 1920s with the addition at back, and your great-grandfather bought it as a revenue property in 1943."

Choy stared at the man who stood in the doorway, blocking the way to his office.

"You are surprised that I know about this house?"

"Are you from Vancouver?" Choy had assumed he was from out of town, because of a reference to the Pan Pacific Hotel earlier.

"I maintain residences in many cities, including Vancouver, but like you, my house is currently undergoing renovation."

What is this guy up to?

Choy relaxed his facial muscles, realizing he was probably looking aggressive.

"I also know that your great-great-great-great-great grand-father was a sailor and a businessman/adventurer who was forced to leave his village south of Canton due to a disagreement with an important opium merchant and went to California in 1847."

A disagreement with an opium merchant? Where did he get this?

"By 1859, fluent in English, Spanish, Chinook and at least three Chinese dialects, he made his way to Victoria and was well placed to become a not insignificant wholesale supplier to the town of Barkerville, the centre of the Cariboo gold rush. His second wife, your great-great-great-great-great grandmother was Metis of Scots and French Canadian extraction."

Second wife? Multilingual? I've got to talk to my father.

"Did you know about his first wife back in China?"

"This is what you made an appointment to talk about with me?" said Choy, annoyed a stranger knew so much about him.

"You do not wish to learn about your ancestor?" said Lee, maintaining an officious, almost inscrutable, smile.

"Someone I never met phones and asks for an appointment to discuss a job, but shows up knowing details about my house and great, great, great, great, great grandfather that I've never heard before. Who does something like that?"

"Someone who wants to be your friend."

"What do you want?" said Choy, probably too harshly.

"My sole motivations were to be helpful and prove to you that I have many sources of information."

"And you need to prove that because?"

Lee strained to maintain a polite smile. Choy felt guilty.

Maybe I've misread the situation.

"Would you prefer if I left?" Lee asked.

At least listen to what he has to say.

"Look, I'm sorry. Please come into my office."

Choy sat behind his desk and pointed to the wine-coloured 100-year-old reupholstered loveseat.

Lee's eyes made Choy feel like he was getting an MRI scan.

"What exactly do you want to talk about?" said Choy, the guilt growing every time he opened his mouth. "What sort of job do you have for me?"

"I'd like you to investigate someone and write a story," said Lee.

"Who?"

"His name is Billy-Bob Baker."

Better Business Bureau? What's going on?

"Who is he?" said Choy, struggling to avoid reacting in a way that revealed he'd heard the name before.

"He and his organization are attempting to become the largest importers of heroin and especially synthetic drugs into North America."

"Fentanyl?" Choy said the first word that popped into his mind, as he thought about the 85-pound corpse currently inhabiting a metal box in Vancouver General's morgue and the slim chance that Lee's appearance at his door with a request to investigate BBB was unrelated to his meeting the day before with Svetlana Borovsky.

"Yes."

"How do you know this?"

"Answering that question would require getting to know you better."

"Which is why you started off by telling me about my ancestor and the house I live in. You want me to trust you?"

Lee didn't exactly shake his head, but a slight shift in his eyes and cheekbones functioned much the same.

Choy too relied on a physical representation of what could have been a verbal "what then?"

"Whether or not you trust me is irrelevant," said Lee. "I must trust you."

Maybe it was a stupid thing to say to a potential client, but before he could consider the wisdom of his words, they came out: "You know because you're an importer of the stuff as well, right? They're muscling in on your territory."

One downside of a continuously inscrutable visage is that the very slightest muscle movement is discernible.

"Don't get me wrong, I don't care," said Choy. "I think the war on drugs has been a complete disaster and addicts ought to be treated for their disease, not locked up."

Lee continued to make like a statue.

"Although I do believe that whoever is supplying the Fentanyl that's been killing people, probably should be locked up for murder, whether that's you or someone named Billy-Bob."

"You have misunderstood who I am."

"Okay. Then who are you?"

"A businessman with various interests: primarily property development, real estate, financial, a little manufacturing, some import export and consulting. The people who have directed me to contact you have their reasons, which you may or may not be interested in."

After a moment of silence Choy smiled at the man he knew next to nothing about and said: "Okay. I'll choose 'not interested in'. Right now it's better if I don't know their exact motivation. And it's better if I am told you are a go-between. If I were to take on your project our relationship should be strictly professional. I'm a journalist and you would become my publisher — my source of income. A contract, much like that used for a single project in the movie business, would be drawn up. If you are in possession of some reliable information and assign me to check it out, I can do that. If I find there is a story, which I and I alone will determine, I will keep digging until I have enough material to write that story. I will then attempt to sell or give the story to whatever media outlet you desire or we can publish it on my website. I can promise to do my best to guarantee your anonymity, but in this country the courts have ruled journalists may be forced to give up their sources."

"So you are interested?" Lee said.

"I don't do anything illegal. I mean other than regular journalistic methods that might, in other circumstance, be of questionable legality."

Lee nodded. "You do follow a journalism code of ethics that prohibits you working for the police or other governmental agency, correct?"

It was Choy's turn to nod. "So?" he said, meaning 'what next?'

But rather than answer, Lee pulled a cellphone from his jacket pocket. "Yes?" he said and no more than a few seconds later stood up.

"We need to go out the back way," said Lee, his voice calm, but urgent.

"What?"

"Someone is currently placing an explosive device on your front porch."

"What?" Choy repeated himself, his voice an octave higher, as he made his way out of the office and turned left to the front door.

"No time to look! The back door!" shouted Lee, as he pulled at Choy's arm. "Now! We don't know how quickly it will go off."

What the fuck? This guy. A bomb?

Choy turned and ran towards the old kitchen and the back door of the house as the older man followed.

"Who phoned?" said Choy, as they entered the hallway of the 1920s' addition.

"My security," said Lee. "He's stationed across the street."

Security? A bomb?

Fragments of thoughts raced through his consciousness. Joy moving here and wanting a baby. A drug dealer who wants him to expose another drug dealer. Better Business Bureau. Reb, her skin so cold to his touch.

"What the fuck have you got me into," yelled Choy as they exited into the back yard.

A bomb?

3.

John Choy sat on the couch, staring at his feet.

"You owe how much?" said his son.

"One hundred and thirty thousand."

"To a bookie?"

His father faintly nodded, head hung in shame.

"Jesus Christ," said Waylon Choy. "And he's been threatening you? Why didn't you tell me?"

"I thought I could deal with it," he answered, without making eye contact because he knew how his words would be received.

"By making another bet?"

His father's head dropped lower.

"But that was when the debt was $65,000, right? Double or nothing, right? On the Canucks?"

"Against them. On the Blue Jackets. Tortorella's new team. After four straight losses by the Canucks. In Columbus. A Blue Jacket win or an overtime loss and I would have been all even," said his father. "But the Canucks beat the Blue Jackets by three."

Waylon Choy felt an anger that had built up over decades surge inside him. He took one more look at his father then walked out of the living room, into the hallway and out the front door onto the veranda.

My father the addict. A gambling junkie who lost most of our family fortune, property that today would be worth at least 60 or 70 million dollars.

Choy felt a tingling sensation from his arms and legs as the anger coursed through his body. He kicked at an empty cardboard box, the remains of a delivery to the electrician who had been working at the house earlier in the week.

He looked out over the scene on Alexander Street as scores of people, mostly men, lined up, clutching bags of dirty clothes, waiting for access to the washers and dryers that the Lookout offered free to use on Tuesday mornings.

Fathers, brothers, cousins, sisters, mothers … addicts end up in lines like this.

He stared at the line-up for half a minute.

My father.

He took a few dozen deep breaths then returned to the room where his father remained in silent reflection of his misdeeds.

"You started with some relatively small bets didn't you, after I sold my house and gave you that five thousand? A couple of wins got you hooked again, then some bigger bets wiped out your cash and you started doubling down. How many times did you do it?"

Silence for a few more seconds.

"Six, more or less," he finally answered and looked up quickly. "I'm sorry. I messed up."

It hurt to see his father humiliated but Choy made it worse by adding: "Again."

"Again." Eyes continued to stare at slippers.

"You promised there would be no more gambling if I agreed to move in with you."

"I know … I thought … I signed over the house to you, so I can't borrow against it," John Choy said, as if to proclaim, 'I did something right'.

After decades of gambling away property all over the downtown peninsula.

The counsellors had made it clear relapses were likely.

Take it one day at a time.

"So you think the fake bomb may have been a warning from your bookie?"

A nod.

"Christ Almighty!" Waylon Choy sat down but then immediately stood up again. "I screamed at my first potential paying customer. Told him he was the target of his drug dealer rivals who put that package there to send him a message."

"I'm sorry," repeated his father.

The son held his left hand over his face as he shook his head.

I have to tell Joy about his gambling addiction because in a few weeks she will be in the middle of it.

"$130,000. What are we going to do?"

"I'm sorry," his father said, sobbing.

A son shouldn't see his father like this.

He sat on the couch beside his Dad. After a few seconds he put his right arm around him.

"Don't worry, I can fix this. I just need to know you've learned a lesson."

"Yes." The voice was weak and sodden with humiliation. "I …"

"I don't want you to promise anything," said a son who had had this particular conversation too many times before. "I just want you to think about the best way to prevent something like this from happening again. Maybe some rules about your spending, rules that you can live with and still feel … Okay?"

His father nodded.

"Okay," repeated his son, this time without the question mark.

Someone has to be strong in this relationship and it's always been me.

"What are you going to do?" asked his father.

"I don't know."

It was a lot of money. He had the cash in the bank but that was to pay for renovations and living expenses.

Everything else is in term deposits, or ... too soon and too dangerous.

Was there another way? Someone he could talk to? In his experience bookies were not forgiving. Maybe the police. If his father testified? Was a debt to an illegal bookmaker legally enforceable? He knew the answer and it was no, but those people had other means ... like a fake bomb on your veranda, perhaps followed by ...

"What are you going to do?" his father repeated.

"Don't worry, I'll figure it out."

I always do.

***

The two men walked along an old logging road in Lynn Canyon Headwaters Park.

"It is good that you care for your father so much," said Mr. Lee. "Even if he does have an unforgiveable gambling problem."

"Again, we would be so grateful for any assistance you might be available to provide," said Choy, burrowing deeper into the thick mud of obsequiousness. "It is a most generous offer."

"It is nothing, a simple phone call, that is all."

"You would have been justified in never speaking to me again after how I treated you. Again, I am so sorry for what I said."

Lee held up his hand to indicate silence. "It has been many years since I have walked in this park. The air is so fresh, the colours so beautiful and the sounds so peaceful. It was an excellent choice for our meeting."

"You said a place where you could be assured no one could plant listening devices. Here, only Mother Nature can listen."

"Yes."

They walked in silence for at least a minute as Choy thought about what had just happened. His first apology to this potential customer led to a discussion of his father's gambling debt, which in turn led to Lee telling him about his private lending business in which he sometimes dealt with problem gamblers like his father and so he had connections in that world. "Perhaps I can help, talk with some people," Lee had said. And that eventually led to: "Perhaps we can help each other with an exchange of favours." Was Mr. Lee rich enough to simply pay $130,000 to the bookie or did he have the connections and power in the criminal underworld to have the debt cancelled? And then what 'favour' would Lee ask of him? Would it simply be to write a story? He thought of the opening scenes in the Godfather where Marlon Brando is bestowing favours on his daughter's wedding day. He had done a little research on who Emerson Lee was, but the only information he could find was that he was a prominent businessman reputedly close to important people in the Chinese Communist Party. From his quick search it seemed Lee's companies were, as he said, primarily involved in real estate development, financial services and investment banking. There was nothing online even hinting he might be a mobster or a drug dealer.

Still…

"Will I or my father need to do something?" Choy asked. "I don't even know the name of the bookie, but I can ask."

"No," said Lee. "Leave the matter to me."

"Can I ask how the matter will be taken care of?"

Lee stopped and took a deep breath. "This forest, so close to millions of people and yet so far away from the problems that plague them."

"It would help me and my father's piece of mind."

"You doubt whether I can do what I have told you I will do?"

"We hardly know each other."

"Yes, we do need to talk, to share a meal, perhaps enjoy a few bottles of good wine."

"That would be wonderful, but perhaps you could give me some indication now, of exactly how …"

"I will fix your father's problem?"

People who finished other's sentences had always annoyed Choy. It seemed either a putdown or a boast, maybe both at the same time.

"You are right to be cautious until I prove to be a man who can make his promises come true," said Lee, in a way that seemed a purposeful affectation.

He's using the stereotype of the "inscrutable Oriental" to appear mysterious and powerful.

"Many people owe me favours," he continued.

"Including the man who ordered that fake bomb be placed on our veranda?"

"While we may never know for certain who gave that order, I can assure you that someone with much higher status in the organization of the person who took your father's bet will be thrilled to please me or someone I know. And they will ensure that your father is never allowed to make a bet, ever again."

Thrilled? Like I'm thrilled you're doing me a favour? Christ, what have I got myself into?

"People, especially the media, focus their attention on violence, but I can assure you that at least 99 percent of what is defined as organized crime is simply based on personal relationships."

Is he acknowledging the business he is in?

"Nothing more personal than having someone beaten up or killed," said Choy flippantly and immediately wondered if his words would annoy his potential benefactor.

"The truth is there is nothing less personal than having someone killed," replied Lee. "Do you really think it is personal when the president of the United States orders a drone strike that kills a hundred people? Or when a general sends ten thousand troops into battle, knowing a quarter of them will die? Or when the

CEO of a railway corporation decides to reduce staffing on every train, even though it will inevitably result in an extra death for every million kilometres his trains travel?"

"It is certainly personal for the victims."

"Yes, I would agree," said Lee. "Dialectics. We must consider the tree as well as the forest."

What does he mean?

"To truly understand the world we must study the whole, the individual and all the interconnections," continued Lee. "The great insight of Karl Marx was that to completely comprehend capitalism, one needed to contemplate its entirety as a system, to go beyond how it seemed from the point of view of the individual capitalist or worker."

An inscrutable communist Charlie Chan.

Choy smiled at this thought.

"You find my words amusing?" said Lee, as he stopped walking.

"Yes," answered Choy. "Someone like you praising Marx. It's not what I expected."

Lee also smiled and started walking again. "Thank you," he said. "For the compliment."

The pace of the hike picked up, which suggested that despite his words, Lee was annoyed. This was confirmed a few seconds later.

"What do you mean, 'someone like me'," he said, stopping again. "You know next to nothing about me."

"That's true," said Choy quickly. "Perhaps I should have said, 'someone who I imagine you to be.'"

The two men stared at each other.

"Like you said, we should get to know each other better," said Choy, breaking the silence first. "So why don't you tell me about yourself. Where did you grow up? Tell me about your family. What have you done in your life? What do you do now?"

Once more Lee smiled. "Yes, that would be good. We should exchange such information. Let us continue along this trail until it becomes too difficult for an old man wearing $2,000 shoes and I will tell you all about myself."

***

Emerson Lee was not who Choy first thought him to be. He was down to earth, intellectually entertaining and raised in rural China, rather than a stuffed shirt upper class Brit twit. While the Oxford accent was not a complete affectation, since he claimed to have attended the famous university, it was admittedly "useful" and could be replaced by a more "Soho-Chinatown" manner of speaking because it was on those streets he learned English.

If even half of the stories he told were true, Lee had already lived a life worthy of a Hollywood epic. The son of a successful businessman who lost everything in 1949, Lee was born in a rural re-education camp a few years after the Chinese revolution. He was a youthful Red Guard who waved Mao's Little Red Book while marching through the streets to denounce the "four olds" — old customs, old culture, old habits and old ideas — but later took advantage of Communist Party connections to write exams that ultimately earned him a scholarship to study Classics, then European history at Oxford in England. He joined the Chinese diplomatic corps after university and travelled the world, becoming a specialist in overseas Chinese communities. For over 20 years he was a diplomat and mid-ranking Communist Party official but after 2001, when capitalists were allowed to join, he resigned in protest and worked as a businessman ever since. While primarily a real estate developer, Lee said certain parts of his business required the bodyguards that travelled with him everywhere. He did not elucidate further, but the implication was close underworld connections. At a minimum he cultivated an image of being a powerful man not to be crossed.

He claimed to remain a Marxist, although one fond of Thomas Hobbes and Confucius as well, more a Chinese nationalist than an actual communist. While claiming not to like capitalism he nonetheless was an enthusiastic capitalist, making money by investing his own and other people's money in whatever business offered the highest rate of return, regardless of ethical considerations.

"Profit is the only consideration when accumulation of capital is the point of your existence," Lee said as they dined at one of Richmond's best Fujian restaurants. "The Party decided that the primary purpose of this period in Chinese history is development of the economy and the best way to accomplish that is through capitalism, so who am I to argue?"

But when confronted by the contradiction that he had resigned from the party whose policy was cited to justify his profit-seeking existence, he smiled and simply said: "Dialectics." That seemed his favourite explanation for the many contradictions that necessarily arose from being a "Marxist businessman." But each time he said it with such a twinkle in his eyes and lightness in tone that it seemed more self-deprecating comedy than mere hypocrisy. Or, as he said, "through the negation of the negation we achieve progress, and also absolve ourselves of sin — a more scientific version of purchasing indulgences from the 13th century Catholic Church."

How could you not like a man who justified his existence with such wit and disdain for conventional morality, and who also loved great food, wine and conversation? A man who argued that chilli peppers actually were native to China, or were brought to China much earlier than Columbus's so-called discovery of the Americas. A man whose eyes sparkled when he said: "As Hobbes informs us 'force and fraud are in war the two cardinal virtues' and 'the con-

dition of man is a condition of war of everyone against everyone'."
A man who told him there was no more need to worry about his
father's gambling debt. It had been taken care of.

***

Despite spending the best part of a week talking to people
around skid row, as well as to connections made over the years in
the police, social services community and film industry, Choy had
come to a dead end in Vancouver regarding Reb. She was almost
certainly in Canada illegally and therefore had no official records.
Without even a proper name, there was no way of tracking down
where she came from and if she had any remaining family. To find
out who she was might require a trip to Los Angeles. He could
try calling the Directors Guild office there for information about
Ken the director friend who supposedly drove her to Canada, but
based on his experience as a reporter, getting anywhere on that
front would mean an in-person visit. In fact, he was almost certain
that a visit to the City of Angels was going to be necessary as soon
as he learned Reb moved from there to Vancouver, but he had to
wait around town until Svetlana Borovsky called him back about
that possible meeting with Billy-Bob, the purported drug dealer,
who Mr. Lee wanted exposed and Choy needed to interview for
his book.

After they had talked four times, twice at dinner, Lee seemed
satisfied that Choy was trustworthy and gave him the name of an
ex-RCMP drug squad member who would meet with him Sunday
morning at the Glad Tidings Pentecostal Church on Fraser Street.
It seemed a strange location for an interview, but Choy said nothing when Lee gave him the place and time. Given the size of the
"favour" the man had done for him and his father, the least Choy
could do in return was follow his instructions. Still, he didn't mention the possible interview with BBB, or his meeting with Svetlana

and was inclined to keep both his secrets, although he did consider the possibility that Lee already knew and, in fact, had first contacted him because he knew. While lying to Lee would not be a good idea, it seemed entirely fair to be as inscrutable as his benefactor. Still, when the phone call from Svetlana came Saturday morning telling him that BBB was available to be interviewed in an hour, Choy did consider calling Lee before heading down to the Movieland Arcade on Granville Street, but decided against it. He was playing poker with unfamiliar opponents, a situation in which it's usually best to reveal as little as possible.

The arcade, a venerable institution on Vancouver's old "uptown" shopping and entertainment street that had been transformed in Choy's lifetime from an area that featured big old working class beer halls where one could buy hashish from Montreal and get drunk on cheap suds throughout the day and evening into the club district where patrons were better dressed and younger while the drinks and drugs were more expensive, but available every night until five hours into tomorrow.

As he entered the arcade, a place last visited a few times over 30 years earlier when it was an exotic spot for a 15-year old to hang out, the pinball machines and video games seemed eerily familiar. But before he could become reacquainted with old friends, Svetlana walked towards him, stopping only momentarily to whisper in his ear.

"Take the machine with no one playing it three from the back, right side," she said then kissed him on the lips, as if they were old friends or maybe lovers, before exiting the arcade.

As Choy watched her leave the weirdness of what had just happened lingered in his consciousness, upsetting his planned cool approach to the man people said was a big-time drug importer. As he walked to the back of the room to take up a position at the end of a 1970s pinball machine, Choy noted that there were at least a half dozen very large muscular men, who looked like they belonged in a prison gym rather than a teenaged boys' hangout. Before he could think through the implications of that, a short, skinny 25-year old playing the pinball machine next to his said: "Russian girls give great head. You ever get any?"

His Deep South accent certainly sounded like it might belong to a Billy-Bob, but he seemed much too young to be a major drug dealer.

"Are you the Better Business Bureau?" Choy asked.

"You want to try something really cool," said the man. "Here."

One of the large men handed Choy what looked like a virtual reality "helmet" that he had seen on TV a few months earlier. The guy with the Deep South accent took an identical helmet and pulled it over his head, demonstrating what to do. As Choy followed suit, pulling the device over his face and ears, he suddenly was on some Antarctic island, surrounded by penguins.

"Pretty cool, eh?" said the same voice that made the crude remark about Svetlana. "It's a new virtual reality device that the people who know about these sorts of things tell me is absolutely impossible to bug."

"You're Billy-Bob?" asked Choy, suffering sensory overload as he was lost in a sea of creatures that stretched as far as he could see, even though he could hear the guy beside him clearly. The sensation was like being up on the screen in the March of Penguins, a film he had taken Samantha to see when she was three, but still able to talk to the guy beside you in the theatre.

"There were three choices of what to experience, this one, mountain gorillas and a white water rafting expedition. I picked this one seeing as how we're up in Canada and all."

Rather than point out there are no penguins in the great white north, but lots of white water rafting, Choy simply repeated: "Are you Billy-Bob Baker?"

"That's what my Daddy named me," he answered cheerfully, obviously enjoying the virtually real three foot tall flightless, but well-dressed, birds surrounding him.

"Svetlana told you why I wanted to interview you?"

"She said you're writing a book about some junkie streetwalker who ODed and want to know how the drugs get from wherever to here. Is that about right?"

"Yes."

"Svetlana is excellent at explaining things," Billy-Bob said. "She's very good at other shit too and seems to really like you. You want to fuck her?"

On the one hand Choy was amazed there was still a social milieu in which it was acceptable to speak about women this way, but on the other hand knew strippers, prostitutes and pimps existed everywhere, including his hometown. "What should I call you?" he said, changing the subject. "What name should I use in the book?"

"The name my Daddy and Momma gave me."

"You're not worried about incriminating yourself or what people might think about you?"

"I'm not ashamed of what I do and the police already know who I am."

"You don't fear the police using what I write in a criminal case against you?"

"It will be my word against yours because you will have no record and I can prove I was not in Vancouver today."

Choy didn't like this means of conducting an interview. He couldn't see Billy-Bob's eyes or hear the subtle inflections of his voice.

"So why are you talking to me? What's in it for you?"

"Market share," Billy-Bob answered. "I'm the new guy on the block. I need the right people to know I have product."

"These 'right people' read newspaper or magazine stories about dead junkies? They want to do business with a new guy who talks to reporters about his business?"

There was no response, but his silence answered the question regardless.

The point isn't publicity but rather to prove his power. 'He talks to reporters but nothing happens to him.'

"How long have you been in the drug business?"

"I could say my whole life, or at least since I was 10. My Momma was a little too fond of methamphetamines and I was holding stuff for the neighbourhood dealer by the time I was in Grade 4."

"You bring drugs into Canada and the United States?"

"California to Alaska."

"What sort of drugs?"

"Whatever people want."

"A lot of drugs?"

"My sales territory has a population of over 50 million people."

"That's how you view yourself? As a salesman?"

"A wholesale sales agent, the middleman who enables product to get from the grower/processor to the consumer. But I also invest in new technology."

"New technology?"

"This is a business that has been very conservative, so I'm trying to bring new approaches, all along the production and distribution system. My speciality is designer drugs. We invest in the latest, best products from the best labs."

"Do you sell Fentanyl?"

"I sell what the customer wants."

"Even if it kills your customer?"

"I'm spending large sums of money to look for safer synthetic alternatives. Besides, obesity kills more people in the United States than all the opioids combined and yet you can go into any store in the country and buy candy bars and chips."

"Do you make payments to police and other arms of the law?"

"Yes sir I do. It's a cost of doing business."

"Do you do drugs?"

"I try not to, but have done so, on occasion."

"Why do you try not to?"

"It's fun, but unhealthy, like having popcorn, Goobers and a soda at the movie theatre. I try not to do that too, but sometimes can't help myself."

"What are your thoughts about the opioid epidemic? About people dying from overdoses?"

"Some people are here for a long time, others for a good time. Who are we to judge?"

"So you don't take any responsibility?"

"I have never once stuck a needle in someone else's arm or made them smoke a pipe or forced them to do something they didn't want to do. I'm a businessman and a libertarian. John Galt would approve of what we do."

Another damn supporter of Ayn Rand.

"Do you object to the use of the term 'pusher' to describe people who do what you do?"

"I offer products that people freely choose to buy. I don't advertise, I don't run marketing campaigns. The people who sell cars and Coca-Cola, those are the real pushers. They spend billions each year convincing you to buy their products."

This kid is not as stupid as I first thought.

"You do acknowledge violence is an integral part of your business?"

"We operate in a free, unregulated market, where everyone understands the state is our enemy. Our constitution gives us the right to bear arms, so we do. Sometime this leads to violence but compared to that perpetrated by the various arms of government, very little at all. Most of our violence would end if the state would simply get their noses out of what people can and cannot buy."

"So you're in favour of legalizing all drugs?"

"It might not be good for my profit margins, but yes I am. Did you ever read the Fountainhead or Atlas Shrugged? People don't hate us because we're violent, or because we hurt people. They envy us. They're jealous of our wealth and the fact we're smarter than them."

As Choy was thinking the interview was going better than he could ever have hoped and was about to move on to questions about exactly how and how many police were on his payroll, the penguins disappeared, replaced by darkness and silence. He pulled off his helmet to see Svetlana whispering in BBB's ear. Her boss was immediately surrounded by a crowd of muscular men, who headed as a group out a door at the back of the arcade.

"It would perhaps be safer for you to leave quickly as well," Svetlana said, taking the helmet from him.

"What's going on?" asked Choy.

"You send email with the rest of your questions at this address," she said, handing him a card that read, "Unique White Cleaners LLC, Los Angeles, California, Email: uniquewhitecleanersllc.net" before turning to join the group that was now in the back alley.

***

As Choy sat Sunday morning in the large hall of the Glad Tidings Pentecostal Church, he tried to remember exactly what the large muscular men from Billy-Bob's security detail looked like. He thought maybe the two six-foot-six-ish, 250-plus-pound, NFL-linemen-looking white guys, one to his left and one to his right, standing against the back wall of the room looked familiar, but couldn't be certain he'd seen them the day before. The arcade's dim light, the VR device over his head most of the time, and the weirdness of Svetlana kissing him had thrown off his usually excellent powers of observation.

If they are Billy-Bob's goons what are they doing here? Following me? Do they know I'm meeting with an ex-RCMP drug squad agent? If so, how? Is someone inside Mr. Lee's organization working for Billy-Bob?

Probably he was imagining all of it. Maybe the two big guys were CFL players. Lots of football players were evangelicals.

If they are Billy-Bob's goons why are they being so obvious? To intimidate me? To intimidate the person I'm supposed to meet?

No one is following me. Nothing is going on.

Variations on this pattern of thoughts raced through Choy's brain for a half an hour past the appointed meeting time. The church was almost packed and the service, or whatever it was called in this brand of religion, was about to begin, when he decided to leave. The guy had not shown up, maybe because of the two goons standing against the back wall, although neither moved or even seemed to notice when he walked quickly between them into the lobby and out of the church.

As he strolled down the hill to where his car was parked in a hardware store parking lot off Grandview Highway, Choy was feeling a mixture of excitement and dread. It was what he imagined climbing a dangerous mountain peak would be like— an immense thrill while constantly questioning why on earth you were doing it.

Upon opening his car door he noticed a piece of paper on the front seat. On it was written: "Drive away now. When you get where you are going, open the trunk. Perhaps we'll meet another day."

4.

All Choy had said was "do you want to go for a ride?" but it triggered a half-hour long rant about global warming by his daughter Samantha, whose new Grade 9 science teacher was a very convincing environmentalist and opponent of the private automobile.

"You have to get rid of that car for the planet's sake," came the directive after a ten-minute preliminary argument.

Strangely, it was less than a year earlier that Sam had made him promise to keep his restored 1965 AMC Ambassador 990 convertible at least until she turned 16 and got her driver's licence.

"We have to abandon a transportation system based on the private car or we are cooked," was one of the few sentences he later remembered.

Initially he had tried to argue, coming up with a feeble "my Ambassador isn't part of a transportation system, it's my hobby", but that only unleashed more invective based upon the many elements of what she called 'automobility' that were destroying mother earth. So, he mostly just listened contritely as the green lecture series continued for what seemed like hours.

Of course he was proud of Sam's rhetorical skills and her passion for a good cause. But he did wonder about the significance of her quoting Mr. Morrison at least 25 times. He wasn't completely comfortable with a teacher promoting such strong opinions in the classroom; on the other hand provoking thinking outside the box and challenging conventional wisdom were exactly what the best educators did.

"So, how is he supposed to get to Los Angeles?" said Benjamin, her younger brother, who had been listening to the conversation from the kitchen. "Fly? That's even worse than driving for carbon dioxide emissions."

Where do they learn this stuff?

"Why are you going to Los Angeles?" asked Sam.

"The story he's working on," said Ben. "All the leads point to Los Angeles. That woman who died, she used to work down there."

"He could take a bus or the train," said Sam. "The train is best."

"Except if he went with a full car," said Ben. "A car can be good if it is full."

"Not a 1965 Ambassador," said Sam. "It spews greenhouse gases. Spews them."

Hard to argue with that. Even after a rebuild, that 287 cubic inch engine is a gas-guzzler.

"How would you know?" said Ben, making a face at his sister. "You're some kind of mechanical engineer now too?"

"I helped Dad restore the car as much as you," said Sam.

"No you didn't," said Ben. "You don't even know the difference between an adjustable wrench and an Allen wrench."

"Like you're some kind of mechanic."

Their bickering seemed a daily occurrence, at least at his house. He wondered if the same was true when they were with their mother but was afraid to ask. Helena had a way of twisting his questions into accusations. Besides he was almost certain that is was normal for teenaged sisters to fight with their brothers. And deep down they cared about each other, despite the regular fusillades of angry words. He was certain about that.

At least the mutual broadside changed the subject, one that made him uncomfortable because accusations of participating in the destruction of the planet seemed, at a minimum, plausible and likely well founded. While he sometimes felt that environmentalism was Vancouver's state religion, it didn't make caring for the planet less critical. He did want healthy grandchildren and not ones whose lives were diminished by global warming. How could anyone be in favour of the destruction of the planet?

A few minutes after he abandoned the living room to his children and sat at the kitchen table to read a hard copy of the *Vancouver Sun* for the first time in a week, Samantha appeared with her hands on her hips, a pose that suggested he was about to get another blast of political invective.

"Are you really going to Los Angeles?"

"Probably," he answered, then looked back down at his newspaper.

"Without us?"

"You have school."

"You promised to take us four years ago."

He had a vague recollection of such a pledge, but it was to a pre-adolescent who was in love with all things Disney, not this version 15.01, who surely had grown out of such childish desires.

"Why would you want to go to the home of freeways where climate wrecking automobility is at its most advanced stage?"

Is this cruel? Maybe, but it's also fun.

He struggled to contain his smile.

***

Despite spending a day and a half going over the two boxes of material that someone had left in his trunk there were still hundreds of pieces of paper that Choy had barely glanced at. In the boxes were RCMP, FBI and U.S. Drug Enforcement Administration files as well as other material concerning Billy-Bob and Svetlana linking them to dozens of corporations that operated in the United States, Russia, Afghanistan, China, Myanmar, Thailand, Taiwan, Cayman Islands and Canada. Among these were generic drug manufacturers, shipping and import-export companies, two boutique banks, a small Asian regional airline, a fish canning factory, a pineapple plantation and cannery, and a trucking company based in Los Angeles that operated in Canada, the USA and Mexico. Plus, there were hundreds of surveillance photos that showed Billy-Bob meeting with various people, including some who looked like police officers, as well as what looked like drugs being packed into tuna sized cans and Tetra Pac juice boxes. Finally, there were translations of what were labelled affidavits from various witnesses about how heroin was shipped from opium-growing regions in Afghanistan, Laos, Cambodia and Burma to packing plants in Thailand.

After he thought about the material for most of two sleepless nights, Choy still wasn't sure how to proceed. How could he confirm the authenticity of the material? Who could confirm it? More important, why would a Vancouver drug squad or any other official confirm the stuff, even if they could? Especially to a freelance journalist, who used to be a fluff-piece feature writer at the *Vancouver Sun*. Then there was the question of exactly where the tentacles of Billy-Bob's organization stretched into various police forces. He had admitted to paying off cops and the pictures seemed to show that was true. Clearly, the material that Lee's informant had assembled came from cops of one sort or another, but Billy-Bob was not in custody. Why? Someone was protecting him or this material wasn't considered sufficient evidence. Or no one police force had seen all the material that Lee's guy had given him. Which raised the question: Why hadn't Lee simply given the boxes to the RCMP or DEA? If he were a rival drug dealer why wouldn't he simply have the opposing operation shut down by police? Did he suspect Billy-Bob had infiltrated both forces? Or maybe, if Lee too was a drug dealer, he was paying off cops and knew that the Better Business Bureau had done the same.

Maybe Lee knows Billy-Bob is protected and wants to expose that by going to a journalist. But then why would BBB have agreed to an interview in which he admitted selling drugs?

He needed to discuss the story with someone. His first thought was Joy, but she was too busy finishing her job in Las Vegas and getting ready to move to Vancouver. Besides, he needed someone who could look over the material immediately, an experienced journalist with connections to the police. The best person he could think of was Jan James, the current crime reporter for the *Sun*. She had covered Vancouver gangs for the past 25 years and had worked at the paper for a decade longer than that. She had a reputation, at least among editors, for being difficult to work with, but Choy had always gotten along with her, especially after the two week strike about 20 years earlier when he had spent a lot of time with her and her then four-year-old son Quentin. She was the most fearless journalist Choy had ever met, having been under police protection at least a half dozen times over her years of exposing the inner workings of various gangs that ran the drug trade in Vancouver and the entire province of B.C. Rumours had circulated in the newsroom that one gang boss had actually ordered her and her son killed a few years earlier. Choy didn't know if the talk was true, but the veracity of the rumour wasn't as important as the fact that she had to work through it and many other threats over the years. He certainly doubted his capacity to continue working in the face of such risk to his kids. Maybe chasing this story would be a test of that.

The two issues he had with calling her were letting the story out of his control and Lee's reaction if he found out. While he could insist that James, before he showed her anything, agree to complete secrecy, how could he even broach the subject with Lee without risking a rupture in their relationship? While the idea of bringing in another reporter to work on the story had not been discussed, Choy had never mentioned a need for outside assistance and he doubted Lee would think it a reasonable request. The man didn't seem to have a very high opinion of journalists working in the mainstream media; in fact he had made a point of mentioning that not being employed by such a news outlet was one of the most important criteria he used to decide who to contact.

On the other hand, perhaps calling James is a way of asserting editorial independence — if Lee finds out and complains, my response will be: "The story belongs to me and I decide how best to proceed. I can't work any other way. If you don't like my rules, find somebody else." How would he react to that?

He needed to think about this some more before deciding what to do.

***

Choy spent three hours on the Directors Guild of America website entering Ken and Kenneth together with variations of last names ending in son, sen, sin, san, sun such as Fensin, Benson, Sensun, Sampson, etc. into the directory search engine. He found six names among the 16,000 members that seemed possibilities. He Googled each one to see if the age seemed right and if there was any mention of having made porn videos or of having worked on a film in Vancouver. Two of the six names belonged to directors over 70 years old and none of the others mentioned working in the "adult entertainment" industry. But three had at least one credit that was a film or TV show shot in Vancouver. He found contact information for two and emailed both, telling them he was trying to find the real name of a woman who was very good at impressions, was known by the name of Reb, had come to Vancouver by car with a man who had a job on a Vancouver shoot and who had died of a drug overdose. But the likelihood of a return email seemed so remote that he booked a sleeping car ticket on the Starlight Express Amtrak train to Los Angeles two days later.

***

"Who said I'm difficult to work with?" said Jan James, in a perpetually bass voice that seemed odd coming from someone who was less than five feet tall.

"Guys on the desk," said Choy. "You know how they talk about any reporter who stands up for herself."

"Assholes."

"Ya."

"The desk had a thing for me right back to the day I started. Twenty-two, a woman, a feminist, African-Canadian and I stood up for myself, I checked all the 60-year-old desker asshole alert buttons."

"So maybe something good has come out of dismantling the desk and shipping all the work to Hamilton," said Choy. "At least you don't need to deal with them anymore."

"I wish," she said. "But it's worse than ever. When they combined the two newsrooms we got two assistant city editors who think no story should be longer than eight inches."

She did like to write long. But to be fair, her stories explaining the latest intrigues among various gangs — who was trying to kill whom — required space that seldom existed in the tabloid *Province*. He'd heard from other former co-workers that the integration of two cultures — tab and broadsheet — had had some bumpy moments. But it wasn't primarily *Sun* reporters clashing with *Province* editors trying to chop their stories. It was also tab reporters wanting to write longer versions of their *Province* stories that now might appear in the broadsheet *Sun*. In Choy's experience few newspaper reporters were ever satisfied that they got enough space for their precious stories.

"And now with the layoffs announced last week, there's rumours we'll be filing everything straight to Hamilton," she added. "No more local editors. Good or bad. None. Can you imagine someone in Ontario trying to figure out the difference between the Westend, the Westside and West Vancouver?"

"Glad I'm gone," said Choy. "Freedom 47. I can write whatever I want, whenever I want, without having to worry about what my editor is going to think."

"I never worry about what an editor is going to think and I always write what I want, when I want," said James, who had a reputation of being permanently serious, but, if she trusted you, sometimes revealed a wicked a sense of humour.

"You never considered a buyout?"

"A single mother of two? My house mortgaged to the max?"

"Aren't your kids grown up?"

She shrugged.

"And didn't you buy the house almost 20 years ago? The mortgage can't be that big."

"Renovations, helping Quentin with a down payment for his apartment, Gaylin's school," she said, looking around his living room. "My father never owned a real estate empire across Vancouver."

She was from Halifax. Choy remembered her stories about a Black mother who was active in the 1960s Nova Scotia civil rights movement and a mostly absent White musician father who she chased to Vancouver, only to discover he was committing slow motion suicide by alcohol and various other substances. Maybe that's why she had gotten into covering the gang scene.

"Besides, what else would I do? I've got exactly the job I want."

"You aren't tired of it? You don't feel like you're writing the same stories over and over again after 25 years of covering gangs? Does anything really new, something you haven't seen before, happen?"

"Everything gets boring sometimes, but no one could replace me. I know stuff, people. If I leave, no one will shine a light on the world I cover. The criminals will disappear into the shadows and the people who profit from exploitation, violence, intimidation and human misery will get richer and more comfortable."

The world is a better place with driven, passionate people like her. You have to admire someone who believes in her journalism so thoroughly, even if she does sound a bit naïve.

"Speaking of human misery, before I show you what I've got, promise again you won't talk to anyone, or write about it, until I say okay?"

"I already promised." She had a way with glares.

"Okay then," Choy said, not entirely convinced this was a good idea. "Come into my office and I'll show you what I have."

***

"You're going to Los Angeles to see if you can find a 'boyfriend' who may or may not be working there now and you don't even know his name?" said his daughter. "Isn't that an awfully long shot?"

"He doesn't have any other leads," said his son, as they played cribbage.

"Thirty-one," said Choy and pegged two points.

"Who do you think Reb was?" said Sam. "Where was she from, what was her background? What made her become a drug addict?"

"Why does anybody become a drug addict?" said Ben.

"I'll bet she was from some small town in Alabama or Mississippi and in high school fell in love with a black guy who was like this great football player," said Sam. "Her Daddy, a Ku Klux Klan member, warned him to stop seeing his daughter, but he refused. A couple of weeks later, in the middle of the night, someone sets the boyfriend's house on fire and he has to rush upstairs to save his Momma. He gets her out, but then goes back upstairs to get his grandma's wedding ring, which he planned on giving Reb, but then has to jump out of a window to save himself. He breaks both ankles and can never play football again. No one ever proves it was Reb's Dad that set the house on fire, but everyone is pretty sure. So the boyfriend grows bitter and Reb's heart is broken and she finds a new boyfriend who is into drugs, but is white, and next thing you know she is a regular user."

"Oh come on," said Ben. "All that is from like movies or Shakespeare."

"I doubt if I'll find anything so romantic," said Choy. "She's more likely to have been a victim of sexual abuse. Apparently that's very common when they look at people who become prostitutes and drug addicts."

Both Sam and Ben became uncomfortable at his mention of sexual abuse. But better a little discomfort than being naïve and vulnerable. He was glad his ex-wife had insisted upon talking to their kids about abuse at an early age.

"Grandpa, do you want to play cribbage?" shouted Ben. "You can be on my team."

Ben's strategy to win any card or board game was to try playing on his grandfather's team. Despite being a lousy gambler he was an excellent card and game player.

"No," said their grandfather as he entered the kitchen. "I'm meeting someone in 15 minutes."

Choy gave his father a look to convey the message, 'I hope you're really meeting a friend and not going gambling.'

"Oh," lamented Ben.

"You'll have to face us on your own," said Choy. "Without the help of the king of cribbage."

Ben's grandfather smiled, then said: "See you later."

"Bye grandpa."

"Bye," said Sam.

Choy smiled, feeling good that his kids were finally getting comfortable living with his father in a neighbourhood that had once scared them.

"Twenty-four," said Sam, putting down her hand on the table, "and I win."

Given that Ben had been beaten at games hundreds of times by his sister, one would have thought he would be used to it, but as always, he was unable to hide his pain, which caused Sam to gloat, which hurt him even more.

"So who do you think Reb was?" Choy said to his son. "And what caused her to become a drug addict?"

Ben shrugged.

"Sam's made her prediction, now you. Let's see who gets closer to the truth. Maybe there will be a prize."

"A prize?" said Samantha.

"You can't change your guess now," said Ben.

"But I wasn't guessing or predicting. I was imagining the most romantic story."

"Dying on Cordoba Street with a needle stuck in your arm is not romantic," said Ben, who was warming to the idea of beating his sister at something.

"It's not fair," said Sam. "You should be told the rules of the game before you start playing."

Choy looked at his son as if to say, 'she has a point,' but he shook his head.

"Why should she get two chances and I only have one?"

Which gave Choy an idea. "You're right. Sam gets one more prediction and you get two."

He looked at his son and then at his daughter. They each nodded.

"What's the prize going to be?" said Sam.

"How about a special dedication at the beginning of my book about Reb?"

"You don't even know there's a good enough story to write a book," said Sam, giving him her special 'I'm-a-teenager-and-know-more-than-you look.' "There's got to be a better prize than that."

"Okay, how about a hundred dollars? You can spend it on anything you want or save it."

Their glowing faces revealed how much they preferred cash.

"But you have to take this seriously," continued Choy. "It's not just a game. This is person's life we're talking about. I'm trying to write a book that will give voice to someone who no longer has one. It's an important story. You know that in the past few months more than two people a day have been dying in B.C. from drug overdoses? I want you both to think about this, do some research, maybe figure out a few experts to talk to and interview them. What is the profile of the typical person who is dying? This will be a big help to me in writing Reb's story. You each get three days."

"You'll be in Los Angeles in three days," said Ben, displeased by learning there might be actual work involved in winning the prize.

"You both know how to email and phone. Maybe one of you will come up with something that points me in the right direction down in California."

***

After arguing with himself for hours, first on one side then the other, Choy finally decided it would be best to inform Lee about his interview with Billy-Bob and the trip to Los Angeles. While it might not be entirely ethical for a journalist to owe someone like

Lee a favour, the reality was he did. The only question was how much that favour was worth. Or to frame the query more concretely, how far out on the limb of poor journalism ethics was he prepared to crawl in order to pay back a man who had rescued his father from a $130,000 debt to violent criminals? The answer, for now, was: Far enough to break the rules of showing no fear and no favour. He was both scared of the position he was in — stuck between one certain and one likely major drug dealer — and enmeshed by a web of liability cleverly spun by someone who was undoubtedly a master of getting what he wanted. Choy was now certain that Lee and the fake bomb supposedly targeting his father arriving at his house at the same time was no coincidence. And the subject of his father's gambling debt coming up during their second meeting was part of a plan. Lee was someone who planned everything down to the finest detail.

After he phoned the number Lee had given him and left a message that he needed to meet, Choy sat in his office looking at a stack of photographs from the files on Billy-Bob that he had previously barely glanced at. The drill with contacting Lee included waiting with his laptop for a half hour, before he would get a Skype call on one of the 20 "clean" accounts he had been given. Each account was used once before moving on to the next on the list.

As Choy killed time by carefully studying each photograph for 10 seconds or so to see if there was something particularly significant in it, his thoughts wandered. Were all big-time drug dealers as charming as Billy-Bob and Mr. Lee? While the older man was more cultured and intellectually sophisticated, the kid from the Deep South possessed a sort of naïve, down-home allure that made you feel he could be trusted. It was probably the accent, which vaguely reminded Choy of old episodes of the Andy Griffith TV show that he watched as an 8-year-old with his grandma Rosa.

As the scent memory of his grandmother passed through his consciousness, something in one of the photographs caught his attention. In the foreground there was Billy-Bob shaking hands with a military officer from somewhere in south-eastern Asia, but in the background was a group of people looking on. One of them looked very much like Amanda Bennett, a prominent American 'alt-right' leader who he had written a series of stories about the previous summer for the *Vancouver Sun*. If she was in the picture, was there a connection between her and Billy-Bob's importation of drugs? He looked carefully at the series of a dozen photos taken at the same location, which looked like a military base. Bennett, or a woman who looked very much like her, was in more than half the pictures. This was an important discovery because Bennett had connections to some people in President Donald Trump's inner circle. If she was somehow connected to a major drug dealer and he could prove it, this was a major story that every newspaper in the United States, probably the world, would be interested in!

In his excitement he completely forgot his misgivings about meeting with Lee, and when he received instructions on Skype to go immediately to Crab Park, he almost ran the block and a half to Main Street and the few hundred metres further on the winding overpass that crossed the old CPR mainline track and neighbouring road to the waterfront green space that Choy remembered from his childhood as the location of abandoned piers and other port facilities.

Emerson Lee was sitting on a bench on top of a small grassy knoll that Choy remembered watching some earth moving machinery create just after Expo 86 while him and a few high school chums smoked a joint.

"Waylon, it is so very good to see you," Lee said, a fatherly smile portending a friendly conversation. "I thank you for your unexpected request that rescued me from a terribly boring evening with some people who were only pretending to be interested in my words because they wish to borrow rather large sums of money. I will trade that for this and a visit with you every time."

As Lee swung his arm to indicate the panoramic view of Burrard Inlet lit by a full moon was the 'this' he was referring to, Choy detected a hint of annoyance in his voice.

"Sorry I interrupted your meeting," he said, "but I have some important news and a few questions that can't wait."

"Yes?"

"Have you seen these photographs?" asked Choy, pulling out the half dozen copies he had made. "Do you recognize this woman?"

Lee shrugged as the poor light made it impossible for him to see. He motioned to one of his two bodyguards. The guy, who Lee always spoke to in Mandarin, sprinted the 25 or so metres from where he had been stationed. Lee said something Choy didn't understand and the guard pulled a flashlight from his coat pocket, which he carefully handed over, then retreated back.

"Who is she?" said Lee, after staring at the picture for a few seconds.

"I think it is Amanda Bennett, the head of the Committee of One Thousand, one of the most notorious right wing ..."

"I know who Amanda Bennett is," Lee answered.

"I've seen her up close and personal numerous times, and I'm almost certain this is her," said Choy. "You realize what this means?"

"Almost certain?"

"She's in the background, a little out of focus, so ..."

"You cannot be certain."

"I might have a way of confirming this."

Once again Lee was giving him that inscrutable faux Charlie Chan look.

"If we can link Billy-Bob Baker to Amanda Bennett there are an awful lot of media outlets that would be interested in this story."

"To embarrass the new president of the United States," said Lee, with concern in his voice rather than excitement.

"*New York Times, Washington Post*, CNN, *Globe and Mail*, we'd be able to pick anyone we want."

"I must consult my clients," Lee said, his lack of enthusiasm dampening Choy's mood. "This may change everything."

"Your clients may not be interested in drawing a link between someone in Donald Trump's inner circle and a major drug importer?"

"This was not the story intended."

"It's a way, way, way better story," Choy said quickly.

"You said you could not be certain it was Amanda Bennett."

"But I might have a way of finding out."

Lee asked him to continue without saying a word.

"I was interviewing Billy-Bob when he had to leave abruptly, so Svetlana Borovsky, his assistant — Russian and very beautiful — gave me this card and ..."

"You spoke to Billy-Bob and Svetlana?" Lee interjected. "When?"

"A few days ago," answered Choy, realizing this conversation was headed exactly where he originally feared it would lead. "It was for my story about the woman I found dead on the street."

"A few days ago? And you didn't think to mention this to me?"

"We haven't spoken and I've been busy. I called you tonight because I realized you'd want to know and also I'm going to Los

Angeles tomorrow morning to work on my story about the dead woman. I thought you'd want to know about that as well."

Lee stared at him for a few moments and then raised his hand, which caused his two bodyguards to come running. As they neared, Lee opened his hand, motioning them to stop.

"Waylon, I am very disappointed in you."

Lee stood up and walked towards his car, the two bodyguards on either side of him.

5.

Even though the ride through Washington and Oregon was uneventful, his conversation with Lee the night before had thrown Choy off balance and put him on constant alert. Rather than enjoying the scenery from the dome car and the soothing, sleep-inducing clackity-clack of the moving train, he stewed over what Lee being 'disappointed' meant.

Was it a threat? Should I respond? At least talk to him about it?

If Lee told me to drop the story linking Billy-Bob with Amanda Bennett would I? It's an important story with international implications. But what happens if I 'disappoint' Lee, again?

It was a question that seemed better left unanswered.

When the winter daylight disappeared in southern Oregon, he ate by himself in a half empty dining car and immediately retired to his foldout bed compartment. An entire Michael Didbin Italian mystery later sleep came, but fitful and ripe with anxiety.

He was having a dream about having a dream. Asleep, but sitting in a theatre watching himself sleep, his randomly firing synapses projected his dream onto a giant curved screen in an Omnimax dome, like the one at Vancouver's Science World. In the movie his daughter Samantha was driving his restored AMC convertible down Cordoba Street along the south side of Oppenheimer Park heading to the block where he discovered Reb's body. Sam was lecturing him about how private automobiles were destroying the planet and how she was really doing him and the world a favour by crashing the gas guzzling, carbon spewing vehicle into the side of the chicken processing plant just a few feet away from where a needle dangled from the dead prostitute's pulseless arm. The version of him that sat in the movie theatre watched the car speed, in slow motion, up onto the sidewalk as he marvelled at the size of the image being projected onto the curved screen above and in front of him. The version of him that was inside the car was being lectured by his daughter that the only people who needed cars in cities were those who could not walk and feeling the shame of his daughter's moral superiority he looked down at his lap where stumps rather than legs were attached to his torso. When he looked up again it was no longer Samantha, his daughter, who was driving the car, but a nude Amanda Bennett, the leader of the extreme right wing Committee of One Thousand. As the version of him who was in the car glanced at her breasts then looked up to her face, she made eye contact and smirked. The version of him who was in the movie theatre watched in horror as Amanda laughed and drove his car across the spot where Reb had died and straight into the cinder block wall of the chicken processing plant.

Choy's pants were buzzing. It was the cellphone inside the right pocket of his jeans hanging from the metal hook on the other side of the small compartment. He almost fell off the bed as he reached for it.

"Is she there? On the train?"

He recognized Lee's voice but failed to understand the meaning of his words.

"Svetlana Borovsky? She's there, isn't she? What has she said?"

On the train. Sleeping. A very weird dream.

Samantha was his ex-wife's choice of a name for their daughter. He had agreed, but never really liked it. It had always reminded him of the witch with that name in the TV series Bewitched.

"Waylon," repeated Mr. Lee. "Can you talk? Is she there, right now, with you?"

"Who?" he finally managed to attain a level of consciousness that allowed him to understand and speak. "I am sorry, I was asleep. You woke me from a dream."

"Where are you?"

"In my compartment, on the train."

Where else would I be?

"Have you reached Oakland?"

"I don't know, I've been sleeping. I don't think so."

He raised the window blind. The signs of urban activity were everywhere.

"It looks like we're just pulling into a station." He looked at the time on his cellphone screen. "If we're on time, this is Oakland."

"Good. She'll be getting on the train once you pull in."

"How do you know that?"

Lee did not answer. He obviously had someone from Billy-Bob's inner circle working for him.

"Are you warning me about something?" Choy said.

"I thought you would like a heads up," said Lee. "That is what you journalists call a notification before something happens?"

"Yes, that's what we call it."

"Do not underestimate this woman."

He called to tell me this?

"She's not to be trusted, very dangerous and devious. You must not speak to her."

I must not speak to her? Did he really just say that or am I still dreaming?

"Please Emerson, do not interfere with how I choose to research my story."

"Your story?"

"It's either my story or someone else's," said Choy slowly, to illustrate his anger at Lee's words and tone. "My story done my way or not. You choose."

His silence suggested a calculation.

"We had an arrangement," said Lee. "I completed my side of the bargain."

"And I will complete mine, if you let me."

Another silence.

"Why do you need to speak to her?" Lee said.

"To find out if the person in the photographs is Amanda Bennett."

"I don't care about that."

"I do." He immediately regretted his tone but what choice did he have? He had to assert his independence.

"We'll see about that."

If he's trying to scare me, he's doing a decent job.

"Well, thanks for the heads up," said Choy trying to end the conversation. "If Svetlana is paying me a visit I need to shake the cobwebs, clean up and eat."

"You are making a mistake Waylon."

"It won't be my first or my last." As soon as he said it Choy realized that Lee could make certain it was his last.

"Please reconsider."

"No one would respect me as a journalist, not even you, if I stopped pursuing a lead simply because someone told me not to."

"You don't understand," said Lee.

"You're right, I don't. Why don't you explain it to me?"

"I have made my expectation clear, have I not Waylon?"

"As have I."

"Good-bye then."

"Good-bye."

Lee was obviously angry, which made Choy nervous. But, while pissing off powerful people was risky, it was what good journalists were supposed to do. That was a comfort. On the other hand, perhaps sensible good journalists were more deferential, or at least careful, around violent, powerful people.

What am I doing?

***

It wasn't until the train was a few minutes south of Paso Robles that the porter knocked on his door and handed him an envelope.

"A very beautiful young lady asked me to give you this," the sixtyish, distinguished looking Black man said with a smile suggesting exactly how beautiful he thought she was.

"Thank you," said Choy, uncertain if he was supposed to hand over some cash for this service, but decided that doing so would be rude, crass and demeaning, even if it was expected, so he simply smiled and opened the envelope as the porter waited. "I understand you wish to speak with me. If five minutes from now in your compartment works for you, please tell the porter, yes."

In my compartment? That's not a good idea.

"Does she know my compartment number?"

"No," he answered, smiling. "But I'll tell her if you want me to."

"Is there somewhere else private we could meet?" asked Choy.

"Not as private as here."

Did he wink?

The twinkle in the porter's eyes suggested any man who had the opportunity to be alone with a woman like her would be a fool not to take it.

If he knew what she does for a living would he be so keen?

He looked at the porter and returned the smile. "Tell the lady, yes."

Choy spent the next few minutes preparing himself for her arrival. Despite the five-minute warning from the porter, he was startled by the knock on his sliding door. He was still seated when Svetlana Borovsky let herself in.

"Waylon, it is good to see you again," she said, kissing him on one cheek and then the other.

He did his best to pretend this was expected and normal. She was again dressed conservatively; a stranger would assume a businesswoman, probably a Silicon Valley executive taking a carbon-light train ride to Los Angeles for an important meeting.

"You're looking very good," she said, her smile sly and suggestive.

I'm imagining that.

"I must take off jacket," she said. "It is too warm in here."

Choy tried to look away as she undid the buttons on the front of her suit jacket, then had trouble extricating her right arm from the sleeve in the small space where both of them remained standing. Struggling with the jacket, her face and breasts ended up an inch away from him.

"I'm sorry, could you please ..."

He froze as the squirming pushed her breasts against his chest.

"Please."

A moment of embarrassment passed as he realized she was asking him to help with her sleeve. He quickly manoeuvred behind her, but she turned in the same direction as if they were partners dancing cheek to cheek. Her breasts remained pressed against his chest and Choy could feel blood rushing to his face. Both of them stopped moving and, as he looked into her eyes, a demur smile appeared.

"Let me, please."

What does she mean?

"You stay still and I will move."

He could not have done otherwise.

Her wiggling movements produced a feeling much like the first time he and Joy were naked in bed together. Scared, but excited.

Finally, after a few more seconds of contortion, her arm was successfully extricated from its recalcitrant sleeve. She looked embarrassed and genuinely flustered and her momentary vulnerability made her appear human, certainly less frightening than a Russian drug dealer. Then the sweet smile that followed convinced Choy she was not as dangerous or unremittingly evil as previously suspected. Even Vaudeville greats like Charlie Chaplin would have required hours of rehearsal to pull off that shtick. Her vulnerability had to be genuine.

"Why I am so clumsy today?" she said, sitting down while fumbling with the folded jacket. "Even my English goes away."

"Let me hang that up," said Choy, gaining confidence as he took the jacket.

"Being alone with man I barely know in tiny room on train."

"We could go to the dome car if you prefer," he said, her vulnerability making him feel manly, gallant even. It was an exotic feeling for someone normally discomforted by women who moved too easily into his personal space.

"No, this good, you are gentleman," she said. "I am correct?"

"Yes, of course."

"Some men I must deal with in this business cannot be trusted — animals — but you I think are safe. Is correct?"

Being described as "safe" was both pleasing and deflating.

"Even my ex-wife, who dislikes me intensely, would acknowledge I always treat women with respect."

"You are divorced? With children?"

"Two."

"Girls?"

"One of each."

I'm six inches away from a beautiful, dangerous drug dealer, discussing my children and ex-wife and it seems so ... not extraordinary.

He smiled. To himself at first, but then invited her in.

"What Billy-Bob says about me is not true."

What does she mean?

"He talks like he is pimp and I am prostitute."

He shrugged and shook his head as if disagreeing.

"I know what he says about me." She touched his arm in a gesture of reassurance.

"He's charming, but very crude," Choy answered.

"Crude is good word for Billy-Bob."

Her fingers remained touching his forearm. Even though it felt comfortable, he remembered Lee's warning.

She is beautiful, but …

He was already deep enough in treacherous water. And Joy.

"How did you get involved with him? And the drug business?" he asked, moving his arm enough to send a message.

"I needed job," she said abruptly, taking her hand away.

"There was an ad in a newspaper?"

"I meet him at meeting."

"What sort of meeting?"

"Political meeting."

"You're interested in politics?"

"I had boyfriend who wanted to show me off, 'tall Russian girl with beautiful white skin', he said. These people at political meeting, white was very important."

"At a white nationalist meeting, that's where you met Billy-Bob?" said Choy excited about this information, which seemed to suggest a link to Amanda Bennett was possible, even likely.

"He was speaker at meeting, very good speaker," she said. "Talked about how white people must stick together."

"I wrote an important story last year about a woman from the white nationalist movement, Amanda Bennett. Very beautiful, like you."

She smiled.

"Billy-Bob is good friend with that woman. You think she is more beautiful than me?"

Saying this she put her hand on top of his.

"Did Billy-Bob tell you to seduce me?"

The humiliating truth.

"Does it matter?" She stared into his eyes as her fingers moved up his arm.

"Yes, it does," said Choy, standing. "I have a girlfriend who I love very much and you are a very smart woman, who should respect herself more than she does."

In an instant, Svetlana's sexy eyes turned into the tips of very sharp spears. "It is just sex. What does that have to do with respect?"

"You know what I mean."

"Da. Men who conquer many women are great heroes. Women who conquer many men are sluts."

A feminist analysis was not what he expected.

"Fair enough, but I still don't want to have sex with you."

"I see the way you look at me."

"You are very beautiful, but I'm a journalist and must remain objective." As the words came out he realized how ridiculous they sounded.

"Why did you ask to meet?"

"Why does Billy-Bob want you to have sex with me?" he answered, quickly.

"To have power over you."

"That's what sex is? A means to get people to do what you want them to do?"

"In my university in Russia there was professor who studied bonobos, close relatives of chimpanzees, but much less aggressive, more peaceful. Why? Because everyone fucks. Males, females, it does not matter, they all like each other after they fuck. No fighting, no wars, just fucking. They are all friends."

An interesting point.

"I think your first answer was the right one; Billy-Bob wants power over me."

"Same thing. Your business schools have name for it: networking."

Another interesting point.

"What else did Billy–Bob instruct you to do, to me or for me or whatever?"

"He does not instruct me."

"After we fucked what were you going to tell me?"

She stared at him for a few seconds before answering.

"We want you to know, as far as we are concerned, you are white man," she said. "Despite your name."

Is she serious? What does that even mean?

"What does that even mean?" he verbalized the second part of his thought.

"You are one of us."

"One of you?"

"Our kind."

He stared, flabbergasted and amazed — not surprised, after all she was a white supremacist — that anyone in 2017 talked like this, or worse, actually believed there was such a thing as a white person, let alone that he was one of them, and calling someone that was a form of flattery.

"Wow, I've never been called a white man before."

She seemed both perplexed and pleased by his reaction.

"You actually think that is a compliment?" he said.

"You find me too politically incorrect for your liberal tastes?"

"I find it hard to believe that someone who seems as smart as you, actually believes there is anything at all to the notion of 'white people'. You do know that there's absolutely no biological or genetic basis to the very notion of race?"

"There are many biological and genetic differences among people."

"Not based on the colour of their skin; certainly not on whether they have white skin or black skin or yellow skin. Read the science. Human beings' greatest genetic variation exists amongst black skinned people living inside Africa, not between what ignorant people stuck in the nineteenth century call races."

"I am not racist," she said. "I am defender of white, northern-European Christian culture against persecution and genocide."

"You're saying, contrary to all economic evidence that shows the descendants of white, Christian northern Europeans are the wealthiest, most powerful ethnic group in the world, white people are persecuted?"

"Jews are wealthiest, most powerful ethnic group in the world."

"But they're not white enough people for you?"

"Whether Jews are white people is much debated. Billy-Bob says we are all part of great Judeo-Christian culture, followers of Old Testament."

"So are Muslims, but I bet Billy-Bob doesn't consider them part of his culture."

The two of them stared at each other.

Does she have a gun?

"You are angry, but I did not come here to have argument," she finally said. "Perhaps I should leave."

"Perhaps you should."

"What about your questions for Billy-Bob?"

"Like you said, I can email them."

"How long will you stay in Los Angeles?"

"As long as it takes to get what I need."

"Where are you staying?"

"Downtown," he knew the name of the hotel, but did not offer it.

"We will be in city for few days. Better to meet Billy-Bob for lunch."

"Sure," he replied, despite having decided not to have anything more to do with Svetlana or Billy-Bob. "Get back to me with a time and a place."

As soon as Svetlana left, he wrote an email to TwoSpiritPhoenix, the cover name for a computer hacker who had offered his or her services six months earlier. Choy needed some information to gain an edge on Billy-Bob and Lee. They were both trying to manipulate him. To what end?

***

The 20-block walk to the hotel from Union Station, pulling his rolling overnight bag, would have been pleasant in the light sweater-ish LA winter evening, except for all the homeless people on the sidewalks and benches. He thought Vancouver was bad, but Los Angeles was obviously much worse. Then the phone call from Lee really soured his mood.

"You didn't call me after you talked to her," Lee said, skipping all salutations and pleasantries.

"Mr. Lee, I can barely hear you. I'm walking on a sidewalk in downtown Los Angeles."

"What did she say, Waylon?" His curtness suggested anger, although he was much too polite to actually raise his voice. "I am paying for your trip. The least you can do is keep me informed."

"Svetlana said nothing important."

"Did she try to seduce you?"

She obviously has a reputation.

"Yes."

"I warned you about her."

"You did."

"So?"

"She tried and I resisted, then we talked, but the conversation ended rather abruptly."

"Why?"

"Because she said I was a white man," Choy said, thinking his words would provoke laughter.

"She said you were white?"

"She said Billy-Bob and her considered me white."

The pregnant silence suggested Lee didn't think Svetlana's racial musings were amusing.

"But you do know who you are."

So who or what does Lee think I am?

"Who am I?" Choy said out loud.

"Chinese," said Lee. "A Choy, the descendant of the fifth son of King Wen of Zhou. Your lineage can be traced back over three thousand years."

Not a smart guy, or a good-looking man, or an ethical person, or a quality journalist, but Chinese.

He had never before considered ethnicity as a defining feature of his being. How could anybody think that important?

Lee, Borovsky, Billy-Bob obviously think it is. What's wrong with these people?

"Are you Chinese before you're a businessman or an intellectual or a lover of fine foods and wine?" he asked.

"I'm a Chinese businessman, a Chinese intellectual and a Chinese gourmand," Lee answered.

"I don't understand this attachment to a generalization as broad as White or Chinese," said Choy. "What does it even mean? White, Chinese, Black, Indian — they all come in different shapes, sizes, degrees of intelligence, emotional empathy, character. Those are the things I judge myself and others on, not race or ethnicity."

"You are Chinese," repeated Lee.

"I'm one-thirty-second Chinese," I got the name, the brand that says Chinese, but not the contents."

"You are Chinese," Lee said for a third time.

This is important to him. Why?

"White, Chinese, what difference does it make?"

"Who you are is not important?" Lee answered, pronouncing each word carefully, to signify their profundity.

"I am neither White, nor Chinese, but I am also White and Chinese. I'm a Canadian, a British Columbian with ancestors from all corners of humanity."

"Your words mean nothing. There is no such thing as Canadian."

"Why? Because we were British or French when the nineteenth century inventors of race divided up the world?"

"Perhaps if you were aboriginal."

"I've got a little bit of that."

"You are Chinese. Be proud of who you are."

"I am proud of who I am, Chinese and every other bit of me."

Why am I even talking to this rich, racist drug dealer? Either of them.

6.

That evening in his Japantown hotel room Choy tried to work on the story Lee wanted him to write about BBB and Svetlana, but it just wasn't there for him. There was no clear angle to take and no obvious lede, the writing of which was sometimes enough to get a difficult story going. All he had was a bunch of details, but even when he thought of them as facts, the essence of the story was missing. He had the who, what, where and when, but absolutely no why. Sure, he could write a straight-up crime story — we have evidence some bad guys did this and that and what are the police going to do about it — but doing so would feel too much like accepting Lee's bribe. He needed a meaningful story to justify his significant lapse in journalistic ethics.

How do I tell Lee I can't write it? How will he respond?

On the 8 a.m. walk to the Red Line station, the 20-minute ride on a train and then a short bus trip to the Directors Guild of America offices on Sunset Boulevard, Choy tried to focus on Reb and a plan of attack that would get the most out of his time in Los Angeles. First up was to get contact information for Kenneth Dobson, or another Ken with the right sounding last name who might have driven to Vancouver with Reb.

Employing an old reporters' trick he'd learned on one of his first assignments with a veteran photographer, he bought four fruit scones, along with a hot chocolate at a coffee shop down the street from the office building where he was headed. As he approached the receptionist, he put his hot chocolate on the counter and took one of the scones from his laptop bag.

"Hello," he said in his most friendly voice. "I don't suppose you want one of my scones. They were two for one, but I can't really eat two of them. It's blueberry and very good."

The treat and his friendliness earned a sympathetic hearing for his tale about a woman practically dying in his arms and how he wanted to tell the world her story but didn't know her real name and how the one person who might be able to help had a first name of Ken or Kenneth, a last name ending in 'son' and worked as an assistant director on a production shot in Vancouver about four or five years earlier.

"You need to speak with Latrice, honey. She's the guardian and master of our database. She can search that thing in a thousand different ways. Let me call her for you."

The second scone went to Latrice, who probably didn't need more incentive than proving her mastery of the database, but certainly enjoyed the pastry as she listened to Choy's story, then immediately tried multiple combinations of Ken, Kenneth, K. with last names consisting of a wildcard and endings with son, soon, sen, senn, sun, sunn, sin, sinn, sann and syn, and synn. That generated a list of fourteen possibilities, but when she cross referenced those with working as an assistant director on a Vancouver-based production in the past seven years, only three names came up, one of which was for a job six months earlier. That was Ken Dobson. Ken Massen worked in Vancouver as an AD in 2012 and Kenneth Poulsen in 2013.

"Is it possible for you to give me their contact information?" asked Choy, employing the friendliest smile he owned.

"You know I'm not supposed to do that? We have a privacy policy."

"Which I fully support, but I'm guessing that if one of these two guys knew Reb, he'd want to help find her family. Don't you think?"

She stared intensely into his eyes, then made a point of making sure he saw her checking if anyone was watching or listening.

"They'll never know it was you who gave me their contact information. I'll tell them Reb's friend remembered their name."

She continued to think about what to do, then wrote the contact information on a piece of paper. She held it out for him to take, but quickly pulled it back.

"How the hell did you get the name Choy?" she said.

"My grandfather changed his name from Bonderoff," he answered, a true statement, although misleadingly incomplete.

"To Choy? Why?"

"Why do you think?" he answered, but seeing the confusion on Latrice's face decided to explain. "Because that should have been his name all along."

"Should have been? Now I'm really confused."

"I had a great-great-grandfather who wanted to pass as White," he answered, the first time he had ever told this part of the story to a stranger. "So he changed his name from Choy to Bonderoff, which was his wife's maiden name."

Latrice nodded. "I heard about that sort of thing in Black families but never knew it happened with Chinese too."

"Chinese-Canadians were not allowed to vote until 1947 and that was only reversed then because the Chinese Exclusion Act had to be repealed when Canada joined the United Nations."

"The White man's world is a cruel, unfair place for the rest of us," she said.

"Amen," answered Choy.

She handed him the piece of paper. "Most people who try to use this data base to find someone run into a big brick wall named Latrice. But I like you. You're a good person. I like people who tell the truth."

"Thank you," he said, embarrassed but enjoying the easy intimacy that had blossomed between them. "You're a good person too."

What do I do now? Just leave?

"Well, go on, get out of here; I've got work to do" she said, returning to her intimidating big woman voice. "Go find Reb's family and write your book."

Choy stood and smiled one more time. He felt like walking over and hugging her but thought it would be inappropriate.

"Go on," Latrice repeated.

"Is it okay if I acknowledge you when I write my book?"

"I'd rather a free copy."

"I'd like to do both."

"Yes, that would be nice," she said, then made a show of turning her attention back to the computer screen.

"Thank you again," he said, feeling like he had not adequately expressed his appreciation.

She waved him away, keeping her eyes on the screen.

He smiled and turned around, thinking about how secretaries and other such "clerical" or "information" workers are holders of many secrets and key to discovering the truth about politicians, bankers, businessmen and anonymous junkies dead from needles still dangling from their arms.

***

Both the ramen in pork broth and the outcome of conversation at lunch with Max Parker were excellent. Five years earlier Max had been a junior *Los Angeles Times* reporter working on a gossip piece about a certain A-list Hollywood star who had trashed a West Vancouver rented house while on a movie shoot in the Lower Mainland and Choy had given him both background and contacts, enabling the *Times* to scoop the *Sun* in its own backyard. Max had been extremely grateful — not that this gift was an act of generosity — Choy hated both this sort of celebrity story and the city editor who had given him the assignment. Plus there was a better, more important and pressing story that required phone calls and an in-person interview, a fact ignored by an editor whose news sense extended no further than watching TV and following orders.

"That's a really great story," said Max after Choy told him about Reb and trying to find out who she was and what had happened in her life before ending up dead on a Vancouver street. "A young white woman, the opioid crisis, fentanyl, prostitution and a Hollywood connection."

"I didn't say she was white."

"But she is, isn't she?"

"Was. She was white. They turn a kind of blue after a few hours in the refrigerator," said Choy, feeling annoyed at too many people's focus on race, the very concept of which was ridiculous.

"I want to do a story about your search for this guy," said Max. "Can you come to the newsroom and we'll get a picture of you at a desk? Maybe some video."

"Now?"

"Yes. This is way better than what I was working on. This is exactly what the managing editor loves. Bottom of the front page in tomorrow's print edition and top-10 in hits online. If this guy is anywhere in southern California, he'll know you are looking for him."

***

When his cellphone buzzed while walking into the hotel lobby and he saw the 323 area code Choy expected the caller to be one of the two Kens responding to his morning emails or phone messages, but instead it was Svetlana Borovsky, who was all friendly again and said she and Billy-Bob wanted to meet with him so he could finish his interview. Despite his attempts to brush her off, she was persistent and insisted on arranging another meeting. She knew where he was staying, which didn't completely surprise him but nonetheless was unsettling, and offered to come to the hotel in a few minutes to pick him up.

"I'm still an hour away," he answered, trying to at least buy some time to think about a more neutral, safer location.

"No you're not," she answered. "You just walked into the lobby."

His immediate reaction was to swing around looking for a tail, but then realized, based on his experience with tracking devices the previous summer, she had probably planted one, or even multiple ones, on him during her visit to the train compartment. All that embarrassing effort to remove her coat in a confined space was cover for attaching miniature antennae to his clothes.

"You're having me followed?"

"Don't be angry," she said in a little girl's voice, almost as if she were parodying Shirley Temple. "It is for protection. People want to hurt you."

"You've moved into the protection racket as well as drugs," he said, looking around the lobby more carefully, just in case she did have someone following him.

As he turned, there was a tap on his shoulder. Svetlana stood two feet away, wearing a smile that would suit a new fiancé surprising her lover.

"Surprise!" she said, throwing her arms around him, quickly giving him a hug and then a kiss directly on the lips. Next she interlocked her fingers into his right hand and pulled him to the nearby sofa where she sat him down and snuggled in beside him. It all happened so fast he had no chance to resist, or perhaps he simply enjoyed attention from a beautiful woman.

Before he had a chance to say anything or pull away, she whispered in his ear: "You see big guy by front desk — don't look — he has letters 'AB' tattooed on hand. You know what that means?"

She giggled as if telling some private joke. Choy discretely looked in the direction of the front desk. A muscular man, late thirties dressed in blue jeans, blue shirt and a leather jacket was reading a sightseeing brochure, or at least attempting to look like he was. He couldn't exactly make them out, but there were definitely tattoos on both hands. Tom Tennyson, who killed his friend Adam the previous summer, had been a member of the Aryan Brotherhood and also had an AB tattooed on his hand.

Perhaps it was best to keep up the pretence that he and Borovsky were an item, so he smiled then positioned himself to speak quietly into her ear.

"Is he a friend of Tom Tennyson?"

"I don't know who that is," she said.

"The white supremacist I put in jail for murdering my gay journalist friend."

"That would explain this awkward situation," she said.

"How the hell does he know I'm here? Did you tell him?"

She giggled again and then it was her turn to whisper. "Your Mr. Lee told him. Well probably not him directly and probably not Mr. Lee, but someone who works for him told one of this guy's associates."

Why would Lee do that? What's going on?

"Why?" Choy said.

"Because you would think Billy-Bob. He wants you to believe we are enemy."

"I hardly need any convincing of that."

She pulled away and smiled at him, then kissed him full on the mouth again, this time her tongue attempting entry into his mouth. As he resisted, she pulled away, smiled once more and whispered.

"Play along to save life. If he learns who I am we are both dead."

"Members of the Aryan Brotherhood are not Billy-Bob's best friends?"

"Don't call themselves that anymore, has been political disagreement."

"They want to kill us both?"

"They might only want to scare you, but for many months I am on 'eliminate' list."

"You're saying I could give you up and be safe?"

She moved in front of him. He smiled then leaned forward to close the three inches between their lips. When he pulled away from the wooden kiss, a frown covered her face.

"Raymond hates race mixers and homosexuals and has killed at least ten people, not counting time in Marines, a few just for fun."

Does she think I am homosexual, like Adam?

"Even before political disagreement Billy-Bob thought this man is crazy."

Maybe she thinks all journalists are homosexuals.

"I can walk away because he thinks I am girlfriend. Is that what you want? Leave you alone with him?"

Why am I not scared?

"We need plan," she said, her face remaining only a few inches from his.

Why would I believe anything she tells me?

"Maybe you should leave me alone with him," Choy finally said, forming his own plan, free from Svetlana's powers of persuasion. "You carry a gun?"

She nodded.

She doesn't scare me anymore. Is that a good or bad thing?

"And you do still travel with one or more of those bodyguards?"

"He comes here with me but no sign of trouble, so I say go have coffee," she answered, pushing her face even closer to his so they appeared to be kissing. "I can handle you on my own."

What does she mean by that?

"But you could get him here quickly, right?"

She nodded slightly.

"So you're going to stand up, lean over and kiss me good-bye and then head for the exit," he whispered. "But first, take one of the two room key cards from my right pocket. Make it seem part of the lovey-dovey act."

He felt her hands begin to roam. It was not a bad feeling.

"I'll go to the gift shop and look at magazines for ten minutes. Is that enough time for you and your bodyguard to get up to my room?"

She kissed him, which he took as a 'yes'.

"You know the number?"

She kissed him again. He could feel her fingers inside his pant pocket retrieving the plastic card.

"What number?" she said.

"Seven oh seven."

"You sure this way is best? He may shoot you in elevator or hallway."

"I don't think so; his kind want to say something first," Choy answered, trying to sound confident despite the onset of a feeling that he was sinking in one of those oozing, dark Port Moody low tide mud pits that he had written a story about years before and which had, for some reason, haunted him in the occasional nightmare since. He needed to know if Svetlana was telling him the truth about Lee sending an Aryan Brotherhood member to scare him and this might be the only way to find out. "You guys hide in the bathroom until he starts threatening to hurt or kill me. I want to ask him some questions first, if I can."

She gave him a quizzical look, stood up, kissed him as instructed and walked straight to the exit. Choy pulled his cellphone from his pocket, pretended to check messages for a few minutes and then headed to the gift shop, where he stood in front of the magazine rack, fondled various publications then purchased a *Wall Street Journal*. He was thinking about how much better he had liked the look of that paper before they began running photos as he tried to give the impression of reading a front page story while walking through the lobby to the elevator.

What if she didn't make it up there? What if she changed her mind and decided to let Raymond do whatever he was going to do?

As he stood waiting for the elevator Choy felt someone come up behind him.

Don't look. It has to be Raymond.

As the bell sounded to indicate the car's arrival, it occurred to Choy that he could safely turn around and walk to the bar or straight out of the hotel, but he didn't. He was determined not to show these bullies any fear. He walked to the back of the mirrored elevator car and turned around. Two young Japanese tourists and Raymond followed him in. One of the two twenty-something women pressed the button for the twelfth floor, while Raymond acted like he was searching his coat pocket for something. Choy leaned forward and pressed the '7' button. Raymond immediately moved to press the same one. When he saw the button already lit he nodded then backed up, taking up a position beside Choy at the rear of the car and took out a cellphone. When the door opened on the seventh floor Raymond stared at something on his screen, cover for waiting until Choy exited and walked down the hallway towards his room.

Stay calm and pretend like everything is normal.

Choy pulled the remaining key card from his pocket. When he turned to face the door Raymond was only about a metre behind him, walking briskly, but with his eyes apparently still glued to the cellphone screen. As Choy pressed the card against the locking pad a green light came on and he put his shoulder into the door as he turned the handle. The man following him had timed his approach perfectly and the shove from behind caused Choy to stumble into his room, almost falling to the floor. When he recovered his balance and turned Raymond stood in front of the closed door, a large black gun in his right hand.

"What do you want? Who are you?" said Choy, trying to act like someone who was about to be robbed.

"I'm a friend of Tom Tennyson. Remember him, you faggot half-breed?"

How to play this, deferential or confrontational?

"Why are you here?" Choy said, backing further into the room.

"Tom asked me to say hello," Raymond said, smiling and waving his gun like a conductor in front of an orchestra.

"How did you know where to find me?"

"We have our sources."

"Who is we?"

"The Aryan People's Party."

"That's the new name for the Aryan Brotherhood?"

He did not answer as he looked around the room.

"What have you got against gay people and half-breeds?" said Choy, trying to distract the guy from looking in the bathroom. "Not that I am either. I'm heterosexual and a mongrel breed. Probably about 40 percent northern European, four percent Chinese and 56 percent from here and there all over the world."

"Fucking race mixer."

"I'm glad you brought that up. I meant to ask Tom about it, when he said the same thing about me. What do you mean by race mixer? You know we're all descended from the same woman back in Africa a hundred thousand years ago, right?"

"Liberal, communist, Jew bullshit."

"Okay, even if you don't believe that, what about all the people who lived on the edges of Europe, between there and Asia, between there and Africa? Were they like race mixers or entirely different races? You see what I'm getting at? How long does it take for what you call race mixers to become an entirely new race? Genghis Khan and his men fucked their way across Asia all the way into Europe a thousand years ago. Were they race mixers and if so what do you call their descendants a few centuries later? Apparently there are millions of them all over Europe and Asia. Or how do you classify the Huns and their offspring? They were nomads moving around from eastern Europe to central Asia for hundreds of years, more than a thousand years ago. You don't think they fucked the locals wherever they went? Or the Roman legionnaires who might have been stationed anywhere from England to North Africa or Syria. You don't think they were fucking around? I mean the whole history of homo sapiens is people moving from one part of the world to another and fucking around. Scientists say we even interbred with the Neanderthals. So everybody must have been race mixers at some point. How long did they have to stay in one spot before you and your Aryan brothers call them a new race?"

The words came out fast with barely any spaces between them and it felt like he hadn't stopped to breathe. Raymond's face grew sour as he pointed the pistol at Choy's chest, then up to his head.

Never argue with a man pointing a gun at you — probably advice worth following.

"Hold on, hold on," said Choy wagging his finger. "Why are you doing this?"

"Because you have a chink name and you're a race mixer and you sent my comrade to jail for life."

"Tom sodomized and beat my friend to death with a pipe."

"Faggot friend."

"You don't think he should pay a price for that?"

"He should be given a medal," said Raymond, his smile returning. "for killing a degenerate, just like I should get one for ridding the planet of a race mixer."

Never argue with a man pointing a gun at you. Unless you think there's someone on the other side of the bathroom door who also has a gun and reason to protect you.

"I need to correct something you said. Tom pled guilty because the people he was working for made a deal with the cops for him to be the fall guy and take all the blame. I never even testified because there was no trial, so how could I have "sent your comrade to jail for life'?"

"Tom was no 'fall guy' and it was his idea to take all the blame for the cause."

"His idea?"

"Ya," said Raymond. "You journalists are all alike, thinking you're so smart and people like us so stupid. Tom got enough money from playing off that traitor Amanda Bennett against the police spy George Mason to keep the Aryan People's Party flush for the next decade. He made a noble sacrifice. He's a hero and all he asked was for us to finish some business he started."

"You mean killing me?"

"You said it, not me."

"Okay, I can buy that, but how did Tom know that I was going to be in Los Angeles and at this hotel when he's in prison?"

"All sorts of stuff can be arranged from prison if you have the right connections."

"There were very few friends who knew I was coming."

"Maybe one of your 'friends' isn't exactly so friendly."

"What are you saying?"

"What am I saying?" Raymond said. "How about maybe even real chinks don't like race mixers. Is that clear enough for you?"

"Emerson Lee told someone in your organization that I would be here?"

"I don't know who the hell Emerson Lee is."

"Some Chinese gang member here in Los Angeles told you I'd be here? What was his name?"

"You all look alike to me," he said, smiling like a six year-old after telling his first knock-knock joke.

"What else did he tell you?"

"To make sure I said hello from Tom and that I'm supposed to scare you but not kill you. But hey, you know what, accidents happen." He again pointed the gun at Choy's head.

"Hold on, one more question," said Choy, expecting the bathroom door behind Raymond to open and a large man with a gun to step out.

What question to ask?

"Why do you call Amanda Bennett a traitor?"

"What's it to you?"

"I'm curious. I was a reporter for 25 years."

"She sold out to the billionaires. She takes their money and does what they tell her. She says Jews are white people and Israel is a European country. She says even race mixers like you can be white, if you have enough European blood. She's a traitor to the white race. Just like you."

As he said that, he once more pointed the gun at Choy's forehead.

"Please, can I use the bathroom before you do that?" said Choy, panic in his voice and thoughts. "There will be a big enough mess with all the blood for the maids to clean up, we don't need shit and piss added to it. Okay? Please?"

Raymond considered the request for a moment and then indicated with his gun that a trip to the toilet was okay. Choy quickly stepped around him, paused at the closed door, turned the brass handle and tried to discretely look inside. As he opened the door wider he discovered the room empty save for a toiletry bag beside the sink.

***

The buzzing of his cellphone was almost drowned out by the noise emanating from somewhere between his two ears. It wasn't really a sound at all, but the absence of it, like when your eardrums have been damaged. Choy could see from the cellphone screen it was Max Parker, the *LA Times* reporter, and he should take the call, because he might have information about the guy who knew Reb, but that seemed impossible right now. His entire being was still shaking, a few minutes, a half hour maybe, after Raymond had pulled the trigger. He had been certain his last conscious moments were about to be spent with an oversized, ex-con, right wing, racist bully and that thought bothered him more than the actual idea of death. Dying was difficult but at least if people you loved were there at the end … instead he had a severely damaged pathetic hulk of a human being who had absolutely no empathy for at least three-quarters of the planet's population.

The realization that no one was about to rescue him, that he never should have trusted Borovsky, was followed by a brief return of hope with the thought that maybe his rescuers were simply late and would burst through the hotel room door any moment, so he had to keep the conversation going any way he could.

"I'm so scared neither my bowels or bladder are working," he had said, sitting on the toilet as Raymond stared blankly. "You ever get that way? In prison maybe?"

There was no answer, only a slight change in his facial muscles that Choy interpreted as a look of disdain.

"Maybe I am a defective human being," Choy added, probably as a way to elicit sympathy. Instead he received scorn.

"You all are," said Raymond. "Mixing of the blood fucks you up inside. You don't know where you belong."

He said it with such conviction that Choy couldn't help his response.

"I sure as hell know I don't belong with people like you," the words came out angry and contemptuous. After saying them he expected to feel the bullet crash into his skull before hearing the crack of gunpowder exploding. When nothing happened he felt emboldened. "You're so pathetically lacking in self-confidence that you have to deny the humanity of billions of people just so you can feel some sense of self-worth. Did your Daddy abandon you as a child? Or was he a KKK member who beat you into being just like him? Were your momma and papa white trash speed addicts who left you as a baby wallowing in dirty diapers in the neighbourhood crack house? Was your mother a hooker who never knew your father and you grew up in foster homes where you were beaten and otherwise abused? Were you gang raped in prison by 40 black guys? I mean what's your story? Is there something that a decent human being can have a little sympathy for? Or are you just a fucking racist asshole with absolutely no redeeming features?"

Raymond was speechless, unable to answer. The hand holding the weapon began to shake. Were those tears forming in his eyes? The vicious giant was becoming a whimpering man boy. He turned, walked towards the hotel room door, then turned back again, pointed the gun once more at Choy's face and burst into tears.

Or more likely none of this had taken place. More likely he had cowardly and silently left the bathroom and stood in front of the bed waiting for death And when Raymond stepped close, placing the end of the gun on the bridge of his nose and pulled the trigger, nothing happened, except for warm trickle of liquid running down Choy's leg. Then Raymond said: "Bang." He put the gun in a holster inside his jacket, smiled and before leaving the room said, "Tom says to remember we can get to you anytime, anywhere" and then he was gone.

Choy was not absolutely certain which version of recent history was true because the moment Raymond disappeared an uncontrollable all-body tremor had begun and his head filled with a noise that he knew wasn't really there.

He could not make himself answer the cellphone.

7.

"I'm the guy you're looking for," said the man on the other end of the waves that none of Choy's senses could detect but nonetheless transmitted the voice coming from his cellphone.

"Who is this?"

"Ken Poulsen. The woman in the *Times* story, I drove up to Vancouver with her, I think. I was pretty messed up back then and the memories are all kind of fuzzy. I was smoking a lot of marijuana, dropping acid, eating mushrooms and swallowing various other pills. My father's connections had gotten me into the industry but then he suffered this massive heart attack and nothing was making sense anymore. I got a job as an AD on a TV series shooting in Vancouver and I was scared shitless about messing up like I'd done with everything else in my life. I'm not making excuses but I was pretty fucked up and the drugs made it even worse."

"Her name?" Choy asked before the guy went on about his troubled life.

"Promise my name won't get into any of this. People who fund my projects don't know about my past and I want to keep it that way. Okay?"

"I promise I won't use your name."

"Everyone called her Orchid, because she had these acid stamps with pictures of orchids — 200 different ones she said. It was the best."

"Her real name?"

"If I ever knew it I don't remember. Everyone called her Orchid. She was part of this scene where people showed up at parties, women and a few guys who were either in or associated with the porn business — nobody used their real names, not just because of the drugs, but also the porn. The women, especially the younger ones, were high all the time — people say it's just a business and maybe it is, but most of the young women never intended to fuck on camera, the drugs draw them in — and Orchid was one of them, high, high, high, like a satellite orbiting Jupiter. Not that she was really into porn. Far as I know she only did one video and that was on a dare. Wanted to be a real actress and was really good. Pretty sure she did acting classes and maybe even studied theatre in university, back home."

"Where was that? Where did she grow up?"

"I don't know," he answered after taking a few seconds to think about it. "She might have told me. Maybe from down south somewhere. She didn't have an accent though, I'm pretty sure of that, although she could do a hell of a southern belle, you know like from *Gone With The Wind*. She would have made a great Scarlett O'Hara if they ever did a remake. She knew all Vivien Leigh's lines and would recite them all the time. It might have been me tripping on acid but I remember driving up to Vancouver with her and she's teaching me Clark Gable's part so we can do scenes from the movie. I think she was getting me to do Leslie Howard and Olivia De Havilland as well. Ya, I remember trying to do like this falsetto voice."

This was useful information to paint a picture of Reb, but not to figure out who she actually was. At least it was confirmation he was talking about the same woman described by her friends in Vancouver.

"Did she do other accents?" asked Choy, just to make sure.

"Ya," he answered. "Did someone else tell you that? She was really good, like some of those classically trained British actors."

Progress.

"Again, it could have been an hallucination, but I don't think so — I remember being in a restaurant with her and the waitress was

Indian, South Asian, and after hearing her take our order Orchid did her accent perfectly for like the next two hours. She had it spot on."

Poulsen stopped talking for a moment.

"Life is shitty and unfair, you know," he continued. "Orchid was beautiful and this brilliant actor and what happens? Then there's these other so called actors who make it big on TV and in film who look good, that's all. Sure as hell don't do accents, not like Orchid."

"How did you meet her?"

"She was holding stuff, mostly acid and pot, for some dealer, maybe a boyfriend but I don't think so. Like most people in the drug business, the only way she could afford to use was by selling."

"You bought acid from her?"

"She gave it me. Had this big stash and was mad at the guy who owned it — I remember now — because he was the one who made the porn video she appeared in. Randy, that was his name. An Indian from India dude. Called himself a producer, but he was a pimp and a dealer."

"Randy what? Do you remember his last name?"

"Randy Randy, that was the name that went on the credits as executive producer. Probably not his real name, of course. A real prick. He owed me a few hundred dollars for directing this other video and when I met Orchid at a party it was like, 'we both hate that guy, so let's do his entire stash and run away together' and that's what we did. I had a job coming up in a few weeks in Vancouver and my father had like six cars he would never miss, and probably would never use even one of them again because he was in hospital in really bad shape, so we took a Lincoln and headed north. We'd smoke up and drive a hundred miles, find some place that looked nice or in some way caught our fancy, then drop some acid, maybe get a motel room and have a party or sometimes we just slept in the car."

"She told people in Vancouver about an adventure crossing the border?"

"Ya, after about a week, we're in Seattle tripping in the Pike Place Market where they throw the fish around and we're like amazed and blown away just standing there watching when she says: 'That's how you'll have to get me across the border because I don't have a passport.' We must have laughed for the next eight hours, just thinking about me throwing her across the border like one of those big salmon. We were walking all over downtown Seattle, tripping and every time we came to a park or an open space I'd pick her up like one of those 40 pound fish and pretend to toss her over the border. We were having the time of our lives, or maybe it was the acid and the weed and I made it all up, but I don't think so. I think we were genuinely in tune with each other's vibes and that was why we were having such a great time. She was a real good person, you know. When I read the story on the *Times'* website and you described how she died, I started crying."

After a short silence, Choy asked. "So how did she get across the border? I'm assuming it wasn't by you throwing her?"

"She hid in the trunk and I drove across," he answered, sadness remaining in his voice. "She did three tabs of acid and we decided that made her invisible. All I remember is that the border guard made me pull over to the office and I had to show my papers for working on the film, then they asked if I was bringing any firearms across. That was it. And they let me drive off with Orchid in the trunk. By the time we got to the motel I was really freaking, thinking maybe she had suffocated or was having a bad trip — I would have — but when I popped the lid, she was lying there giggling. She was convinced the trunk was a cave where the Greek god Hypnos lived and he was feeding her drugs made from the poppies that grew around the entrance. That was like the first time I realized she had also been doing heroin."

Again he remained silent for a few moments.

"Did she talk a lot about Greek or Roman gods?"

"I don't know," he answered. "Maybe. I think so, yes. Why?"

"Just something she said to me a few times," Choy said. "'Go with the wings of Mercury.' I'm wondering if it is significant, like maybe she studied classics in university."

"Pretty sure she was well read. Smarter than me, but I can't remember anything else about Greek or Roman gods. I was really into myself back then and didn't pay attention to anyone else. A selfish bastard. My father was in intensive care and I stole his car and disappeared. Pretty fucked up, right? You ever look back on stuff and think 'wow, that's such a different person from who I am now'?"

Never.

"To this day I haven't told him I'm sorry. My Dad. And he's never said anything about it. I wrecked that car up in Vancouver and he never once asked about it or said anything. I was a complete dick and he was a saint."

"How long were you in Vancouver?"

"Two months. I was supposed to be there six but everything fell apart because of my drug use. People covered for me, because of my Dad, but I was too fucked up. Then I got sick, an infection. Best thing that ever happened, because losing that job made me see I was ruining my life. When I came back home my Dad was out of hospital and he put me in rehab. I've been pretty straight since then. A little medicinal marijuana, that's it. But I could have easily ended up like Orchid."

"Did you hang out with her in Vancouver?"

"Until we finished her stash. I had an apartment rented for me in the West End and it was party central. There were like thousands of foreign students in Vancouver taking English courses back

then and dozens of them lived in the same building as us. We'd drop acid and invite the Koreans and Mexicans and Brazilians and Japanese over and it was like a trip around the world, or at least that's what we told ourselves."

"She lived with you?"

"For a few weeks we were a couple, but when I caught her shooting up and she asked me to try it, I got scared. Something about needles. Tried to give blood one time and fainted. Anyway, I wanted her to stop, but turns out she had been using heroin off and on for a few years. Claimed to be able to stop anytime because she had done it before, but that was all bullshit. After that everything was different, even the way she looked. Before, she was young, pretty, even glamorous, and a lot of fun, but after seeing that needle stuck into her bulging ankle vein she looked older, sadder, worn out, dangerous. All I could see was a junkie, I guess. A junkie committing slow suicide. Seeing her like that was my first step to recovery, so I guess she did me a favour."

"How long did she stay with you?"

"Another week or two. She started bringing home other guys, dealers, real scum bags. They were stealing things from the furnished apartment, the microwave, a cheap sound system. Then one of them pulled a knife and took all my cash. So I kicked her out. Told her I'd call the cops if she ever came back, but she did, looking for money. Had to get another apartment and then I never saw her again."

"That's it?" said Choy. "You don't remember anything else? Stories she told you about growing up?"

"No. I thought we were so close, but really we were tripping in our own separate spaces. I see that now."

"Other than Randy Randy, was there anyone else who might have known her real name?"

"I don't know," he said. "Maybe. There was this porn actress who I think was friends with Orchid. Went by the name of Alpha Bett, but her real name is Mary-Ellen Randolph. She was in rehab with me. She's a real estate agent now specializing in downtown lofts. Her office is not far away from the *Times* building. She was the listing agent on an apartment I looked at before buying the place I live in now."

***

Svetlana Borovky's failure to show up in his hotel room played on a loop in Choy's consciousness. Had something happened that prevented her? Was she playing some sort of game? Why had Lee told the Aryan Brotherhood or whatever they were called now where he was? He felt like the meat in a three-foot-long sandwich that was being devoured from both ends in an eating contest that no one told him he was participating in and didn't understand the rules.

The only information his hacker 'TwoSpiritPhoenix' had gathered for him so far was that both Mr. Lee and Billy-Bob were very security conscious. Their companies' and their private networks were designed by professionals using state-of-the-art hardware and software. It would be possible to hack them, but it would take time.

He needed to go back to the beginning.

Why did Lee contact me? To write a story, exposing Billy-Bob's connection to the drug business.

His plan was to expose a rival, gain an advantage, something politicians, businessmen, professional athletes, movie publicists, even wealthy estranged spouses did all the time. They used journalists and journalists used them.

Nothing strange in that. The six months I spent in Ottawa writing features about the new B.C. Reform Party members of the Official Opposition was full of calls from aides of the two B.C. Liberal cabinet ministers offering information or story suggestions.

Governments, businesses, institutions all try to shape the news. Why not drug dealers? Public relation is the only growth sector of "journalism."

So, Billy-Bob finds out what Lee is doing and decides to play friendly with me, seeing if he and Svetlana can turn the tables, use me to get at him, or at least deflect his attack. That would make sense. But how does telling me that a crazy white supremacist is about to kill me, promising to help, but then not helping make any sense at all?

Unless she knows he's only going to scare me and that's what suits her purpose. Like a gang running a protection racket, she wants me to be scared and to believe I need protection from lunatic white supremacists getting information from Mr. Lee.

Or maybe it was all a set-up, Tom's so-called Aryan Brotherhood comrade was in fact working for Billy-Bob.

On the other hand, maybe she ran across the street to find her bodyguard and was hit by a car. Stranger things have happened.

There's no way around it, I have to contact Svetlana again and Emerson Lee won't be happy.

***

A Google search and two phone calls revealed Randy Randy, the porno producer, was now going by the name of Rajinder Singh, and owned two popular northern Indian restaurants, one in downtown Los Angeles and the other in Beverly Hills. Since one was only ten blocks from his hotel and he was hungry, Choy decided to go there before the dinner crowd arrived. While most Asian cuisines were best experienced with a large group of friends or family, North American Indian restaurants often offered vegetarian and meat thalis, which made dining solo tolerable by providing a selection of three or four small dishes plus rice and a bread. Northern Indian breads were one of his favourite foods; a naan or stuffed paratha fresh out of a tandoori oven from Tandoori K. King in South Van-

couver, with their butter chicken sauce for dipping was a weekly craving. Perhaps the owner of Indian Clay Oven would be on site and if Choy were even luckier, the restaurant would serve a decent onion kulcha, his absolute favourite Indian stuffed bread.

Within two minutes of his arrival at the chic, minimalist space in a pre-First World War building the target of his inquiry had been pointed out.

"Yes, I remember Orchid," said Singh, who Choy was surprised to see wearing a turban and kirpan, symbols of his Sikh faith, when the waitress identified him sitting at a back table covered with papers. "Before I returned to my religious roots I would have told you she was a pain in the ass. What has she done that brings you to me?"

"She died."

"I am so sorry." He seemed genuinely disturbed by the news, as if he had in fact cared about her. "Please sit down."

As Choy pulled up a chair, Singh stacked the papers into a single pile.

"She died in Vancouver — that's where I'm from — pretty much right in front of me on the street, a fentanyl overdose they think. No one there knows her real name or where she was from or really anything at all. The government of British Columbia has declared a health emergency because of all the opioid deaths and I want to write a book about the woman people on the street in Vancouver called Reb and people down here knew as Orchid to help personalize the crisis."

"You're the guy the *Times* had a story about?"

"Yes."

"I heard some of the waitresses talking about it. I never have time to read anymore. Pornography provides more free time than the restaurant business."

Choy's quizzical look was involuntary but enough for Singh to get the point.

"How does someone who is a baptized Sikh come to terms with once having been a pornographer?" said Singh. "That's what you're thinking?"

"The thought did cross my mind," answered Choy, who was interested in the answer but worried the conversation was being diverted away from Reb.

"Seven years of my life are proof that we live in a time where the Five Thieves dominate the world," said Singh. "Do you know anything about Sikhism?"

"I was a reporter for 25 years in Vancouver."

"So you have written stories about parades and festivals?"

"And about how the temples are always open to anyone who is hungry."

"Well, did you know that we believe lust, ego, greed, anger and attachment to worldly things distract us from knowing God. Until three years ago I was living embodiment that this belief is true. The Five Thieves we call this and they stole my life, but I have set myself free by returning to my religion. I cannot deny my past, I can only learn from it. Do you know what Sikh means?"

"I was told it means 'learner'."

"Yes, exactly. I am a learner."

"Me too," Choy said quickly, to avoid a religious discussion, although he knew Sikhs did not proselytize. "I need your help to learn about Orchid."

"Yes, but first I should remember my manners and ask if you are hungry?"

"I am."

"If you are from Vancouver you probably know Punjabi cuisine."

"Enough to tell you I like it — breads, especially stuffed ones, fresh out of the tandoor, a fragrant dal, tikka, bhindi bhaji, baigan bharta, butter chicken — pretty much everything, except dishes heavy on fenugreek. Something about that spice upsets my stomach."

"I am impressed," he said, while motioning for the waitress to come to the table. "Do you also cook?"

"Recreationally," answered Choy. "Mostly Cantonese, Szechuan and Indian for my girlfriend."

"You are part Chinese, I assume from your name?"

As Choy nodded, Singh whispered into the waitress's ear.

"Did you have a mother or father who passed down family recipes?" said Singh, after the waitress nodded and headed to the kitchen.

"My mother's borscht was the best I ever tasted. I still make it sometimes and my daughter loves it. My son, on the other hand, has a thing about beets."

"So your interest in Chinese and Indian cuisines is purely gastronomic?"

Choy was pretty sure he knew what Singh was getting at.

"I'm an eighth generation mongrel-Canadian — Chinese, European, North American Indian, Hawaiian, African — whose parents were an atheist and a lapsed Methodist. I was a journalist for 25 years at the *Vancouver Sun* and now am trying to make a business out of writing books and other shorter pieces. You?"

"Second generation American Sikh. My family came to Canada in the early 1970s, then a few years later bought a farm in the Central Valley, where I was born. I hated farming and first chance I had moved here. Wanted to get into TV and movies, but ended up in porn, then got out of that business and into restaurants. This and another one are quite popular right now, but I understand the fickleness of popular taste and am diversifying into real estate. I will soon open my third restaurant, but through a corporate structure, which allows me to capitalize on my current success."

"Congratulations."

"But you don't really care about that at all, do you?" said Singh, smiling.

"My focus is Reb, or Orchid as you knew her."

Singh seemed to appreciate his getting down to business. He continued to smile and said: "Thank you for considering my busy schedule and not trying to be all faux friendly with me. Surinder will soon bring some food to our table and I hope you will share it with me, given that we both require nourishment, but other than that we must focus on helping you learn what I know about Orchid. Okay?"

"Thank you," said Choy. For a former pornographer, and who knew what else went along with that, he was a decent guy.

"There's really not much to tell," he said. "I slept with her, like I did with all my 'actresses', but only once because she was not the sort of woman I enjoyed."

"What do you mean?"

"She was not submissive, the exact opposite in fact, extremely wilful and obstinate. A 'western woman' as my father would say."

"Can you elaborate?"

"The women who are attracted to pornography are, in general, damaged goods, in one way or another. Often sexually abused as children and drug addicts they have self-esteem problems and those in the business exploit this damage. I can admit this now, after years away. Yes, there are some women who choose porn as a business they can succeed in, but in my experience this is rarely their primary motivation. The business acumen only comes once they become accustomed to the exploitation. I can acknowledge now that I exploited many women, but it was never like that with Orchid. You know the difference between a candy with a soft centre and a hard one? Orchid's centre was hard. I don't know if this was because she overcame a horrible childhood or later suffered an injury that caused her to turn to drugs for relief. "

The waitress carried a tray with a half dozen dishes and spread them across the table.

"Would you like a beer? We have local craft brews on tap."

"No thank you. Water is good for me."

"Please enjoy," said Singh, signalling with his hand to begin eating.

Two naans, an aloo paratha, an onion kulcha, a red sauced dish, likely butter chicken, lamb tikka, daal, an eggplant bharta and pieces of okra in a rich dark sauce. Singh offered the exact dishes Choy had spoken of.

"I hope you will find our recipes to your liking. Except for some of the spices, we use all local organic ingredients. That sets us apart from every other Indian restaurant in the city and is what makes us so popular."

"Wow, this is really good," said Choy after dipping a piece of onion kulcha into the butter chicken sauce. "The bread is absolutely perfect."

"Like with an Italian brick pizza oven, the trick with a tandoor is the very high temperature — that and the special Punjabi variety of wheat grown especially for me in the Central Valley by my father."

"The okra is amazing," said Choy. "It's crisp but tender. That is the best bhindi bhaji I've ever had."

"It is my mother's recipe and the okra is also grown by her."

"Outstanding. Congratulations to you, your chef and all your suppliers."

"Thank you."

The texture of the breads, the wonderfully aromatic taste of the fresh ginger, garlic and onion, together with the individually identifiable influence of coriander, cinnamon, green cardamom, cumin, cloves, nutmeg, and mustard seeds blended together in a seamless whole that was more than the sum of its parts.

"I am very impressed," Choy added between bites.

"There is no greater pleasure than making others happy," Singh said. "Especially through their senses of sight, taste and smell."

As the buzz from the wonderful food wore off, Choy's thoughts once again turned to Reb. "You were saying that Orchid had a hard centre?"

"Perhaps the better word is strong. She had a strong and grounded centre, unlike most women involved in the pornography business who lack any centre at all. They are seeking something or someone to fill that space and the men who exploit them understand this weakness. With Orchid there was no weakness."

"Yet something caused her to do a lot of drugs and get addicted."

"Drugs have been with humankind for millennia; elephants and monkeys seek out inebriation, something I have seen for myself in India. Drugs deaden pain or make some people feel especially good and they become so habituated that we give it a special name when it comes to certain substances. Why is that? Why if someone needs aspirin, or acetaminophen, or insulin do we provide it, sometimes under medical supervision, other times no questions asked at all, but if they need opioids of one sort or another, we call them drug addicts and try to prevent access to what they need to live normal, productive lives?"

"I support the legalization of all drugs," answered Choy. "Certainly the war on them has been an absolute failure."

"Unless you're a drug dealer, or a cop," said Singh, who then leaned closer to his tablemate. "I'll tell you a secret."

Choy mimed zipping his mouth shut.

"The original source of capital for my videos, restaurants and real estate was buying and selling illegal substances, so I know what I am talking about. You know why they don't make all drugs legal? Too many people have a stake in keeping them illegal and I'm not just talking about the dealers. The jobs of hundreds of thousands, maybe millions, of cops, prison guards, lawyers, and judges depend on drugs remaining illegal. Our system of entrepreneurial capitalism depends on the access to super profits that illegal drugs provide. Our system of institutionalized racism against people with brown or black skin depends on drugs being illegal so we can incarcerate about one third of them, mostly in private, profit-making prisons."

"Would we have Nirvana if drugs were made legal?"

"Some people's lives would be made better, that is all," said Singh. "What we have today is a drug distribution system that in-centivizes ever more violent gang warfare, the ill health that stems from the adulteration of product, and the expansion of the addict base by compelling people who need drugs to survive by convinc-ing others to buy from them in order to afford the cost of their addiction. Giving drugs to addicts like we give prescriptions to sick people would end all that. It might not be heaven, but it sure would be an improvement over what we have today. Did you know that almost 400,000 Americans have died from opioid overdoses over the past 20 years? Most of them started off on legal drugs and then once addicted moved over to illegal drugs. Four hundred thousand! Think about it, read some books, like I have, and you will come to the same conclusion."

"As I said, I support the legalization of all drugs and treating addicts through the healthcare system. But they damage people like

Orchid and that would probably be true if her dealer was the government heroin store or some street dealer."

"All drugs, including legal ones have adverse side effects," said Singh. "Do you blame the doctor and call him a pusher when his patient on chemotherapy loses all her hair and is violently sick?"

"I think we have gotten side tracked and need to get back to Orchid."

"I am making a point about her. She was a grounded person, not the sort to be a victim of a drug pusher, or pimp, or pornographer. If Orchid was a victim at all, it was of a political and economic system that creates illegality. Call it the war on drug addicts."

"That's an interesting point but with all due respect to your obvious culinary and philosophical talents, you've barely told me anything at all about Orchid," said Choy, who couldn't help the annoyance in his voice. "Instead you've given me your opinions on a variety of subjects."

Singh kept an angry gaze in the general direction of Choy in a silence with many possible outcomes, but finally his shoulder muscles relaxed as he exhaled.

"To understand why a particular tree in the forest has died, you must consider the individual and the forest," Singh said in an obvious allegory that reeked of condescension. "To grasp what killed this woman, you must look at both."

"I understand your point and can assure you that when it comes time to write about Orchid both the tree and the forest will be part of the story. But the way I work is to gather as many details about my subject as possible and then fit these together into a bigger picture that, to your point, includes the forces greater than an individual human being."

Strange how I can like somebody one moment and then find him a condescending know-it-all the next.

"Orchid had an opinion about everything," said Singh, "as I do, so that is perhaps why we clashed so frequently."

He half smiled and Choy reciprocated.

A know-it-all who understands how others perceive him is more tolerable than one who only gazes outward.

"She was feminist and an actor — somehow these two things were intertwined in her mind, like acting enabled her to be anything she wanted and so did feminism."

Something new.

"She talked a lot about acting, about how an actress must become the character she is playing. She was willing to try anything once in order to accumulate the experiences necessary to become a great actress."

"Did she use the word actress or actor?" Details like this were telling.

He thought for a moment. "She used the word actor. Is that significant?"

She was a feminist.

"Perhaps it reflected her feminism," said Singh, in step with Choy's thought.

"Did she talk about that? About what feminism meant to her?"

"She mostly criticized my sexist behaviour. She saw how I controlled the actresses in my videos. She was very perceptive and understood all my tricks. She watched people to learn their strengths and weaknesses, just like I did. In my videos I specialized in fresh faces, women who had never done pornography before, what we called the 'amateur genre' and this required convincing women to have sex on camera. I was very good at it. She commented about how I used flattery on some women, guilt on others, and monetary inducements to a few; how I could be abusive to those who required that and kind to those for whom that was necessary. It was all about listening and watching, picking up clues. She listened and watched me as I was listening and watching them."

"What did it take to convince Orchid to have sex on camera?"

"An intellectual argument about acting," answered Singh, quickly and possibly a bit smugly. "I told her, 'what if you were up for a part about a porno star?' and proceeded from there. Ultimately she agreed that doing it would be a useful addition to her 'basket of experiences'."

"Was that how she justified taking drugs as well?"

"I'm not sure. I never had to convince her to pop a pill, smoke a pipe or stick a needle in her arm — she was already well into all that before I met her."

"She ever say anything about her parents or where she grew up?"

"Somewhere in suburbia or a small town I think."

"Why do you say that?"

"Because I remember her saying something about her mother being suffocated by 'suburban housewifedom' — that was the term she used and I'd never heard it before. Perhaps she made it up or maybe she learned it in some women's studies program."

"You think she went to university?"

"She was educated, no doubt. Used allusions to Greek and Roman mythology. Maybe she went to acting school. I've met hundreds, maybe thousands of young actors here and you can always tell the ones who went to a university theatre program. Over-analytical and they try to impress you with historical perspective on film and theatre."

"Orchid was like that?"

"Yes. Made me sad, because I knew success in this town has very little to do with any of that. Mostly it comes down to looks and who you know."

"Do you think she understood that?"

"And maybe that was what turned her towards drugs?" he answered. "I do remember thinking that might be true. She had a cynical edge about her and used it to try to protect the younger women around the edges of the business."

"A mother hen?"

"More like a clever, extremely cynical drug-addled lawyer. She tried to be their advocate, but she was almost always under the influence."

"You have any sense of how old she was?"

"Early thirties, so if she were alive today, mid-to-late thirties."

"Christ, she looked past fifty at the end," said Choy.

"Street heroin and hooking will do that to you."

"Can you think of anyone I could contact who might know more about her?"

"Nobody that I would have any idea about how to contact," he said. "I really did leave that life behind."

"Is there anything else? Anything at all?"

"She had one of those laughs that is infectious," he said after thinking about the question for a few moments. "I remember telling her to call a guy I met at a party who did laugh tracks."

"Did she laugh a lot?"

"No, but when she did the whole room would join in."

"Is that it?"

"That's all and I really must get back to work."

"Thank you so much for your time and the wonderful meal," said Choy, as he handed Singh his card. "Call me if anything else comes to you."

"I think I will choose to remember her laugh," Singh said, as the two men shook hands.

"I wish I had heard it," said Choy.

8.

Although he'd seen bigger mansions on southwest Marine Drive in Vancouver, or on the water in West Vancouver, the house where he met Emerson Lee had a long driveway that passed between tennis and basketball courts and the grounds reminded Choy of his visit to Versailles, outside Paris.

"Quite a place," said Choy as they walked through art deco influenced rooms to a backyard pool patio.

"It was built by a movie star in the 1920s who has long been forgotten," said Lee. "I purchased the house three years ago. It was quite run down."

"You've done an excellent job on the renovation," said Choy looking at the delicate walnut mouldings emanating from massive bookcases that covered two walls of the reading room, which overlooked, through massive French doors, the backyard. "It must be very expensive. My much simpler renovation of a house one sixth this size is eating through my bank account."

"This is a city where one must demonstrate his wealth and power to gain entry to certain circles."

"Rich people and their houses are like ten year-old boys standing in a circle seeing who can piss the furthest," said Choy, purposely sarcastic.

The phone call earlier in the morning had been full of tension and Choy remained upset over what Lee had said. The conversation had ended with an "invitation" to a face-face meeting in two hours and Choy had stewed about how to respond for over an hour in his hotel room, a half hour in the lobby and a 20-minute limousine ride during which the driver disappeared behind an opaque, perhaps bulletproof and soundproof, window. Maybe it was time to quit and find another way to pay off his father's gambling debt.

And he didn't want anything more to do with Billy-Bob and Svetlana either. On the other hand, defying drug dealer danger had its attraction. The thought of risking his life for a good story excited, not frightened, him. Maybe it was the same kind of rush his father got from gambling.

"I agree there is something primitive, primal even, in the urge to impress," responded Lee, who remained outwardly friendly. "We are like peacocks with their displays or rutting elk butting heads to prove who is more dominant."

The same with your threats and violence.

"Please sit down," said Lee, pointing to a set of wicker chairs surrounding a teak table on a patio overlooking a large swimming pool.

A rather large Chinese man appeared from inside the house carrying a tray with plates, utensils and a large bottle of water. He put the tray down, then set the table.

"Merci, Henri, C'est bon," he said, then turned to Choy. "We shall enjoy a wonderful lunch. Henri has come straight from Paris where he apprenticed in various Michelin starred establishments for the past five years. The Chinese diaspora is a marvellous resource, don't you agree?"

"Do you speak French?" asked Choy.

"Fluently, along with English, Spanish, Portuguese, Russian and the important Chinese dialects," answered Lee. "And I can get by in four or five more languages."

Full of himself. Maybe that's the route to get some honest answers.

"I'm impressed," said Choy, smiling. "You're an impressive man, living in an impressive house, surrounded by impressive things and impressive servants."

"I detect a scent of sarcasm."

"I learned long ago that despite choosing my words carefully, people interpret what I write or say in surprising ways," said

Choy. "We may think words, allusions, metaphors are solid, easily looked up entries in a dictionary, but in fact many of them are slippery, amorphous entities that change meaning over time and signify different things to different people."

"What are you trying to say Waylon?"

"I understand I am being used and can accept that as part of the job but this game you, Billy-Bob and Svetlana are playing, have the journalist pin the tail on the drug dealer — I don't like being blindfolded and told to play without even knowing the rules."

"I do like your colourful way of expressing yourself. But you are headstrong, unwilling to be directed and full of an illusion you call journalistic ethics. If you're not careful we'll soon see how creative you can be under fire."

"Under fire?" repeated Choy. "Is that simply a metaphor?"

"Was it a metaphor who killed your journalist friend and tried to kill you the last time you ran into these types of people?"

"What are you telling me Emerson? Who is going to be firing at me?"

"Hard to tell."

"Emerson, please help me. What have I got myself into? What's going on between you and Billy-Bob? What do you want? Please help me understand the movement of pieces in this game where I find myself a pawn. Not even a pawn, I'm the race car on a Monopoly board. Who is rolling the dice and moving me around?"

Lee stared at him for a few seconds before speaking. "You were a reporter during the second Iraq war. And the bombing of Libya?"

Choy nodded. "I didn't cover it, but I was a working reporter then."

"Did you pay attention to what was in the news before, during and after?"

"'One of the most important jobs of a newspaper reporter is to read newspapers and know the news.' My first managing editor was fond of saying that when he introduced himself to a new reporter."

"So you did? Pay attention?"

"Of course."

"What would you say were the common characteristics of the period leading up to both conflicts? From a news content perspective?"

Choy understood where Lee was going with this.

"A flood of stories about how savage and terrible Saddam Hussein and Muammar Gaddafi were. Reports about weapons of mass destruction, slaughters of innocent people, that sort of thing."

"And do you think such stories appeared because intrepid journalists just so happened to dig them up at those particular times?"

Choy shrugged. He had frequently been on the receiving end of Hollywood's and the music industry's PR machine and knew how it worked. Sports, entertainment, business, political parties, banks, governments —public relations professionals attempting to spin the news like it was an advertising campaign. This was the way of journalism. He had no doubt that military, intelligence and foreign affairs departments in Ottawa, Washington or London worked exactly the same way.

"How many people do you think the U.S. military and intelligence services employ to shape the news?" said Lee. "Tens of thousands."

"What are you saying? That you and Billy-Bob Baker are like generals getting ready for war? That what you're doing is part of some big psychological operations program aimed at destabilizing the other side? Are you saying I am about to be in the middle of a war between rival drug gangs?"

"I'm having an interesting conversation about how the news came to be the news during two periods of recent history with a journalist friend, that is all," said Lee. "One can learn much by studying the past. It's a shame your education system is deficient in teaching young people about what has happened and why."

"You're saying drug gangs, preparing to fight over control of a certain territory, are like countries conducting foreign relations?"

"I'm saying that to be successful in any competition one must understand psychology, politics and the application of force. Clausewitz said, 'War is the continuation of politics by other means.' He, Machiavelli and Sun Tzu are relevant to all organizations in competition with others."

"The same message as that scene in Godfather when Michael tells Kate his father is like all powerful leaders who have their own armies and she says comparing a Mafia Don to the president is naïve, but he retorts back, 'who is being naïve?'"

"I remember the scene somewhat differently," said Lee, pouring himself a glass of water and offering another to his guest. "But your essential point is correct."

Choy took a sip of water as he thought about the implications of Lee's words. "So, right now in the lead-up to this inevitable war, which is diplomacy by other means, between you and Billy-Bob, both sides want something from me, which gives me a certain power."

"An illusion shared by many journalists. Do you really think the Saddam's weapons of mass destruction story depended on any one journalist?"

"So, if I were to walk away, abandon this project, you'd simply find another journalist?"

"If I allowed you to walk away, there'd be no problem finding another one. Perhaps she or he wouldn't be as good as you, but as much as I know it pains to hear, none of us are essential."

"Not even you?" This guy's weak spot was his ego and the route to a successful interview had to be through his exaggerated sense of self-worth.

"I may soon be one of the 5,000 richest people in the world and therefore much closer to essential status, but no, not even me. Not even the president of the USA or richest person in the world is essential for the survival of the system, and after all, that is ultimately what we are talking about."

"I thought you were a Marxist who understood the system would be replaced by another just as feudalism was replaced by capitalism."

"I am a Marxist who understands that Marx was right about many things, but not about the longevity of capitalism. It will survive long past our lifetimes. If we want to have a meaningful impact on the course of history, today it is essential that we be capitalists."

"I just interviewed a man who argues that illegal drugs are an essential part of our current economic and political system."

"Hard to disagree with that assessment."

"Is it true about the CIA's involvement in drugs?" said Choy. "The Nicaraguan Contras, the Kuomintang, Air America, all that stuff?"

"Every intelligence service of any consequence uses whatever tools are available to accomplish its goals. All is fair in love and war. Are drugs any more illegal or unethical than bribery or electoral interference or assassination?"

"Are Billy-Bob and Svetlana connected to Amanda Bennett and powerful people inside the U.S. government?"

"Who won the election a few months back? You think it a coincidence that Billy-Bob began expanding his operation a week later?"

Keep him talking that's the trick.

"And you know this because you have connections inside this country that allow you operate," said Choy, guessing.

"Allies," answered Lee. "I have allies."

"People who are enemies of Donald Trump, the alt-right, Billy-Bob Baker and Svetlana Borovsky," said Choy. "But that's the part I don't understand. I follow your arguments about the similarities of conducting a drug business to conducting the foreign affairs of a country, and the nature of war, but what I don't understand is why your interests and the interests of Donald Trump's internal enemies currently coincide. You are a Chinese nationalist and a self-professed Marxist-Leninist who near as I can tell remains close to at least certain circles of a Communist government."

"'Alas, the storm is come again! My best way is to creep under his gaberdine; there is no other shelter hereabout: misery acquaints a man with strange bed-fellows.' Do you know where that comes from?" asked Lee.

"Shakespeare's *The Tempest*," said Choy, who had seen the play six months earlier at Bard on the Beach. "I forget the character's name, but he gets under Caliban's cloak after saying that."

"Very good."

"And the miserable storm is the current president?"

"Excellent, an 'A-plus'."

"This has something to do with Hillary Clinton and the Russian stuff, right?"

"You are very perceptive."

"I've read a few stories about how the Deep State is against the president, about how the CIA and the rest of the security establishment is trying to undermine him, of how Clinton was their candidate."

"Do you believe everything you read?"

"I admit to having less than expert knowledge about any of this, but my interpretation of what is going on is that the State Department, the intelligence community and the American establishment, whatever you want to call it, had a certain foreign policy path laid out and the election of Trump has thrown the country off that path. I think the white nationalists and the people they are close to in government want to be less anti-Russian and more anti-Chinese, but the Americans on your side sees this as a mistake because engaging with China and promoting capitalism there has been extremely good for American business."

"One dimensional thinking is the problem," said Lee. "That and propagandists drinking their own bathwater, having forgotten all the perfume they dumped into it."

Is he saying the extreme right believes the mythology created about the land of the free and making America great again, while the people he deals with are realists?

Why is he telling me this stuff? He's telling me what story to write.

Lee continued on yet another tangent. "Did you know that American historians argue the South's aggressive push to respect the property rights of slaveholders everywhere in the country was a primary cause of the Civil War and hence the end of slavery?"

"When the right wing becomes too powerful it is the author of its own demise?" said Choy. "That's what is going on right now with Trump and the Tea Party and white nationalists? They will provoke a reaction that will not be good for American capitalism?"

"That would be a vast oversimplification of a complex subject, which also involves foreign policy theory, the Great Game and other matters of geopolitical significance, but the sentiment expressed is essentially correct."

"The Great Game? The battle for control of the Silk Road routes from China to Europe?"

Lee nodded.

"You're saying that's part of understanding the current conflict inside the American establishment?"

"Yes."

He's directing me.

There was nothing worse than obvious spin. It insulted the intelligence of even a half decent reporter. That's why Choy hated his brief time in Ottawa covering politics. The manipulation, back scratching, propaganda — all of it was so damned obvious. How could any journalist aspire to cover that?

Time to turn the table, to take control of the interview. Time to go for the prize.

"Interesting, but I want to move on to a different subject. Let's say you were back working for the Chinese intelligence service. And someone came to you wanting to know the best way to get a fiercely independent journalist to write the story you wanted. What would you tell him or her?"

"Devise a plan to convince the journalist that he had written the truth despite all your best efforts to sway him," said Lee. "Or, even easier, take your 'scoop' to another journalist who cares more about making a name for himself than about the truth. There are many of those."

"How about if a colleague came to you and said: 'Here's a scenario I'm looking at. I'm assigned to the Somewhereistan desk and my job is to develop contacts inside the government. I learn there are two rival ministers who hate each other. How do I take advantage of that?'"

"A common scenario," said Lee quickly. "The wrong answer is to approach one of the ministers with information about the other. The right answer is to find a way to get one of the ministers to contact you because they believe you have a certain expertise in finding dirt about their rival."

"The key is to make sure your target thinks he initiated the contact," said Choy, having an 'uh huh' moment. "If someone thinks they came up with an idea they are much more likely to take owner-ship of it. If you take the idea to them, they will feel manipulated."

"Especially if they're smart," said Lee.

"Like you, or me?"

Lee nodded. Choy smiled. His tablemate reacted with a puzzled look.

"What do you think the likelihood is that Svetlana Borovsky, a Russian agent willing to use sex and violence to get her way, told me about you and your American friends?" asked Choy. "That she told me about how certain elements inside the CIA and State Department were actively working against the president, together with certain elements inside Chinese intelligence and was I interested in that story?"

Lee was pondering the implications of this scenario.

"I mean that would be a pretty good story, right? After all the heat Trump has taken for supposedly being too close to the Russians? There's a lot of ways you could spin that story and all sorts of media outlets would be interested, especially if it also in-volved illegal drugs. I'd want to confirm that story as best I could, right? I'd probably want to meet with you and try to figure out if there was anything to it. And, like you said, 'the right answer is to find a way to get one of the ministers to contact you because they believe you have a certain expertise in finding dirt about their ri-val.'"

It felt good to take back the steering wheel.

"Perhaps I have underestimated you," said Lee, leaning back in his chair.

"Perhaps you have," said Choy, doing his best to maintain his poker face, despite the strange mixture of triumph and fear that was bubbling underneath.

He's buying my bluff.

***

Next up was quickly speaking to Borovsky, despite the almost certain danger involved. But he also had to assume he was being watched and could not appear to be acting in panic. He had to make Lee, Borovsky and Baker think that his was a position of strength. He still had the telephone number Borovsky left in his pocket, but rather than call it immediately he would proceed with his day as planned. If his phone was being monitored they would know he had a 3 p.m. interview with a real estate agent downtown. Mary Ellen Randolph was preparing a loft apartment for an open house and told him he should come over then.

"When you called and told me about Orchid dying I was so upset," said Randolph, as soon as she opened the huge metal door to the artist's studio. "That could very easily have been me. In fact, when we knew each other I was much worse than her, much worse. I did more drugs; I was doing all kinds of unprotected sex in those porn videos; I was much closer to the bottom. There but for the grace of God."

Choy was still standing just inside the door when she paused.

"Oh, I am sorry, what terrible manners," said the pleasantly plump 40 year old wearing a real estate agent uniform that consisted of a white blouse and greenish skirt. "Come in, sit down. I just made some coffee with the French press."

"No thanks, but a glass of tap water would hit the spot," said Choy, looking for someplace to sit.

"Are you sure?"

Choy nodded. The choices for sitting seemed either works of art constructed from industrial materials one might find in dumpsters outside factories, or pieces of exercise equipment from a gym.

"I find that weight bench most comfortable," said Randolph. "You can adjust the back part so it stands up and lean against it. I've been too afraid to try any of the pieces of art, although I have been assured they are perfectly functional."

"I've never seen a room furnished quite like this," he said, adjusting the back of the weight bench. "A unique loft in a unique building. What was it, a factory?"

"A fruit packing facility. Apartments here are highly sought after. And the owner is willing to sell all the installations. He's one of the hottest young artists in the city."

"Wow. Unfortunately I have no plans to move to LA."

"You never know what a client will like," she said, handing him a glass of water. "I've done well in this business by keeping an open mind; that and developing a niche expertise. I specialize in the affluent artistic gay urban male loft market."

"Interesting," said Choy, although it really wasn't. His thoughts were still occupied by how best to contact Svetlana.

"If Orchid were alive and could see me now."

"What would she say?"

"Orchid was always very kind, so despite her disapproval she'd say something supportive."

Choy was so lost in his thoughts that he failed to immediately notice Mary Ellen was crying.

"Why do you think she would have disapproved?" He was on interview cruise control mode — repeat something in the previous answer and turn it into a question — as he tried to work up a plan.

"She wanted me to be an artist, like her. There was nothing more important to her than art and she would think I have sold out. I'm certain of it."

"Art?"

"Her art was acting and mine was painting," she said through the tears. "But I haven't put brush to canvas since … It's been years.

I suppose the same is true for Orchid, although she used to say she acted every day of her life. Maybe she would claim to be playing the part of a drug addict and a prostitute, to see what it was like. Maybe even dying …"

Mary Ellen's sobbing finally got Choy's attention.

"I'm sorry, if this is too painful …"

"I loved her," she said, the pain in her voice making her meaning clear. "I loved her, but she never knew. There I was, making pornography, touching, kissing, doing the most intimate things with men and women I barely knew and certainly never cared about, but I never kissed the one I loved."

Choy stood up and offered his seat to her. It seemed the least he could do, but it meant he was now standing awkwardly in front of her. The "installation" a few feet away had a small platform that looked like a trap set by the menacing man-eating metal flower behind it. He hesitated.

"I'm so glad that you're telling her story," she said after recovering her composure. "I wish I could help more, but I don't know her real name, I don't know where she was from. She never talked about any of that and even if she did I was probably too stoned to remember. All I remember is how beautiful she was when we first met. Venice Beach, people dropping acid and she was there. I remember watching her. She took off a pink blouse and blue jeans to swim in her bra and panties."

"Was she a lesbian?"

Mary Ellen shook her head and started crying more heavily again. "No, although I think she tried one time, but not with me. She always said she'd try anything once. She was brave and adventurous. Always willing to take risks, never afraid, especially when it came to standing up for people against bullies. She always confronted them even when others backed down."

As the elements of a plan regarding Svetlana, Lee and Billy-Bob came into focus, Choy could finally spend a greater portion of his consciousness on the interview he was engaged in.

"Mary Ellen, I need to ask you a question I haven't asked anyone else. I need to ask you because you're obviously smart and sensitive."

The crying diminished.

"Would you say that Orchid seemed a damaged person?"

"I'm not sure what you mean."

"People say many drug addicts and prostitutes were victims of some form of abuse — do you think Orchid might have been?"

"I was raped by my uncle," said Mary Ellen. "I never told my parents, I never told anyone until my drug treatment psychiatrist. And now I told you."

Joy once told him that she had gone into forensic science because there was too much pain in the world to deal with living people. He understood.

"I wish I had told Orchid," she said as the sobbing returned.

"Mary Ellen, I need your help."

She looked at him then used her sleeve as a handkerchief.

"No, I don't think Orchid was damaged, at least not in the way you mean. I think maybe she suffered some great pain, maybe the loss of a person close to her, but I don't think she was abused as a child."

"Why do you say that?"

"Because I saw her happy, I saw her sad, and I saw her neither. I think damaged people are always kind of sad. I think I'm always kind of sad, but I've come to accept that and keep myself busy. Earning commissions, that's become the focus of my life. Making money, that's how I survive and that's what Orchid would disapprove of. She'd say I should be braver. She'd say I should do what

I want, do my art and not seek approval from other people or the system."

She smiled at Choy.

"You know the other reason why I don't think Orchid was a damaged person? Because she was happy when she stood up for other people. She liked a good fight and I saw her angry. It was always a happy angry. Do you know what I mean?"

"I think so," he answered, worried that he had reached a dead end in his search for Reb. Even though this woman had provided some interesting background, without a name or a hometown he had nowhere else to go, no one else to interview.

"If you are damaged at your core, I don't think you can be happy like that."

Choy nodded, but his thoughts had again turned to Svetlana.

"Mary Ellen, is it okay if I use your cellphone? I need to call someone who might not answer if she sees it is me, but it is really important that we talk. Really important." It was not exactly a lie, but he still felt guilty about using her this way.

"Yes, of course," said Mary Ellen, pulling her phone out of her purse and handing it to him. "Go into the bathroom over there if you need some privacy."

"Thanks." As he took the cell and turned towards the bathroom, Choy realized he hadn't asked one of the most basic questions of any interview. "Anything else you can think of that might be helpful?"

She shook her head.

"Is there anyone else who you think might know something helpful? Someone else part of your group?"

"You talked to Randy already?"

He nodded.

"I can't think of anyone else," she said. "Except maybe …"

"Who?"

"There was a counsellor in my drug rehab program who spoke to me privately after I shared a story about how much I loved Orchid, but never told her. This counsellor said she knew Orchid."

"Knew her?"

"Said Orchid had been in rehab with her a few years before. She was going to tell me all about her, but then we were interrupted and that night I got really sick and was taken to hospital. Never had a chance to speak with her again."

"Do you remember the name of that counsellor and where she worked?"

She nodded. "Go make your phone call to your girlfriend and apologize for whatever it was you did. I'll write her name and the facility on the back of my card."

Choy entered the bathroom, feeling even guiltier.

9.

"I miss you."

It felt good to hear Joy's voice.

"Where are you?"

"Still in the hotel in Los Angeles," he said.

"Do you want me to come there for the weekend? If I leave Vegas after work on Friday I can make it downtown by 10, maybe earlier if I get lucky with traffic."

"That would be nice," said Choy, uncertain what to tell her about the events of the past few days. "I have a nice room and … But it may not work out."

"What's wrong?"

"Nothing," he lied. "It's just very intense. A few hours ago I spoke with a woman who was in love with Reb, who she knew as Orchid, and she cried through most of the interview. I'm still shaking."

"Poor dear."

"Maybe I could go to Vegas for the weekend," he said, an idea coming from left field like an accurate throw from a Gold Glover to home plate. "Rent a car and I could help you get ready for the move."

"We could go to a show, or just hang out in bed together."

"Anything with you is better than a trip to the top of the Empire State Building." They had said this to each other a few times before and it had become one of their private signals of affection. "I'm not a hundred percent sure I will be free, but I'll know better tomorrow. If I can't then you come here."

"How's your story coming?"

"Even though the people I've interviewed have helped me paint a picture of what Reb was like, it's still very abstract. Mostly

I've run into dead ends, nobody knows her real name or where she was from. I have one more lead and am going to Malibu to speak with her tomorrow."

"And what you're working on for Mr. Lee?"

Don't lie to Joy. Once you head down that road it's difficult to turn back.

"That's gotten very complicated," he answered.

"And?" There was insistence in her voice.

"And some white nationalists are now in the picture."

"Like the white supremacist who tried to kill you last summer? Why?"

"I shouldn't say more on the telephone."

"What is going on?"

"Don't worry, everything is under control," he said and immediately hoped it didn't qualify as a lie, but there certainly was very little truth to the statement. "I can't very well write about rival drug gangs without talking to both sides. Right? You understand how journalism works."

Is a half-truth also a half-lie? Or an entirely different species of obfuscation?

***

"How fast can you have these clothes cleaned?" Choy asked, as instructed by the card that had been slid under his hotel room door.

The large, muscular man standing behind the counter at the Echo Park drycleaners held up a sign and indicated with his head to step behind the counter.

"Take off all your clothes quickly," the words were printed in crayon on a piece of cardboard. "And don't say anything more."

"I could have this done for you in three hours," said the man, in what sounded like a heavy eastern-European accent. "Just fill out this form."

On a chair behind the counter were sweat pants, flip-flops, a T-shirt and a canvas shopping bag. A second large muscular man stood beside the chair. Once Choy had undressed, he took his cellphone out of his pants pocket, but the second man held his hand out and once he had possession put the phone, wallet and all his clothes, including shoes into the bag and walked past the counter, out the storefront entry. The man at the counter waited for the second man to disappear and then pointed at a door to the right.

"Through there," he said. "Down the stairs, through the blue door and along the blue hallway. There will be a door at the end of it. She's waiting for you there."

Once Choy had dressed, he followed the instructions and entered a short narrow hallway that led to stairs. He walked down the stairs into a basement room with three doors. He took the blue one into a small room that had two hallways leading from it. He took the blue one and at the end of it was another door, which he opened and stepped inside a dimly lit room with music playing. It was Roy Orbison singing Blue Bayou. As his eyes grew accustomed to the low light he saw that he was alone, but a moment later another door, on the other side of the room opened and Svetlana Borovsky stepped out.

"Again Waylon, I am so pleased you asked to meet," she said, motioning for him to follow. "This way."

She led him through the door and up two flights of stairs into what looked like the living room of a 1920s second floor apartment above a storefront.

"I am sorry for security, but things have heated up."

"With the Aryan Brotherhood?"

"You mean the Aryan People's Party?"

Choy shrugged.

"They, and many others, are currently displeased with us," said Borovsky, sitting on a comfortable-looking Depression-era green plush chair, part of a set that included an identical chair and sofa.

Choy sat on the matching chair just as Billy-Bob Baker entered the room.

"What is so important that we had to meet as soon as possible?" asked Baker, his smug smile suggesting he had the upper hand in the 'force the journalist to take my side' sweepstakes.

"First I need to ask Svetlana about the other day when she didn't show up in my hotel room," said Choy, determined this discussion would go according to his plan. "Why?"

She smiled and held up her hands in the cowboy 'I give up' pose. "I plead guilty."

"Your guilt is obvious; it is the question just posed that requires an answer."

"Why did I abandon you to fate? Because it served my purpose."

"Which was sending a message about my vulnerability in the face of many hostile forces and about how I need your protection?"

"If you understood message, my 'crime' was a success."

"Did you know he wouldn't kill me?"

"Best guess," she said, a slight sly smile escaping the corner of her mouth. "One cannot be certain with people like this but is risk I am prepared to take."

It was impossible to resist Borovsky's impish grin

"You and Billy-Bob were close to people like him not so long ago."

"We've moved on from some of our more extreme positions," said Baker, returning from the kitchen with two beers, offering one to Choy.

"Closer to Amanda's Committee of One Thousand and your new president?"

"Yes," said Baker, who glanced at Borovsky on hearing Bennett's name.

"Is that for real?"

"You don't believe we've moderated our positions?"

"Why would you?"

"Because we have been convinced that real power is within our grasp, that we are no longer playing on the fringe, that our current president has opened up new possibilities to reach a much greater proportion of the population."

"So ideological purity is no longer important to you?"

"Less important than considerations of mass appeal," he said. "The point has never been to have the right ideas, but rather to achieve the right results."

"Politics is much less about ideas than about power?"

"Exactly."

"So you are no longer a racist or a white supremacist?"

"These are labels applied to us by enemies of our people. I have always been against the racism facing those with European Judaeo-Christian backgrounds. In the name of identity politics laws are passed that discriminate against us."

"I see you include Jews in your new 'we'. When she left me alone with that whacko in the hotel, he expressed his displeasure with that fact in particular."

"There is much we can learn from Israel — how to build a state for our own people, how to protect ourselves, how to stand up to the so-called United Nations, how a country for one people and one religion can thrive and be strong."

"Okay," Choy interrupted him to make a point about how little he cared for his ideas. "I understand how dropping your overt racism and anti-Semitism were the price to pay for the Committee of One Thousand, or whatever you call yourselves now, to be allowed into the Washington corridors of power, but how does involvement in the drug business fit in?"

All traces of Baker's smile and cheerful demeanour vanished. He studied Choy for a moment. "Who told you about Amanda Bennett?" he said.

"I have files, photographs, video, copies of money transfers," he said, pressing relentlessly. "Someone inside your organization provided Mr. Lee with very damning evidence. But you already know that, because you have someone inside Mr. Lee's organization."

Baker smiled again.

"According to Lee, you and he are about to go to war and seek to gain some advantage by manipulating the media, represented by me. Of course, attempting to control and shape the flow of information is something all organizations do, so this in itself does not bother me. But when accompanied by threats to my safety, mere manipulation moves into another realm and becomes blackmail."

"In my experience a threat of personal harm has way of making people see more clearly, helps to understand essential from merely desirable," said Borovsky, joining the conversation. The juxtaposition between her faintly child-like demeanour and the meaning of her words was startling. "Life is all we have. We do what we must do to preserve it. This is central imperative that motivates us all. "

Choy's apparent reaction to her threat, a weak poker face, allowed both Baker and Borovsky to assume a moment of triumphal intimidation. Exactly what he was hoping for. "I am guessing one of your heroes is Ollie North," he said to Baker. "Have you met him? Did he give you advice? He was an American hero right? A true patriot? He did what was necessary to serve his president and his country."

Once more Baker's smile disappeared.

"I know what Lee is up to," continued Choy, certain from Baker's reaction that this track would lead to the place he wanted to go. "I know what you're doing in response has the tacit approval of people in high places. But we both know this tacit approval also comes with built-in deniability and you are well aware of the biblical goat sent into the wilderness carrying the sins of the Jewish people."

'A good journalist knows everything there is to know about the derivation and meaning of the words he uses.' An instructor at Langara College where Choy attended the one-year journalism program had offered this good advice and it had stuck with him. If nothing else it meant multiple ways he could warn someone they were at risk of being made a fall guy.

Baker and Borovsky stared at him, glancing occasionally at each other before responding.

"Why did you ask to meet with us?" said Baker.

"Do you know the true story about the guy the CIA recruited to run drugs into the United States as cover for reconnaissance of the Sandinistas and other guerrilla groups? I understand Hollywood is making a movie about him, starring Tom Cruise. Makes me wonder how they are going to have a happy ending if they stay true to the book because he dies in the end. A horrible beating, very painful, meant to send a message."

"Why did you ask to meet with us?" Baker repeated.

"I thought it important to let you know my understanding of the various balances of power amongst the players involved," Choy answered. "I understand my role and I understand yours. I have no moral objections to working with you or against you. As I told Mr. Lee, the truth, elusive as that may be, is my guiding principle. If it is in your self-interest to tell me certain truths about him, I will listen, learn and write about it, if the veracity of the information can be confirmed by other sources."

"You are trying to play us off against each other?" said Baker.

"Not trying to play, I am playing you off against each other. To uncover the truth about matters of public interest. That is what good journalists and historians do."

"You will help us if we help you?" Borovsky said.

"If my interest in uncovering the truth coincides with a particular interest of yours we would be fools not to cooperate."

"It wouldn't bother you to further our cause?" said Baker.

"If a journalist writes a book about a horrible murder spree, does he further the cause of psychopaths by interviewing one?"

"You are making same offer to Lee?" said Borovsky.

"He has already supplied me with information about you for reasons that have become obvious and it is only fair I extend the same opportunity to you," Choy answered. "Otherwise I could be accused of taking sides. Choosing one drug dealer over another."

Baker's smile was ominous, but entertaining. "And we should go along with this journalist-playing-off-both sides rather than simply intimidating you into silence, because?"

"Because you have more to lose travelling in that direction and more to gain going my way," Choy answered. "You don't know exactly what I know and who I've told. If I were to suddenly fall victim to a crazed speed addict killing me for the ten dollars in my wallet, a story very much favouring one side in this dispute might come out and you would have lost the opportunity to make sure it is fair and balanced. Something I have uncovered may be very embarrassing to powerful people, who may decide they are no longer your friends."

Choy's smile was larger than Baker's, but not by much.

"I do like you," Baker said after a few seconds of silent thinking. "You have what the Hebes call Chutzpah, I'll give you that. You do realize my supporters understand you and your kind write fake news?"

A smile staring contest lasted half a minute before Baker gave up first.

"Perhaps we can do business," Baker said. "But Svetlana and I need to discuss this first."

I have them.

"We will be in touch, soon," Baker said, standing up. "And I'm serious."

"About?"

"Liking you."

A war was about to start between two drug dealers and rather than get as far away as he could, he had planted himself between them. Incredibly he felt good about it.

***

The trip from Union Station to the drug rehab clinic in Malibu took almost two hours, but Choy enjoyed the ride on the Red Line subway, then two buses. Unlike when he had driven in Los Angeles, he actually had an opportunity to see the city. And it was not like public transit was substantially slower than a car, given how the freeways were more like parking lots throughout the day. His daughter and her teacher were right about the private automobile, they are bad things, best avoided. Urban areas should be designed around walking, cycling and public transit, not just for the sake of the climate, but for many other reasons as well: Aesthetics for one, all the world's most beautiful cities were laid out before automobiles; Health for another, driving instead of walking is one of the greatest risk factors for obesity and all sorts of other diseases; Sociability for yet another, driving induces stress and alienation, whereas walking and cycling make you feel friendly and part of the crowd sharing streets with you.

The realization that he had learned from his daughter felt good. He decided to text her. "Thinking UR right about cars as I ride streetcar in LA. All is well. Miss U"

In between watching the city go by and thoughts about how urban life could be improved by getting rid of cars, Choy focused on where he was at with Lee, Baker and Borovsky. It felt good to have stood up against their bullying, but there was still a missing piece of the puzzle, something about the relationship between Baker-Borovsky and Lee.

Thinking about drug lords and their victims made Choy think about Reb/Orchid again. For some reason drug rehab was big business in Malibu. It was home to dozens of facilities, ranging from the very posh and expensive to the quite utilitarian, according to a few Google searches Choy did while riding the bus from the Hollywood/Highland station. The one Mary Ellen had directed him to was in a slightly rundown old mansion on spacious, nicely landscaped grounds on a cliff looking out over the Pacific Ocean. It didn't look luxurious, but certainly wasn't cheap either. The 15-minute walk up from the beach road had revealed bigger, more spectacular homes, but the location alone must have ensured the facility was only attended by the extremely well off or people with excellent insurance plans.

At the gatehouse, which served as a small office, the receptionist glared at him when he asked to speak with Dawn Roberts.

"Do you have an appointment?"

"A former client of yours, Mary Ellen Randolph, told me the best time to talk with Dawn would be around 5 p.m. when the afternoon sessions were done."

"What is this about?"

"I'm writing a book about the life of a woman who died in Vancouver of a drug overdose and there's a possibility that Dawn might have some information that would be helpful."

"You're the guy from the story in the *Times*?" The look on the receptionist's face changed when he nodded. "Sit down just outside there and I will call her."

It took Dawn Roberts about 20 minutes to appear outside the gatehouse. She was fiftyish, a severe looking woman, wearing a skirt and jacket, who seemed annoyed rather than friendly. "I understand you are looking for me."

"Dawn Roberts?"

"Yes."

"I am Waylon Choy," he smiled and handed her his card. "I'm writing a book about a woman known around here as Orchid who recently died of a drug overdose in Vancouver, where she was known as Reb. Mary Ellen Randolph told me that you told her you knew Orchid. Does any of this ring a bell?"

"No," she said abruptly then made a point of crumpling the card he had given her. She looked inside the gatehouse at the receptionist. "We do not speak to journalists here. Never. No matter what or who it is about."

Perhaps there was nothing to it, but as he walked back down the winding road to the highway along the ocean Choy wondered why Roberts had only pretended to throw the crumpled business card into a wastebasket while the receptionist watched. Then as he was considering whether to get something to eat at the Jack in the Box across the road from the Malibu Pier, his cellphone vibrated.

"Mr. Choy?"

"Yes."

"This is Dawn Roberts," the voice was almost a whisper. "Are you still in Malibu? Can we meet? I'm walking to my car."

Five minutes later she pulled into the Jack in the Box parking lot and motioned for Choy to get in her car.

"Where are you parked?" she said, looking around the parking lot nervously.

"I don't have a car," he answered. "I came by public transit."

"Where are you staying? Can I give you a lift as we talk?"

"Downtown. Japantown." He could tell from the look on her face that her offer of a ride didn't extend to a location that far away. "But anywhere near a bus stop or a Metro Line would be fine. Where are you going?"

"Santa Monica. I could drop you at the downtown station. It's about 50 minutes from there to where you're going."

"Perfect."

"I'm sorry about what happened back there," she said, the car still parked. "But you must understand what's been going on and the clinic owner's problems with journalists. I can't be seen talking to one."

"What sort of problems?" said Choy.

She looked at him carefully, as if deciding what to say. "You really don't know? It's been all over the news."

"As I told you, I'm from Vancouver, Canada."

"This may take more time than I thought," she sighed.

"I could buy you dinner," he said, curiosity about the clinic owner added to a long list of questions about Reb. "Anywhere you want to go." But as soon as he said it, he thought about restaurants catering to the Hollywood crowd that could cost hundreds of dollars per person. This dinner would be on his tab, not Lee's.

"I'm a creature of habit," she answered. "Thursday is my deli day. It's not far from the downtown Santa Monica station."

"Perfect. I love deli. I'm buying."

She nodded and put the car into gear. "Okay, where do you want to start?"

"Did you know Orchid?"

"Yes I knew her. She attended one of my group sessions. Her real name is, was, Julie Christie. Just like the actress. In fact I believe she was named after her."

***

The meeting with the counsellor who had known Julie Christie convinced Choy that he had to move forward with his plan immediately. When he got back to the hotel he stripped off all his clothes, put on the bathing suit he bought earlier in the day, then the hotel bathrobe, before heading down to the business centre on the second floor. He signed into one of the PCs then logged on to his special Skype account and called the contact number for TwoSpiritPhoenix, left a message and then waited for the return. He then called Jan James back in Vancouver to give her the go ahead to do a story about Billy-Bob Baker's foray into drug dealing based on the material Lee had given him and he had shared with her. Then he called Max Parker from the Times at home.

"Max, it's Waylon Choy."

"I almost didn't answer because I didn't recognize the number on call display."

"I'm using a Skype line that I am assured is pretty secure."

"What's going on?"

"Are you interested in a story about a major importer of heroin and Fentanyl from China and southeast Asia who has connections with both the Chinese and American governments?"

***

Choy needed to sleep but couldn't get his brain to shut. TwoSpiritPhoenix's hacks revealed that both Billy-Bob and Lee had connections to various intelligence agencies which seemed to be running, or at least protecting, their computer systems. He finally had Reb's real name, Julie Christie, or at least that was the name Orchid/Reb had been registered as when she checked into the Malibu Shores Recovery Center for the first time eight years earlier. Dawn Roberts said Julie was from Butte, Montana, the daughter of a miner and a wife who had wanted to go to Hollywood and become a movie star before she got pregnant and married. If Dawn could gain access to Julie's file she would confirm this biographical information and other details, but because Peter Smith, the owner of the rehab clinic, had been the subject of numerous stories by a reporter at the *LA Weekly* newspaper, it was unlikely she would be given that access. One of the accusations was that beginning eight years earlier some Malibu Shores clients had worked for a drug distribution ring at least partly run by the same Peter Smith who owned six local rehab clinics. And Dawn suspected Julie Christie was one of those clients. If this were true and if he could track down Julie's parents to confirm it, this had the makings of one hell of a good story, even sadder with this extra wrinkle of Reb/Orchid/Julie also being a victim of a drug-dealing, drug-rehab-clinic owner.

Twelve Christies were listed with phone numbers in Butte, but it was too late to be calling strangers, especially since it was one hour later in Montana.

On the other hand it was only 11 p.m. in Vancouver. Maybe he should call James again; she always worked late; newsroom talk was she worked all the time. Whatever James wrote he hoped the story came out soon. He wanted to spend his time searching for Reb/Orchid/Julie's family and other people who had known her. Dealing with dodgy drug dealers was too dangerous, too stress inducing, with nothing that could possibly make him feel good as a result of writing what they wanted him to report.

Something had happened that caused Reb/Orchid/Julie to need drugs regardless of the harm they did to her. The war on drugs really was a war on drug addicts. How does it make sense to throw millions people into prison? Because drugs are bad for people? Then why stop at drug addicts? Why not alcohol, tobacco, coffee and sugar addicts? Lock up obese people to protect them from themselves. Obesity was a bigger health problem than heroin or all the opioids put together. Why not send the pushers of overeating, sugary drinks and sedentary lifestyles to jail?

The thoughts spun around Choy's brain like an out of control kid's top on a polished hardwood floor.

How will Baker and Bennett react when the story naming them both drug dealers comes out? They won't be happy and will definitely blame me, even if the story has another reporter's name on it. So? Bennett has been mad at me before. And Lee? What would he do when he found out a Times reporter was digging into his connections with the U.S. deep state? You can't be a good journalist and worry about how much the bad guys would dislike your stories.

That was bullshit of course. Every reporter with a brain should worry about how drug lords would react to their stories. Three hours south of Los Angeles journalists were killed regularly by the Mexican cartels.

Maybe I should change hotels. Maybe Max Parker could arrange for all my clothes and other stuff to be checked for electronic devices.

Could Lee be as violent as Baker and Bennett? He seemed so cultured, but to succeed in the drug business there must be another side to him.

I still haven't let Joy know that I won't make it to Las Vegas this weekend. Will she want to come here? Better make sure the front desk knows she might be coming.

Maybe the story about Reb/Orchid/Julie would work best as a novel. In a novel you could get inside the parents' heads; in real

life, or more to the point, in journalism — certainly not real life —
all you could really report is what they said.

Truth is seldom found in what people say.

On the other hand, how can you ever really know what
someone is thinking? There's no way to be certain.

I wonder if Joy is still awake?

I need to shut my mind off.

Why did I give the two stories to James and Parker?

The dust devil of spinning thoughts was finally tamed by a
buzzing cellphone. It was Joy.

"I was just thinking about calling," he said.

"I was getting worried."

"It's been crazy here. Things have gotten even weirder."

"What's wrong?"

"Nothing," he said, despite knowing he sounded as uncon-
vincing as he felt.

"Waylon?"

He didn't want to make her more worried than she already
was, but a lie wouldn't work; he had to tell her something believable.

"I finally got a break this evening. Reb and Orchid is really
Julie Christie."

"The British actress?"

"Apparently this Julie Christie was named after that one. She
was from Butte, Montana. There are 12 Christies listed in Butte and
I'm going to call all of them tomorrow. Maybe I'll go there."

"That wouldn't be too much out of the way if you drove
with me from Vegas to Vancouver."

"That's a great idea, but I may not be able to wait two weeks.
You know, if I get on a roll with phone calls tomorrow …" He realized how evasive he must sound. "The parents may want to come
to Vancouver right away, you know, to claim the body. Maybe I will

fly back to meet them and interview them there. Or maybe I'll still want to go to Butte, see the place where she grew up, talk to friends, so driving up there with you could work out, I don't know. I really can't say until after I talk with her family, if she has any. I mean I don't know if she does. She may have, but she may not. Or maybe they've moved or died. Everything is still unknown."

"Waylon, tell me what's wrong."

"What do you mean?"

"You start babbling when you're scared."

"Am I babbling?"

"Yes. Tell me what's wrong."

"My phone and probably my clothes have bugs in them," he answered, not wanting to keep things from her, even if he had a good reason to do so.

The silence lasted a few seconds.

"It might be Emerson Lee or it might be Billy-Bob Baker or the Russian woman who works with him, but it's probably all of them. They seem to know where I am and where I'm going to be."

"And they know that you know you are being monitored," she said.

"I don't really care; I've got nothing to hide. I just want to get out of their way, I don't want to be caught in the middle of a war between two drug gangs."

Had he told Joy about that before? He may not have. Now she'd really worry.

"Have either of them threatened you?"

"Not exactly."

"Be careful."

"I will," he answered, knowing that in the circumstances Joy had nothing else she could say over the phone, but that she would definitely try to help. "And you be careful too. I have this under control."

"We shouldn't be talking anymore," she said in a take-charge tone that confirmed Choy's suspicions about her intentions.

"Okay."

"I love you."

"I love you."

"Bye."

"Bye."

As Choy pressed the "end" button on his screen, he felt even more anxious than before Joy had called. This was going to be a long night.

10.

At 7:30 a.m., eight-thirty Mountain Time, Choy began phoning Christies in Butte, Montana. Forty-five minutes later, he ran out of people to call. At eight of the numbers no one answered, which wasn't a huge surprise on a Friday morning, and none of the other four knew anything at all about a Julie Christie, although three made comments about the famous actress. At least everyone was friendly and sounded willing to help if they had known anything helpful. In Choy's experience when you phone a stranger and start off the conversation by explaining you are a journalist working on a story, most people find that intriguing enough to want a conversation, even if they have no useful information. When he first started as a reporter he found calling strangers intimidating, but if you just did it instead of worrying about what people might say, it was often fun and enlightening.

At nine, as he was on his way through the hotel lobby to grab some breakfast, his cellphone began buzzing. He looked at the screen and it was Emerson Lee calling. He let the call go to voice mail and a few minutes later it was Max Parker, then Jan James and Emerson Lee again. While he was curious about the spurt of calls and whether they could all be related, he had told himself that the morning would be devoted to Julie Christie and anyone who had known her in Montana. He'd wait until noon to check his messages and instead, when he got back to his room, would phone the local Butte newspaper and police department.

The editor of the *Montana Standard*, a daily paper with a circulation of just over 12,000, was also one of three reporters. Although Choy was hoping to speak to somebody who had worked at the paper for 20 or 30 years and knew everything about everybody in town, it turned out Wendy Murphy had only worked in Butte for three years but was the senior person in the newsroom. The explanation was not a surprise: "The pay is too low to keep anyone for more than a year," she said. "Most reporters only last a few months. I made it this long because my husband grew up here and works as a high school teacher."

The name Julie Christie didn't ring any of her bells but she was willing to punch the name into the newspaper's database, which had been online a little over 10 years. There were no hits on Julie Christie, but a 21-year-old J. Christie was mentioned as a survivor in a story about a car crash that had killed three in a high school graduation day accident 10 years earlier.

"Nothing else?"

"Sorry."

"Thanks for your help."

"I love Vancouver, by the way," said Murphy. "A beautiful place and so many people from all parts of the world. I'd love to move there if I could get a job, you know get away from Donald Trump."

"There's lots of jobs, but places to live are kind of expensive," he answered, trying to be realistic, but not discouraging.

Similar conversations were happening a lot on this visit to the United States. People wanted to escape the new president. So far Choy had thought it was just California where hardly anybody voted for Trump, but here was someone in Montana where he garnered 55 per cent support.

After offering his phone number and asking for the best person to call at the local police department, he thanked her again, repeated his offer to buy her and her husband dinner if they ever did come to Vancouver and said good-bye. Next up was John Murphy, Wendy's brother-in-law who had recently been made a detective with the Butte-Silver Bow Law Enforcement Department.

"Julie Christie? I knew her. She was three years behind me in high school. A very pretty girl," said the detective, who Choy had asked to check if she had ever been reported missing. "She's dead? From an overdose?"

"Pretty sure it was Fentanyl, but the toxicology report wasn't available last time I checked."

"Was she a junkie?" asked Murphy.

"A prostitute as well on Vancouver's skid road."

"That's terrible. I remember her as smart and good looking. I think she was like a child actor or something. That's it. She was in a play when she was about 12, the Miracle Worker, I think it might have been the first play I ever saw. It was at the Mother Lode right after it opened— that's an old refurbished theatre here in town."

Certainly sounded like the Reb or Orchid people had described.

"Do you know anything else about her or her family?"

"I'm afraid not," he said. "I think they had an acreage out of town, but like I said she was three years behind me in school, so … I could ask around, but I don't see anything coming up when I punch in her name. She's never been reported missing here; she's never been arrested or charged with anything in Montana. You want me to try the FBI database?"

"Sure, if you can."

"I'm working on a case with an agent right now. I'm pretty sure she'd run the name for me."

"That would be great. Tell your agent friend I want to tell Julie's story, make her more than just another dead junkie streetwalker. We've had way too many of those in Vancouver and we need to let people know who exactly is dying, where they grew up, who their families are, you know, if we ever hope to get governments to do anything about all the overdoses."

"Hope you have better governments up there than we do down here. We just seem to go from bad to worse."

Choy took this as another anti-Trump comment. Other than Billy-Bob Baker, no one he had spoken to on this visit had anything positive to say about the former reality TV star.

John Murphy was very helpful, even though he didn't know much about Julie. He was familiar with Butte's drug scene, the kind of substances that a young woman growing up in a small city would have been exposed to — marijuana was most common, usually starting in high school, but sometimes earlier, prescription painkillers had been a huge problem, starting over a decade earlier, cocaine, speed and heroin were around, and Fentanyl had recently been killing addicts, especially "Indians" but a fair number of "white middle class kids" as well. He also spoke about the dead-end prospects for kids growing up in Butte, about how mining and other good industrial jobs had all but disappeared. He saw this as a factor in the growing drug problem facing the entire country.

After the cop conversation was over Choy immediately made another round of calls to the eight Butte Christies who so far had not answered their phones, but no one picked up. Once again he left messages with his phone number, email address and what he was calling about.

Finally he decided to check his voice mail. The first was a simple "call me" from Emerson Lee, then a "I have some news you'll want to hear" from Svetlana Borovsky, Max Parker saying, "I've set up an interview with a high level Southlands drug distributor who is willing to talk about Emerson Lee and I was wondering if you wanted to come along. Call me in the next 10 minutes if you do." The message was almost two hours old. Next up was Jan James: "Thought I'd give you a heads up that my story is going to be the line in tomorrow's *Sun*. Hope you like it. Thanks."

It was good that things were moving fast; it would keep Lee and Baker off balance. He hoped.

What do drug dealers do when thrown off balance? Kill people.

On the other hand, once the stories came out, what would be the point in killing anyone?

To send a message.

And he had to do the same. Send a message that he was not scared of them. Both cared about their public image. Why would they have contacted him if they didn't?

But which public do they care about?

They care about their rivals. Killing an annoying journalist would be just the sort of thing to impress other drug dealers.

What the hell have I gotten myself into?

Think about something else.

He decided to call Max Parker, but from the house phone in the lobby, in case he had anything confidential to say, but there was no answer. Back in his room he called Lee, who picked up immediately.

"Waylon."

"Emerson."

"I expect prompt replies from my people," he said, politely irritated. "It's been over two hours."

"I've been on the phone with police and media." If Lee were indeed listening to his cellphone conversations he would know, or could find out, it was with a cop and a reporter in Butte, Montana, but Choy didn't care. His use of "my people" in reference to him was completely out of bounds and Lee knew it.

"I need that story about Billy-Bob to be published as soon as possible," said Lee. "Events have made it imperative."

"How about tomorrow?"

"I beg your pardon?"

"A story exposing him and Amanda Bennett as major drug importers will be in tomorrow's *Vancouver Sun*."

Lee's silence spoke of his surprise and hopefully confusion.

"I told you not to mention Bennett," he finally said.

"I didn't. I gave the story to another reporter who works at the *Sun*."

An ominous silence.

"What events?" Choy asked. "What's happened to make it imperative that the story comes out?"

More silence.

"You do understand that I have never worked for you?" Choy said. "Certainly not in any employee-employer relationship. You did me a favour and in return I am doing one for you. But, given your lack of trust as evidenced by tracking my whereabouts, monitoring my phone calls, threats of violence if I do not do as I am told, your condescending description of our relationship and placing me in an extremely dangerous position between you and Billy-Bob, I am afraid I must cease to have anything to do with you."

The silence continued, but as he was about to end the call, Lee spoke.

"You are right, my friend. I have behaved poorly."

Despite his sincere tone, Choy was certain there was white hot anger inside a volcano seeking a route to the surface where it would eventually erupt.

"Our relationship must be based on trust," continued Lee. "And I have not acted in a trusting manner."

"You most certainly have not."

"I did not mean to insult you."

"You did not mean to insult me *again*," replied Choy.

"Yes."

Both sides were silent.

"There is a reporter here in LA working on a story about me," Lee said. "That is the event making the story we agreed upon imperative."

"Max Parker at the *Times*. A friend of mine."

It would have been better to have this conversation in person because it would have been easier to gauge exactly how angry Lee was.

"What did you tell him?"

"That you showed up one day at my door looking for someone to write a story about Billy-Bob Baker getting into the drug business, that you probably have connections high up in the Chinese Communist Party, that my guess was you too were a drug dealer, but I had absolutely no proof, and that you were a gentleman who was a wonderful dinner companion."

"That was all?"

"I also mentioned you are collaborating with some elements in the CIA and other security agencies."

Choy let this sink in. He knew it was unlikely to be his last conversation with Lee, but was determined to act as if it was.

"It's been interesting working with you Emerson," he said. "I won't say I enjoyed it, because honestly I did not. Good-bye."

As he pressed the hang-up icon, Choy's heart was racing.

I've just seriously dissed a big-time drug dealer.

***

The phone call from a lobby phone to Svetlana Borovsky also went about as expected. She claimed to have information about Lee and asked to meet again, but he refused, saying he'd look at whatever information she had, but only if it were dropped off at the hotel's front desk. He feigned only modest interest and told her that he had just gotten off the phone with Lee and didn't expect to be seeing him again. But Borovsky put Baker on the phone and he said their information was the "sort that could only be given in person" and would "blow your socks off and turn your long pants into short ones" so he agreed to at least consider meeting with Baker or Borovsky, if he wasn't too busy on the story about the dead woman, which he said, was now his fulltime job. But once the call ended Choy admitted, to himself at least, that he was very interested. The more dirt he had on Lee the safer he would be. Or it could be equally true that the more dirt he had, the greater the risk Lee would kill him.

***

To avoid useless dwelling on what may or may not happen next Choy focused on Julie Christie. On his fourth round of phone calls, just after 4 p.m. Mountain Time, he finally found someone who knew her parents.

"She's dead of a drug overdose?" said Andrea Christie, the former wife of Julie's father's cousin. "Oh dear, I knew something like this would happen. Julie was such a good girl until that accident."

"Were you close?"

"Before my divorce, when Julie was little, yes. But after she was ten, no."

"So you really didn't know her for over twenty years?"

"No one around here knew her for the last ten years, because she moved away to Los Angeles, after the accident. Not even her parents."

"Are they alive and still living in Butte?"

"I'm afraid not. They moved some time ago. I'm not sure exactly when and why. There were stories about Gwen starting to drink and taking pills after Julie left, but I don't know if that's true. She was such a lovely woman."

"Gwen was Julie's mother's name?"

"Yes. She was the most beautiful woman in Butte. And not stuck up like some with her good looks. She was kind and down-to-earth. Nothing fancy for her. And her two daughters were the nicest girls you could ever meet."

"Julie had a sister?"

"Jane. Named after Jane Fonda and her sister after Julie Christie, Gwen's two favourite actresses. She always wanted to be a movie star and she had the looks believe me, but after her marriage she put all her energy into the two girls. Julie even studied acting."

"Do you know where?"

"In Missoula at the university, until the accident. I'm told she was very good, an excellent student. Jane, on the other hand, was the athletic type, like her father.

"Where does she live now?"

"You don't know?"

"Know what?"

"It was so sad. Jane and those two boys were killed in a car crash on Jane's graduation night. Julie was driving the car and it went off the highway and rolled and the three were killed but she survived because of being behind the wheel, or so people said. Walked away with barely a scratch, although I also heard she had tremendous pain from a crack in her spine or something. But then others said the pain was all in her head, from guilt at killing her boyfriend, her sister and her sister's boyfriend. I really don't know the truth, because people make up stories."

"Julie was in a lot of pain after the car accident?"

"That's what I heard."

"But you don't really know? You never spoke with Gwen or Julie's father? What was his name?"

"Thomas. Tom and Gwen never spoke to me after the divorce. The break-up with my husband was very bitter and they took his side, which was understandable under the circumstances. I mean my husband was Tom's cousin."

From the tone of Andrea's voice, Choy was almost certain she had been having an affair and that was the circumstance which caused Gwen and Tom to break with her. Not that it mattered.

"You said Gwen and Tom moved away from Butte?"

"Yes, a year or two after the accident. To Boise, I think. Tom refused to work non-union and there just weren't enough union jobs in Butte anymore. Tom transferred to the union down there, I heard. He was a heavy equipment operator, even though he was first in the family to go to university. All miners before him. He went to university for one year before dropping out. He met Gwen up there."

"Did Gwen or Tom have any brothers or sisters?"

"Gwen was an only child. Tom had an older brother and sister, but they're both dead. I saw the notices in the newspaper, the sister about five years ago and the brother a few years before that."

"Do they have any family or friends left in Butte?"

"I don't think so. The only relatives I know about are dead and if they had any friends my guess is they moved away long ago. There are fewer people in Butte today than in 1920. Everyone who can has left."

"Is there anything else about Tom or Gwen or Julie that might be helpful?"

"Even though they were very angry at me over the divorce, I never stopped thinking they were good people. They were excellent parents, very loving. Tom was an Episcopalian who converted to Catholicism to marry Gwen, but neither were particularly religious. They were Democrats, but then most people in Butte used to be Democrats. Even in the last election most of Butte voted for Clinton, not that big hair crazy man Donald Trump."

"Anything else about Julie?"

"From a very young age, maybe five or six, she would mimic people's accents and was very good at it. She loved performing. She was in that play about Helen Keller when she was 12. It was after my divorce so I wasn't invited to opening night but I went anyway. She was very good."

"That's all? Is there anyone else in Butte I should call who might have more information about where Gwen and Tom live now?"

"Well, I'd say the company that Tom worked for here, but they went bankrupt years ago. Maybe his union."

"Do you know which union that was?"

"The Operating Engineers, I believe, same as Marty, the guy who lives next door to me. But I don't think there's anyone left who would have known him."

After giving Andrea his contact information, Choy thanked her and said good-bye. He was further ahead than a few hours earlier with Julie's parents' names and the knowledge they had once lived in Boise, but he had hoped for more from Butte. From the little he knew about the city it would have been a perfect place for a Reb/Orchid/Julie drug addict prostitute to have come from and for her parents to still live. It was a once glorious mining town that had fallen on hard times by the 1960s, the perfect metaphor for a victim of an opioid crisis in the era of Donald Trump. If he were writing fiction Julie's parents would still live in Butte, maybe in a house that overlooked the Berkeley Pit, a flooded open pit copper mine that he read was one of the largest Superfund contamination sites in the USA. A man-made toxic lake: that would have been a perfect detail for a story about the life and death of Julie Christie.

As he was gathering his thoughts and going over notes his phone vibrated. The screen said the caller was Max Parker, but when Choy answered there was only silence. "Max? Is that you? Max? Hello? Hello?" Finally, a voice that he didn't recognize said: "Chinga tu madre, esse." He couldn't tell if the person was saying this to him or someone else. Then the call ended.

It was weird that Max would have called the cellphone number given he knew it was most likely bugged, but maybe he was excited about something that had come up and called without thinking, then remembered he was supposed to email and wait for a call back. Maybe he was in a room with other people and one of them told another to 'fuck off'. Choy put his phone back into his pocket without thinking too much about it but expected an email in the next few minutes from his *LA Times* reporter colleague.

Again his cellphone vibrated. It was a 406 area code. Butte, or somewhere else in Montana.

"Waylon Choy," he answered.

"It's John Murphy in Butte," said the cop he had previously spoken to. "I have a little more information."

"I appreciate it."

"After we talked I couldn't get the image of Julie Christie playing Helen Keller in A Miracle Worker out of my mind. It's good you are telling her story, people should know who is dying from all these overdoses."

Unsolicited help from a cop? A pleasant surprise. Must be an American thing. Cops in Canada seldom are friendly with reporters.

"Here's what I've been able to find out," he continued. "Julie Christie was born July 4, 1985, in Missoula, so she would have been turning 32 this year."

But looked 50.

"Her parents were Gwendolyn Henderson and Thomas Christie. They were married August 5, 1985."

Born on the Fourth of July is a good detail. Parents not being married when she was born even better. Must have been attending university in Missoula.

"Julie was here in Butte from Grade 1 to 12 and then attended the University of Montana for three years where she was enrolled in the School of Theatre and Dance. She won at least two scholarships and was an excellent student."

Once upon a time it wasn't so hard to think and take notes.

"If you want to track down someone who knew Julie there I'd suggest you call a Ms. Bolan who works in the admissions office. Very friendly and accommodating. Tell her I told you to call. Apparently Julie was working in the university summer children's theatre repertory program around the time of the car accident."

"In which her little sister and two young men were killed," said Choy. "I found a cousin by marriage who still lives in Butte."

"All three of the deceased were drunk and stoned," said Murphy. "Julie had no trace of alcohol or drugs in her system, so she must have been the designated driver. According to the investigator, Julie was driving the deceased home from a graduation party when they began passing around a joint, which she refused to try."

How do you go in 10 years from a designated driver children's repertory actor refusing a joint to a dead hooker with a needle dangling in your arm?

"Somehow the lit joint ended up falling onto her lap and in the ensuing panic, the car went off the road, flipping twice and only the driver was wearing a seatbelt, as well as only the driver position having an airbag that deployed successfully."

What are the chances someone in the same repertory company now lives in Los Angeles? I need to call this Ms. Bolan.

"Julie was reported missing twice, in December 2009 and then three years later. The first report was filed to the Boise police department, but then she was found three months later. The second report was simply withdrawn a few weeks after it was filed, with no explanation. And that is the last record I could find of her. No passport, no driver's licence, no income tax filing, my friend at the FBI says absolutely nothing."

"Not surprising if she was in LA, living on the beach and selling acid."

"So she did make it to Hollywood? She was a great actor, at least at 12."

"I was told she lived here for at least a few years," said Choy. "She attended a drug rehab centre, people say she was in one porn video and that she sometimes sold acid. That's all I got so far."

In Choy's experience the best way to get people in positions of power, or anyone for that matter, to tell you all they know was by sharing what you know with them. Of course that wasn't always possible, but if you could make someone feel like a participant in uncovering the truth, they were more likely to help.

"A porn video, my word, that makes me sad."

"If it's any comfort I'm told she did a very small part more or less on a dare and never did it again. And she only sold acid to her friends at parties."

"She became a prostitute up in Vancouver?"

"From what I know so far, yes. You know people call it Terminal City?"

"Vancouver?"

"Ya, because it was always the end of the line on railways and highways from the east and the south. But it also was always Terminal City in the other sense too. People came to die, commit slow suicide with alcohol or drugs, after running away from whatever crap happened to them somewhere else. The end of the road."

"I guess there's a little of that everywhere. Even in Butte."

"That was everything you could find?" Choy said, even though the answer was obvious. "I don't suppose you checked the databases for her parents."

"There's nothing here and I can't ask my friend at the FBI to run names of living people with no probable cause. You never know when that causes trouble. Some people are very sensitive."

"Even when it might mean learning that your daughter has died?"

"You never know," said Murphy. "Maybe they had a bad falling out. That's pretty common with addicts and their families."

"Even to the point of not wanting to know they've died? I can't imagine not wanting to know how, when and where at least."

"If you're a good reporter, you should be able to find them now that you have their names."

"Probably," Choy said, in a way that he hoped had just the right amount of doubt in voice. "May I call you back if I can't?"

Murphy was silent for a few seconds before answering. "I'll think about it."

"Thank you. You've been a big help already."

"If you get the book published let me know, okay? I want to buy a copy."

"I'll send you one for free, I promise."

As soon as he got off the phone he spent half an hour organizing notes, then grabbed his laptop to look up the number for the University of Montana admissions department. As he was doing that his phone buzzed.

The screen again said Max Parker.

"Hello. Max?"

"Who is this?" said the voice on the other end.

"Who is this?" answered Choy.

"Detective James Carroll of the Los Angeles Police Department."

"You're calling from Max Parker's phone?"

"It appears I am."

"Why?"

"This was the last number called from a cellphone found at the scene where we have four dead people," said Carroll. "Now who is this?"

11.

Despite the shock of the phone call Choy managed to compose himself enough to call Ms. Bolan in the admissions department at the University of Montana, but she had left for the day, so he left a detailed message and told her to check the *Los Angeles Times* website for more background. Then, as he walked out of his hotel room he noticed a piece of paper that had been slipped under the door. There was a printed address on it, "today at 8 p.m. — I have information about AB and BBB", and the initials EL.

He didn't have time for Emerson Lee's games but kept the note. By the time he was going through the hotel lobby on the way to grabbing a cab he was thinking about how much more to tell the police about what Max Parker was working on. He decided to call the *Times* city desk and was put through to the assignment editor, Francine Pelletier.

"Max Parker was there? And he's dead?"

"That's what a Detective Carroll just told me. I agreed to meet him at the house. I'm on my way there now."

"You were the source of the tip Max was given? That had him go to the house where the shooting happened?"

"No, I'm a former reporter at the *Vancouver Sun* in Canada — I helped Max a few years back on a story — who passed on some information I learned in the course of working on something else. I don't have a clue about that house or who he was meeting."

The conversation had been quick and unsatisfying. Pelletier did not handle the shock of a dead reporter well and, it seemed to Choy, was not thinking clearly about the big picture. He had wanted to talk about how much he should say about the story Max was working on, but she was only interested in discussing details about what had just occurred, a subject he knew little about.

After telling the cop the basic outline of what he knew, Choy made out like he had more important information, but didn't want to discuss it on the phone and agreed to be interviewed at the site of the killing, so he might have more details later for the city editor, but the paper had already sent a reporter to the address upon learning of four dead in a shooting while monitoring the police radio.

The site of the shooting was about 25 minutes away from his hotel in a rundown neighbourhood with commercial signs mostly in Spanish. The cab could only get within about a block and a half of the address and Choy had to report to a uniform cop that he was there to meet Detective Carroll. After five minutes another cop, this time a woman, came to the spot where he had been told to wait and accompanied him to the corner of the block where the shooting happened. The area was cordoned off as investigators searched pavement, grass and sidewalks on both sides of the street.

"This is the guy on the other end of the phone you found," said the woman cop to a tall man in a suit.

"You're Waylon Choy?" he said.

"You're Detective Carroll?"

"Ya," he answered. "You have some ID?"

Choy made a show of being irritated as he pulled his passport from his pants pocket and opened it.

"A Canadian? Is Choy a common name up there?"

"Not uncommon for people of Chinese descent," he said.

Carroll leaned down and looked more closely at Choy's face, as if still not believing that someone who looked like this could have that surname.

"Not at all what I expected," the cop muttered.

"Black men like you should understand, better than most, the dangers of stereotyping," said Choy, making sure a big smile appeared on his face.

"Got me there," answered Carroll. "So what do you know about why Max was here when the shooting happened?"

"You're welcome," said Choy.

After a few seconds Carroll asked: "Did I forget to thank you for something?"

"For coming here to answer your questions and spending $25 on a cab."

"I could get you a chit, but it probably won't be paid for a couple of months."

"A thank you would be sufficient."

"Thank you. Guess what? A dead reporter apparently makes this a priority investigation."

"I should hope so."

"You are a journalist friend of the victim?" he asked, looking at his notes.

"I worked with Max years ago in Vancouver, gave him a story about a movie star who trashed a house, but I wasn't really a friend."

"But this latest story you gave him was about drug dealers? That's what you said on the phone."

"It was a tip, nothing more. While working on something else I came across information that I thought would interest Max."

"Why him?"

"He is, was an ambitious reporter. If the story pans out it would be very good for his career."

"I'd say that's unlikely to happen."

"And I feel horrible, guilty even," said Choy, making the mistake of telling the truth to a cop.

"Why do you feel guilty?"

"Because my tip probably led him to this place."

"Tell me again, why Max? As far as I know he's not a regular crime reporter."

"He did me a favour on another story I'm working on, about a dead junkie in Vancouver, that really helped, so I figured I owed him one."

"What sort of favour?"

"He wrote a story that was on the front page of the *Times* a few days ago."

"I saw that. That was you? You have any luck in identifying the woman?"

Choy nodded.

"So what was the tip you gave Max?"

"That a guy named Emerson Lee shows up a few weeks ago in Vancouver wanting me to write a story about a guy named Billy-Bob Baker getting into the drug business. This Mr. Lee probably has connections high up in the Chinese Communist Party, and probably also is a drug importer. I told Max he owns a house here."

"That's it?"

"More or less."

Carroll's unhappy look was purposely intimidating.

"You might be better off not knowing the other bit," said Choy.

"I'll be the judge of that."

"I could get the *Times* management involved regarding journalistic privilege and that might be a real pain in the ass for you, especially for something that's not relevant and you won't believe anyway."

"Now I'm intrigued."

"If I tell you everything, will you tell me what you think happened here, off the record? I won't tell anyone you told me and won't pass on the information to any other journalist. I really do feel guilty that I somehow caused this. I'd like to help you find who killed him and whether or not it had anything to do with me. "

***

Because the interview with the detective lasted only another 15 minutes, Choy had time to make it to the address on Lee's note. In fact he had time to kill, so he asked the woman beat cop who Carroll ordered to give him a lift to drop him off at a coffee shop about a block away from the restaurant Lee had chosen in an old warehouse district that looked to be not far from Japantown.

Time to kill, an interesting phrase with multiple possible meanings.

The longer he worked with words the harder it got to use common turns of phrase without reflecting upon them and questioning their literal meanings.

Time did kill and obviously someone had chosen a few hours earlier as the time to kill four men sitting in that house. Maybe Max just chose the wrong time to be there, but this is not the time to simply shrug my shoulders and say what bad timing. Instead I need to kill time productively, by going over recent events. Time. Killing.

While coincidence was always a possibility, it was best to assume there was a connection between the information he had given Max and the drive-by shooting. The obvious possibility was that Emerson Lee didn't want a story about him to be written and had arranged for Max to be murdered in a way that the police could dismiss as an important person being in the wrong place at the wrong time, but fundamentally just another gangland slaying. To give the detective his due, Carroll seemed intrigued by the possibility that a reporter had in fact been the target of a gang hit, not simply a coincidental innocent victim. But in Choy's limited experience with police investigations they would ultimately buy whatever plausible explanation was the least work. So it would be up to him to steer Carroll in the right direction and the only way of doing that was by telling him everything he knew about Lee, which, in fact, he mostly had already done. Some actual evidence, or at least information that pointed in his direction, was needed for the detective to spend any of his precious time investigating someone rich, powerful and probably well connected to protectors in the police department. Unfortunately Baker and Borovsky were the only people he knew who might be able to provide something good enough for Carroll to seriously investigate Lee's possible connection to the shooting. But the story about their activities related to the wholesale illegal drug business and its connection to notorious alt-right leader Amanda Bennett was going to be in tomorrow's *Vancouver Sun*, which they might like or it could seriously piss them off. If angry they might send a hit team rather than offer dirt about Lee.

Then an alternative scenario occurred to Choy. What if Baker had arranged the shooting himself because he knew the murder of a fellow reporter by Lee would drive Choy into getting back at him?

I'm being paranoid.

Choy hated the certainty of uncertainty. His previous experiences with people involved in the murky, so-called intelligence world had left him without doubt that he would always doubt whatever seemed apparent about any of them. He didn't want to be sucked back into the world of dangerous shadows, yet here he was, heart pumping, feeling … if not good, at least stimulated, like after a good run. The closeness to death made him feel alive.

Again Choy thought about his father's gambling addiction, becoming more convinced that it and whatever he was feeling were connected. Gambling with the highest stakes possible: his life.

Should I see Lee? Or should I go back to my hotel, check out, take a bus to Las Vegas and spend the weekend with Joy?

Or he could stay and start searching for Reb's parents and then first thing Monday morning call the University of Montana. They might have contact information for her parents. Or a lead about a friend from school who is now an actor in Los Angeles. Working on a story about the life and death of a drug addict at least offered the possibility of uncovering the truth. Unlike talking to Lee, where the only certainties were more lies and a frustrating opaqueness.

Still, he couldn't stop himself from leaving the coffee shop and heading up the street to what looked like a restaurant popular with young *trendoids*, the ranks of whom stretched in a line of a few dozen out the large wooden sliding door of an old factory. He had to ask Lee about Max. That was the minimum owed to a fellow journalist.

Curiosity kills cats and journalists.

As he walked straight to the hostess station at the front of the line, smiling at a young woman who could easily have been a model or the next hot young movie star, Choy was not full of determination, but rather an uneasy realization that he might be the next murdered journalist. The hostess led him through a room with a high exposed wood ceiling to a set of stairs that led to a small private room that was probably once a foreman's office, since it overlooked the large open space below. Lee was seated alone, back to the wall, at a table big enough for at least a dozen. There were two open bottles of wine on the table and more on a cupboard that ran the width of the room.

As he stepped through the door his cellphone vibrated. He pulled it from his pocket and looked at the screen. The University of Montana; it had to be Ms. Bolan answering his message. Choy looked up from the screen to Lee, held up the phone and then one finger as if to say, give me a minute, then turned around. As he walked back to the landing at the top of the stairs, he spoke into the phone: "Hello, this is Waylon Choy."

"Mr. Choy, this is Merilee Bolan, at the University of Montana. You left me a message earlier."

"Yes. Thanks for returning my call."

"I remember Julie Christie very well. I've seen every play produced by the theatre department over the past 29 years and she was the best actor who ever attended our school. One performance in particular has stuck with me all these years: an all-woman performance of King Lear set in the civil rights era South with Julie in the title role. My hobby is attending Shakespeare festivals around the world and I have never seen a better Lear. Her Alabama accent was spot on and I grew up in Montgomery. When Julie dropped out of university after that horrible car accident we were all so sad and there have been many conversations over the years about her, so, when I listened to your message, the memories came flooding back."

As Choy stood on the landing overlooking the large room below he noticed two rather muscular Chinese men who looked out of place in this restaurant filled with cool twenty-somethings. Both were discretely keeping an eye on people approaching anywhere near the stairs and constantly glancing up at him.

"I read the *Los Angeles Times* story online and it made me very, very sad. What a waste of a wonderful talent was my first reaction and then realized her death need not be for naught. Her story could teach us all a lesson. So, for the past three hours I have been calling everyone I could think of from the theatre department who might have known her back then and maybe later. Everyone I have spoken to has been absolutely shocked to hear about her tragic end, absolutely shocked."

"Yes," Choy said as he tried to concentrate on the voice coming from the cellphone but was distracted by the thought he was standing in a vulnerable spot that the bodyguards below, who must be there for a reason, could not easily defend. He re-entered the private dining room and again smiled at Lee.

"I tracked down Julie's best friend from that time, Abigail Munro. She was also a very good actor and knew Julie for a time in Los Angeles. In fact Abigail told me just now they lived together for almost a year. I think she is the person you need to speak with."

"Yes, she sounds like exactly the person I've been looking for," said Choy. "I thank you so much for your help."

"I can give you her phone number. Do you have a pen?"

A text message would have been preferable given where he was, but she had called from an office phone, so that would not be convenient. He grabbed the emergency pen that he always carried in his shirt pocket, but the only writing surface available was the back of his hand.

"Go ahead."

After adding the ten numerals under her name and making eye contact with Lee, he did something that he really didn't like to do. He ended a conversation before being certain she had told him everything she knew. While he apologized and wrote Ms. Bolan's home phone number on his other hand and promised to call her back tomorrow, he hoped she didn't feel her assistance had been rewarded with rudeness.

Finally Choy formally greeted a now standing, smiling Lee.

"Thank you so much for coming," said the least-easy-to-read person Choy had ever met. "I'm certain you will find this a worthwhile use of your valuable time."

"Sorry about the interruption, but I've been waiting hours for that phone call and the person on the other end has done me a huge favour, so answering her call was the least I could do."

"I too am doing you a favour."

"We'll see."

"Please, sit down," said Lee. "I've taken the liberty of order-ing some dishes. The chef once worked for a very important family in Lima and is a master of Peruvian coastal and creole cuisine. Another member of our Chinese diaspora. I hope you like seafood. The ceviche and escabeche de pescado are the best you will find in North America."

"Wonderful," he answered but was not quite sure what the second dish was. As both men smiled, Choy understood it was necessary for him to take charge of the conversation, because Lee soon would. "I really don't mean to be rude but as you noted I am in the middle of a very important story and my time is currently quite limited, so please skip the pleasantries and get straight to the point."

Lee's smile froze as if he was about to get angry but quickly recovered his air of detached refinement. "It is refreshing to deal with a straight shooter such as yourself. To be surrounded by sycophants is tiring."

As Choy was thinking it 'takes one to know one' his tablemate poured him a glass of white wine. "An Alsace Grand Cru that I find goes particularly well with Chef Chow's ceviche."

As Lee was pouring the wine a young waitress, another beauty in a restaurant where good looks were common to both the served and servers, appeared with two plates, each covered with artfully arranged pieces of marinated raw white fish. After she had placed dishes in front of both men, Lee motioned with his eyes for her to leave the room.

"I find a chew or two of a generous piece of fish, a swallow, followed by a sip of wine produces a most satisfactory sensory experience," said Lee who then proceeded to illustrate his instructions.

When in the city of angels, do as the angels do, so Choy quickly mimicked the man seated a few feet away. Both the food and the beverage were delicious.

"The chef's secret is aji amarillos, garlic and onions all grown from Peruvian seed in a rather large Santa Monica backyard by a man who learned to farm on the coastal plain just outside of Trujillo," said Lee, showing off. "The climate of both places is similar enough that the resulting taste here is indistinguishable from such a dish made there, if the chef uses limes flown in directly from Lima."

Choy couldn't help but smile and repeat the ritual of fork, then glass to his mouth. Then again and again and again until the plate in front of him was bare, save for some liquid and a few stray pieces of onion and pepper, as his host spoke of the proper technique to marinate white fish in the right combination of citrus juices and other culinary matters. Lee took a piece of bread from a bowl on the table, broke a piece off, rubbed it across the plate to soak up the remaining juice, then motioned with his eyes for Choy to do the same. Again it was advice worth following.

Twenty minutes after trying to take control of the conversation Choy realized he had fallen under the influence of Lee's charms. What was worse, he didn't care. The food and drink were some of the best he ever had and when the waitress returned with two plates of much different looking fish, he could only smile contentedly as a half bottle of the best white wine he had ever tasted had produced a mellow buzz that made the world seem quite wonderful.

"Ah, the escabeche, for that we must switch wines," said Lee, half to Choy and half to the waitress who he directed to an open bottle of red on the counter at the end of the room. "This is a special bottle from the finca of a very good friend in Argentina. A 1976 Malbec — blood red — an extremely good year in Mendoza according to the retired general whose family has owned the vineyard for over one hundred and fifty years."

Choy was not yet drunk enough to miss Lee's understated reference to the year Argentine generals took power and began the Dirty War against left wing "subversives" that resulted in 30,000 deaths.

"You know the difference between ceviche and escabeche de pescado?" asked Lee but didn't wait for Choy to answer. "Both are pickled fish, but ceviche is put into the acidic liquid raw while escabeche is cooked first, so the textures are entirely different."

"The crispness of the carrots and peppers contrasts perfectly with the flakey firm flesh in the escabeche versus the somewhat better held together buttery softness of the fish in the ceviche," said Choy, sounding like he had gotten the food critic beat he applied for many years ago.

"A very good description my friend."

What am I doing?

Something about Lee's tone, a mixture of condescension and solicitousness, woke Choy from his sensual slumber. He pushed away his not quite finished plate and put his hand over the glass when Lee tried to pour him more wine.

"Is something wrong?" asked Lee.

"I am sated," stated Choy. "Thank you. The food and wine were wonderful but now we must get down to business. Who ordered the hit on the *Los Angeles Times* reporter?"

He had Lee's attention but could not read whether or not his adversary knew about the drive-by shooting. Was the marble-like stillness an attempt to cover-up guilt or surprise?

Lee pushed his chair a few inches more away from the table. "I warned you about the war that was about to break out."

"I can make a plausible case for Baker or you being behind the shooting of Max Parker."

"Someone has killed your associate? An *LA Times* reporter?"

"The journalist friend of mine who was working on a story about you and the Chinese government's involvement with current and ex- U.S. intelligence service personnel in the importation and distribution of illegal drugs."

Lee slowly took a sip of wine before he spoke. "I see."

"What do you see?"

"That it would not take much paranoia or belief in conspiracy theories to conjure up all sorts of suspects if one believed such lies."

"So you know absolutely nothing about who did it?"

"I would need to know who did it before I could answer that question truthfully."

"But you don't?" Choy said, trying to get a straight answer out of a man who specialized in avoiding them. "You don't know who killed him?"

"How could I know who killed him if never knew him or the fact that he was dead?"

Ask a direct question.

"What do you know about the death of Max Parker?"

Lee smiled as if he enjoyed playing this game, especially after a bottle of wine. He took another big mouthful of the Malbec. "Let's see. I know that reporters who investigate drug dealers, certainly ones who might have links to the Mexican cartels, are often murdered. I know that the so-called war on drugs has claimed the lives of many journalists. I know that the supply of illegal drugs into the United States has grown since Ronald and Nancy Reagan made their famous declaration of war. I know that the United States has long been the largest, most lucrative market for illegal drugs in the world. I know that countries with large black markets, or underground economies such as that which buys and sells illicit drugs, always have a significant level of corruption in their law enforcement, judicial, political and other governmental systems. I know that every intelligence agency in the world exploits this sort of corruption to its own ends, whether to gather information or to influence policy through the use of tools such as blackmail, bribery, or murder."

With almost a bottle of wine affecting his brain Choy was having difficulty following what Lee was telling him. He seemed to be saying he had some connection with the Mexican cartels and that corrupt cops or politicians or the CIA might have ordered the murder of Max Parker. Or maybe it was a Chinese intelligence agency.

"I know that if the war on drugs has not, in fact, reduced the supply of drugs then it must serve some other purpose or purposes that are either hidden or unstated. I also know that the so-called war on drugs is now used as cover for other policy objectives in countries all around the world. I know much that couldn't otherwise be done can be accomplished in the name of fighting this so-called war."

What does that mean?

"What does that mean?" Choy repeated his thought aloud, as Lee grabbed another bottle of wine and offered to pour him a glass.

"A Premier Cru Sauterne," said Lee. "You will regret, for the rest of your life, not tasting it. It is from Thomas Jefferson's favourite vineyard in all of France."

What the hell!

As he nodded his assent to another glass of wine, Choy failed to comprehend what Lee meant by 'a cover for other policy objectives'.

"What do you mean by 'other policy objectives'," he asked.

"I know that in Colombia coca and other drugs were more likely to be found growing in areas with mineral wealth that mining companies were interested in developing. I know that under Plan Colombia and the Merida Initiative a significant portion of U.S. funding was spent on re-writing laws that made both countries much friendlier environments for foreign investment. I know that in both Colombia and Mexico funds from one war were used to fight another against subversive guerrillas. I also know that in Mexico the war on drugs was used to push the government to rewrite its constitution to undermine the control of collective farms over vast areas of valuable land."

"You're talking about ejidos?" said Choy, who had read many books about the Mexican Revolution and its accomplishments. "They're cooperatives run by the peasants who live on the land, not collective farms owned by the government."

"A barrier to capitalism, whatever you call it."

"You're saying the war on drugs is a cover used by neoliberals to create a world more to their liking, sort of another form of the shock doctrine as described by Naomi Klein?"

"I'm saying the expansion of capitalism has always been accompanied by violence, death and a massive disruption of the existing order. Change is never easy. Short term pain is inevitable for long term gain."

"Whose long-term gain?" asked Choy, after taking a sip of a delicious sweet wine, finally able to understand why people were prepared to pay hundreds of dollars for a half bottle. "Peasant parents must lose their land or be killed so their children can have cellphones and Type 2 diabetes?"

"I am not making a moral defence of capitalism, but rather describing a reality. From the enclosures in 18th century Britain to refugees from Dust Bowl Oklahoma making their way to California through to the small farmers squeezed off their land in 21st century Mexico, people must be made to flee the old economy in order to flourish in the new. That is the way of capitalism, your economic system."

"Mine?"

"It has provided you with a good life, the best food, wines, anything you want, because you were willing to work hard."

"I don't believe in capitalism, or socialism, or communism, or liberalism."

"I know, the only 'ism' for the great Waylon Choy is journalism. Unfortunately that is a very limited and shallow belief system."

"Why did you invite me here? Not to talk politics."

"To enjoy some food, wine and conversation," answered Lee. "One last supper. And to make the point that you too can enjoy the good life, if you make the right decisions."

The right decisions?

"And if I make the wrong decisions I may end up like Max Parker, whose body is probably on some coroner's table as we speak?"

Lee lifted his eyebrows, puckered his cheeks and raised a hand off the table as if to say, 'you said it, not me.'

"What information do you have about Billy-Bob and Svetlana?"

"They, together with Amanda Bennett have just made an alliance with the Russian mafia, a deal brokered by a coalition of Eastern European right wing nationalist groups."

That would certainly be a story I could sell. The alt right making deals with the Russian mob.

"Your proof?" Choy said.

"Some photos of Bennett meeting with various people, an anonymous background briefing from someone high up in the DEA, a heads-up on a few of the targets that the Russians have agreed to eliminate."

"So Bennett and Baker have brought in the Russians, who are white like her and Donald Trump, to fight the inferior Mexicans and Chinese, led by Emerson Lee?"

"Something like that," answered Lee.

His smug smile irritated Choy.

"And now you have finally decided that it is in your self-interest to expose Amanda Bennett's ties to the drug business."

"I have always wanted to expose her," he answered. "My only concern was timing."

As Choy was about to object, the phone vibrated in his pocket. He pulled it out to look at the screen: A Vancouver number that he didn't recognize, maybe one of his children.

"I must take this," he said, not caring about, perhaps even enjoying his rudeness toward Lee. "Hello."

"Waylon?"

"Yes."

"It's Simon Randolph."

"Simon!" said Choy going overboard with his friendliness to further irritate Lee. Randolph was a former colleague at the *Sun*. "How the hell are you? How are you enjoying all the meetings now that you're city editor and ..."

"Waylon," he interrupted, "Jan James has been killed."

The words didn't quite register, perhaps because of the wine.

"We have the story she wrote based on your information ready to go for tomorrow's paper. Front and four pages inside. But I thought I better call and ask if there was any way this story and her death could be connected? I mean she had a lot of enemies and we know from court testimony that various gangsters have discussed killing her over the years ..."

"How?" it was only word he managed to get out.

"A stabbing in the Bay parkade," said Randolph. "It might have been a robbery or a random attack by a violent mentally ill person, the police don't know yet. They're looking for video footage."

"Jesus Christ!" said Choy with a lot of emotion packed into the two blasphemous words.

"Ya."

Choy looked over at the still smiling Lee as the silence on the phone lasted a few seconds.

"So what do you think?" asked Randolph. "Is there any possibility that this could have been in retaliation for tomorrow's story?"

"Ya," said Choy, glaring at Lee. "It's a definite possibility."

"Will you be a target if we run it?"

"Maybe.

"So what do you want us to do?"

"They killed Jan and now you're asking me if you should kill her story too? No damn way! And I just might have a follow for Monday's paper that ties Jan's murder to the killing of a *Los Angeles Times* reporter earlier today. There's a war breaking out between rival gangs, one with links to right-wing extremists in the U.S. and the Russian mafia and the other to Mexican cartels and Chinese and American intelligence agencies."

He smiled at Lee, who stood up from the table. At that moment Choy remembered and understood the significance of the words spoken a few minutes earlier. 'One last supper,' Lee said.

My last supper. He's going to kill me.

12.

On the way back to the hotel in a taxi Choy called Joy.

Do it. For her sake. Just do it.

"Listen, I hate to tell you this now after you've given notice at your job and gotten a new one in Vancouver but I've been thinking a lot about us and I don't know if it's going to work. My kids, my Dad and you, I don't know if I can handle it all."

"What are you saying?"

"My Dad is a gambling addict. I mean a serious gambling addict. It wouldn't be fair to put you in the middle of the stuff going on right now. He lost a lot of money and it's caused some serious problems. I didn't say anything before because I was embarrassed and … I need some time to think. So can we take a break, maybe a couple of weeks?"

"You want a break?"

"I need some space. To think. Both of us. Do you really want to get in the middle of a dysfunctional family?"

Her response was silence.

"Okay?"

What is she thinking?

"A break? I'm in the car, half way to LA."

"Go back. I don't want you here. I'm sorry but I need space."

She's hurt. But she'll figure it out. She knows they're listening.

"I'll call you next week, okay?" he said.

"Okay."

When Choy got back to the hotel he stopped at the business centre to call his ex-wife from his Skype account. He outlined the bare bones of his situation and told Helena to take the kids out of school and he'd pay for a last-minute vacation to Cuba or Jamaica — anywhere but Mexico — or if she couldn't find anything leaving in the next two days to take the kids to her mother's place on Vancouver Island. She was pissed but didn't say much. She had planned to take the following week off anyway, for Spring break.

Next, Choy took off all his clothes, put on his new bathing suit, grabbed the bag with new jeans, shirt, light jacket, sandals and underwear that he had purchased earlier in the day and put his cellphone into the pocket of the hotel bathrobe. He rode the elevator down to the pool level and did a few dozen laps before changing into his new clothes and heading back up to the room, where he put the cellphone on his bedside table. He took the prepaid cellphone bought earlier out from under his pillow and copied some numbers from his old phone to the new one. Next he grabbed his emergency supply of U.S. cash, his passport, driver's licence, the iPad he bought yesterday and credit cards but left his wallet, old cellphone and laptop on the bedside table. He was in the room no more than five minutes before abandoning it and everything else that might have a tracking device on it or in it.

Choy had seen an old hotel of the sort that probably only accepted cash about eight blocks away and he walked there as quickly as he could, checking behind and around him every few seconds to make sure no one was following. Ten minutes later he was in a tiny, but clean room five floors above a busy street and on his new cellphone with Detective Carroll who he told all about Jan James, the latest news from Lee regarding Bennett, Baker and Borovsky as well as the fact he was now hiding from them. Unexpectedly the cop took him seriously and agreed to meet the following morning for breakfast.

At 8 a.m. after a night of fitful sleep, partly from the noise outside his room but mostly from a chronic dread that permeated every attempt at thinking about something pleasant, Choy called Ms. Bolan and the Butte policeman who had been so helpful, giving each of them his new contact number. An hour later he called Abigail Munro, but she did not answer so he left a message.

Because the hotel did not offer a wireless connection Choy headed for the nearest coffee shop that did. He ordered a camomile tea, grabbed a table, opened the new iPad and immediately went to the *Vancouver Sun* website, reading the story that James had written. It was okay, certainly not great. It focused on the connection between White nationalist groups and drug dealing but avoided any mention of links to police or intelligence agencies. It focused on the sensational rather than the systemic. All in all it was about what he had expected from James. Was it enough for someone to have her killed?

Next he started searching for information about Gwendolyn Henderson and Thomas Christie. A half hour of searching confirmed that Julie's father had lived in Boise, Idaho, and had been a vice-president of the Operating Engineers local, but neither of the two T. Christies nor the G. Christie or the G. Henderson still living there were the parents of Julie or knew anything about anyone who was.

A few minutes before 10 he left the coffee shop and walked 12 blocks to a 1950s-style diner to meet Detective Carroll. He was seated with a woman at a booth in the back of the restaurant.

"Waylon Choy, this is my partner Detective Martinez."

"Nice to meet you," said Choy.

Martinez did not offer a hand to shake and merely nodded her hello. After a moment she simply said, "Choy?"

"Says his great, great, great, great, great grandfather or something like that was Chinese," said Carroll.

Martinez grunted and continued staring.

"I've been to Mexico, South and Central America more than a few times and I guarantee there are Martinezes who look like all three of us and Chinese too," said Choy. "Plus every shade in between."

The Black Carroll smiled while the Chicana Martinez looked grumpy.

"I think he's trying to tell you not to judge a book by its cover," said Carroll, smiling.

"Carroll told me your story and quite frankly I have my doubts," she said, getting straight to business.

"Doubts about what?"

"Pretty much everything."

Choy shrugged.

"You know there's more than a few white guys in the LAPD who don't like you," said Martinez. "Something about a story you wrote last year that caused an investment they made to go sour."

"They would have lost all their money if we hadn't exposed Amanda Bennett's skimming as soon as we did," said Choy referring to the events around the death of Vancouver's former police chief the year before.

"That's not the way they see it," said Martinez.

"Would these be right wing racist cops who voted for Donald Trump and like bashing heads of young African and Latino Americans?" said Choy. "The readers of alt-right websites and maybe quiet members of one neo-Nazi group or another?"

Again Carroll smiled and this time Martinez almost joined him.

"You can't prove any of that stuff you told Carroll, can you?"

"I can prove there's one dead reporter here and another in Vancouver and both were working on stories that involved major drug dealers who seem to have connections high up in various government departments in more than one country. I have copies of the files that a story in this morning's *Vancouver Sun* was based on, the writer of which died mysteriously yesterday. I can show them to you if you want to come to my hotel room, in which I did not spend the night because I'm worried I will be the next victim of a coincidental death."

"We'd like to take you up on that offer," said Carroll. "We'd like to check your cellphone and look through your stuff to see if you really have been bugged. Martinez here has all the equipment necessary and is one of the department experts on electronic surveillance."

Choy suddenly realized he had fallen into a trap planned by the two detectives to get him to allow them to look through his stuff. There was information on his cellphone and laptop that he wouldn't want cops to see. On the other hand, if they really could assure him he wasn't being bugged, or remove the bugs if he was, that would be useful. It was not like he had anything illegal or even really sensitive.

Twenty minutes later they pulled up in front of his first hotel in an unmarked police car. After a stop at the front desk to show his identification and get a new room entry card by explaining he had left his in the room, the three of them headed to the seventh floor.

"Just so we're completely clear on this," said Martinez as they rode up the elevator. "You are voluntarily letting us look through your clothes, cellphone, laptop and other belongings we find in this hotel room."

"Yes," answered Choy. "So long as you promise to get rid of any electronic listening or tracking devices you find. You promise?"

"Yes."

"Okay, then I give permission for you to look through all of my stuff in the room."

As soon as he said it, Choy got a bad feeling, a cold shiver that started in his toes and made its way up to the top of his head. Something he would regret was about to happen. What if someone had broken into his room and planted drugs or something else to incriminate him?

Choy pressed the card against the electronic sensor, then pushed the door open, allowing Martinez and Carroll to enter before him. As he did so the hairs on every inch of his body stood at attention.

"Chinga tu madre," shouted Martinez.

"Fucking hell," said Carroll, an octave lower.

As Choy stepped into the room he could see what looked like a body covered in blood-soaked sheets on the king-sized bed.

"Back off!" said an angry Martinez to Choy. "This is a crime scene!"

"Who?" Choy said, frozen to the spot just inside the door.

What the hell is going on? A body? Who?

"A woman," said Carroll, who had put on a pair of disposable plastic gloves pulled from his jacket pocket before carefully lifting up the sheet covering the body.

Martinez surveyed the room from a foot in front of Choy.

"Do you recognize her?" asked Carroll.

Choy didn't realize the detective was asking him a question until Martinez turned back and motioned for him to move a little closer. At first, his brain stalled, failing to process the meaning of the scene he was witnessing.

The detective wearing see-through plastic gloves, like a server at a hotel buffet, holding up a corner of the sheet saturated in reddish black, mostly dried blood. Underneath a naked woman with stab wounds all over her upper torso and neck.

"Do you recognize her?" repeated Carroll.

"I …" The telephone line between his brain and vocal cords was down, toppled in the tornado that was picking him up and spinning him around.

Joy.

The two cops were staring at him, but it seemed like minutes before he could form the words. "It's my girlfriend Joy. She's supposed to be in Las Vegas."

***

The questioning went on for hours. While Choy could understand the necessity of ruling him out as a suspect in the death of his girlfriend, a civilian employee of the Las Vegas police department who he admittedly had broken up with the night before, what had really happened was obvious. After his call, made from a cellphone that she knew he thought was bugged, she had decided to continue her drive to Los Angeles. She must have been concerned about his safety. Two days earlier he had told the front desk to add her name to his as those staying in the room so she would have simply needed to ask for a room card when she arrived late at night to surprise him. When he wasn't there she would have assumed he was out working or visiting with a friend and fell asleep waiting for him to return. Someone had broken into the room to kill him and stabbed a sleeping Joy instead. She always slept with a pillow over her head and a white noise machine running, a habit she had picked up as a child when sleeping in the same room with her older sister, who woke up constantly to read books, so an intruder would have had an easy time sneaking up on her.

She's dead because I let dangerous drug dealers into my life.

Detective Peter Worthington had asked Choy to repeat the story four times over the previous eight hours, but this time when he sat across from him, he simply shook his head.

"Where ever you go journalists seem to die," he finally said. "One last year, two this year. Not that I mind. Journalists are scum as far as I'm concerned. Low-life leeches who thrive on the misery of others, creators of fake news out to topple the first president who actually wants to solve our nation's problems."

Choy defiantly kept eye contact with Worthington throughout his short rant.

"Are your personal feelings about journalists really relevant to Joy's murder? Shouldn't you be out somewhere chasing down the killer rather than in here spouting off about how much you dislike me?"

Worthington smiled, then leaned forward and lowered his voice. "So who do you think killed Joy Lee?"

"I told you, a professional hit man, hired by Billy-Bob Baker, or Emerson Lee, or whatever the Aryan Brotherhood is now called, but he made a mistake and stabbed Joy instead."

"And this Baker and Lee want to kill you because?" said Worthington, who picked up his notepad and looked at it as if searching for the answer.

Motive was complicated, perhaps even subtle, Choy had to admit.

"This Mr. Lee's motive to hire a hit man was that he hired you to write a story about Baker, but you didn't," said Worthington, as he looked at the notepad. "Instead you gave the story to Jan James, a reporter at the newspaper in Vancouver you once worked for and, according to you, Baker ordered someone from the Russian mafia to kill her but make it look like a random act of violence in a Vancouver parking garage. So, this James gets killed because she wrote the story but you become the target of Lee because you didn't. And if this Baker ordered your killing it was because he thought you might still write another story about him and someone named Bennett."

Worthington made a show of dropping his notepad on the table between them. "Give me a fucking break."

"Maybe Amanda Bennett ordered me killed because she doesn't like me."

"That I could believe."

"She knows I know too much. I did write those articles last year exposing her neo-Nazi Committee of One Thousand. Did you check that out?"

"Yes."

"And what about the Aryan Brotherhood or whatever they call themselves now? I told you one of them threatened me with a gun right in that same room."

"Which you never reported until you're a suspect in your girlfriend's murder."

"Okay, I don't know why someone wants to kill me, but they do. But how could you think I killed Joy? We've never even had an argument."

"If my wife and I don't argue at least once a week both of us get nervous. Most couples fight, some don't. Maybe the ones who don't let off steam are more likely to kill each other."

"Even if you don't believe I loved her, I had nothing to gain, no insurance policy, no quick way out of a bad marriage, we didn't even live together yet."

"Lovers, ex-lovers kill each other in jealous rages every day."

"But she wasn't seeing anyone else and neither was I."

"So you say."

"Good luck finding evidence for something that never existed."

"I had a case 10 years or so ago where the guy beat his wife to death because he thought she was cheating on him, but she wasn't. It was all in his head."

"And 20 years ago I wrote a story about an innocent man who spent 10 years in jail because a cop decided he was guilty of rape and murder and never bothered to follow the evidence that would have led to the real killer."

The two men glared at each other.

"Look, I've cooperated with you for eight hours, answered all your questions, repeated my story four times and what do I get in return? Bullshit conjecture, an 'I hate journalists' attitude and a complete lack of empathy for someone whose girlfriend he loved was murdered."

Choy silently refocused his glare at the detective to emphasize his point, before continuing. "I'm a secondary victim in this crime and it's about time you treated me with a semblance of sympathy and some goddamn respect."

Worthington mimed a sad face and tears running down his cheeks.

Choy thought about saying, "I am not without means of publicizing the way you are treating me," but decided not to. Worthington was old enough to retire and probably didn't care about complaints made against him. And he was the sort of lifelong bully who saw himself as Dirty Harry administering rough justice to whomever he thought deserved it, damn due process and the liberal media, so threatening to expose his tactics would only validate his prejudices.

After a few more perfunctory questions Worthington got up from his chair and walked to the door. "I've got nothing else to ask you right now, but your buddies tell me they'd like to speak with you."

Buddies?

"You are staying here in Los Angeles in case something comes up?"

"Maybe, maybe not. I have more people to interview but I don't know where their answers will take me. And I'll have to go to Oakland soon to visit Joy's parents. But call me. I'm always eager to answer any of your penetrating questions."

Worthington gave him the finger as he left the room.

After a few seconds Choy stood up and headed for the exit, but just before he reached it the door opened. Carroll, followed by Martinez, entered.

"What a fucking asshole!" Choy said.

"He's your biggest fan in the department," said Martinez smiling. "Claims to have lost $50,000 because of your story last year."

"So, that's what this waste-of-time interrogation was all about?"

"You hungry?" asked Carroll. "You want to go back to that diner where we were supposed to have breakfast?"

"Anywhere there's decent food will work for me," said Choy. "I'm starving and sick of this damn place."

"Aren't we all," said Martinez, now sporting a friendly look towards him. "But us two have a hell of a lot more years of assholes tormenting us in this place than you, so quit your whining."

***

Dinner with the two cops was interesting and almost enjoyable, even though the primary topic of conversation was the killing of his girlfriend. Every time one of them said her name a pounding surf of sadness swept over him; the only way he could keep his head above water was by focusing on his work, which now included exposing whoever murdered Joy.

Both of the detectives hated Worthington and spoke freely about the case, which belonged to a man, they said, who was widely known inside the department as a white nationalist who undermined cops of colour every chance he got. Because they had found the body and because a connection to one of the gangs they were experts on was possible, they were assigned to the investigation notwithstanding the protests of Worthy, as he was known inside the LAPD. Despite his daylong grilling, Choy was never a primary suspect. Apparently three other guests in the hotel, two on the same floor where Joy was stabbed, had reported items stolen from their rooms sometime during the night and master pass cards for six floors were missing from the housekeeping department. The most likely explanation of what happened was that Joy woke up when the burglar, who had already robbed three other rooms, was near the bed and he panicked, stabbing her five times in the neck and chest. Preliminary analysis of the blood spatter pattern suggested Joy might have been sitting up when some of the knife thrusts entered her body. Other details of the investigation that the two detectives shared with Choy over excellent soup, sandwiches and beer were that Joy had asked the front desk for a key at 1:13 a.m. and that the stabbing likely occurred between 3:33 and 4:01, based on video surveillance that showed a couple of images of a muscular but small man wearing a baseball cap on the seventh floor during that time. Martinez's theory was that the robber had been trying doors with the master pass and entered rooms where the latch had not been set. Of course Joy, who was waiting for Choy to return, had not latched the door.

While Choy was relieved that the police had a working theory of the crime that did not involve him, he felt certain the burglaries were just cover for an expert hit man who had been hired to kill him. While Carroll seemed to take this possibility seriously, Martinez dismissed a gang hit as paranoid fantasy, saying she agreed with Worthington on that one. But she could only shrug when Choy asked which was harder to believe, that it was simply a coincidence when three people with direct connections to him and the story about two powerful drug wholesalers were killed within 24 hours of each other, or that someone sent a hit man to kill him, but he failed and stabbed Joy to death by mistake? Then Martinez admitted she had looked through Choy's possessions, just as he had given her permission to do, and found three tracking devices, one in his laptop, one in a shoe and another in his jacket. As well, she confirmed that his phone could have been tracked and his conversations listened to even though there was no actual bugging device in it. Apparently his cellphone provider in Canada, along with many others around the world, had weak protection against sophisticated hackers who could use the means by which the companies communicated with each other, something called Signalling System No. 7 or SS7 to track his location and listen in on his calls from anywhere in the world. It was a flaw in the international communications system that was well known and exploited by intelligence services, and police. Lately it was being used more frequently by high tech criminals. Still, she said, all that did not justify an LAPD investigation into Baker, Borovsky or Lee. That was the job of the FBI or DEA or NSA or CIA, or the internal affairs departments of one of those, if as Choy alleged, insiders from one or all of the above were somehow involved. Such an investigation was well above their pay grade and outside the jurisdiction of two detectives working the South Central gang detail.

Choy acknowledged she was right. He understood power and the lack thereof. He understood some people gave orders and others followed them. He understood that two detectives in a police department of over ten thousand sworn officers were just shy of impotent against the kind of people he was up against.

His words embarrassed both detectives, which upon reflection, was the point of saying them. He hadn't planned to make them feel guilty, but once he had, he knew it was exactly what was needed. Everyone could do the right thing, under the right circumstances, if she or he was motivated. Even cops.

To Martinez's credit she was the one who asked what Joy was like, how long they had known each and how he was feeling. When answering her questions all the emotions pent up because he had refused to let the asshole Worthington see him cry were suddenly released. By the time Choy got to the part about how he had not yet met her parents and was now facing doing so in order to explain what he believed really happened to their daughter, his tears were flowing. While the release of his feelings was painful, it was also cathartic. She was gone and he would miss her. To uncover the truth, to learn from what happened — the fundamental point of history and journalism — that was all he had left.

In fact, he now owed four people the truth, or at least the telling of their stories, because in reality that's all a journalist could offer. He owed Julie Christie, and the people who had told him about her, the best, most truthful story he could come up with. He owed Jan James and Max Parker. And he owed Joy.

***

The hotel, which Choy guessed was concerned about a possible lawsuit, gave him a suite with a security guard devoted solely to the top floor and told him there would be no charge for as long as he needed to stay. Management also offered to put up Joy's parents for free if they needed to come down to Los Angeles to deal with the coroner or police or anything else, but Choy's sense from a short phone call was that they were too frail to deal with any of it, and that her brother would be heading west from New York, but to Las Vegas to take stock of her possessions that were already partially packed for the move to Vancouver. A funeral home would make the arrangements for her body to be sent to Oakland when the coroner was done with it. The conversations with Joy's family had been awkward and left Choy feeling that her brother blamed him, which was certainly not an unreasonable emotional response to his sister's death. Afterall, he blamed himself.

After a few minutes of staring at the ceiling, then turning on the TV before almost immediately turning it off, Choy realized he needed to call down to the front desk for toiletries because it was too late to go out looking for a drug store. Martinez and Carroll had explained that he was not likely to get any of his personal possessions that had been in the room, including the laptop and cellphone, back for weeks or even months because they were evidence in a murder investigation. There was some possibility that the killer had rifled through his suitcase, so it and all its contents would have to be thoroughly checked by the forensics experts, which was sort of ironic because if the murder had occurred in Las Vegas that would have been a job Joy might have been tasked with.

Lucky I made back-ups of all my important files and took the USB stick with me.

Upon hearing that the police had taken possession of his belongings the manager on duty not only personally brought up a toiletry set, but also offered to pay for two pairs of pants, two shirts and some underwear from the high-end clothing store that leased space from the hotel when it opened again in the morning. He also offered the use of a laptop, which even though it was a clunky cheap Windows machine, would be perfectly fine for writing. Having heard Martinez's explanation of how skilled hackers could track any cellphone for which they had the number, Choy felt safer with one that very few people knew he had.

But after the past two days events he did not feel safe and, despite what was now approaching a chronic lack of sleep, at best he got a half hour. The image of Joy, covered in blood, dead in the hotel bed, was stuck in his brain. Then when he finally did sleep he woke almost immediately because of a dream that replaced Joy with the image of Ben and Samantha under the blood soaked sheet. He turned to reading, finishing *Chasing the Scream*, a copy of which he had taken with him because he was certain no one would bother to put a tracking device on an actual printed book.

As the sun came up Choy was awake in bed, thinking about the nature of addiction, the failed war on drugs, the obvious solutions to the Fentanyl crisis and Julie Christie's life. A happy ending to her story was possible, at least in the sense of finding the people who knew her and offering them closure. Abigail Munro had left a message inviting him to call her after 7 a.m. She indeed knew Julie, in fact they were best friends for a time and had lived together in both Missoula and Los Angeles. She was eager to meet with Choy and tell him everything she knew.

13.

Abigail Munro was waiting inside the cafe in Japantown when Choy arrived. She had picked a place near his hotel, saying it was one of her favourite breakfast restaurants, the best Japanese greasy spoon diner in the entire city. She looked right past him as he entered, but Choy recognized her from his Google search for the moderately successful actor who had appeared in numerous TV series and even had a few small parts in important films. In her mid-thirties the ebony-haired, blue-eyed, tall and thin alumnus of the University of Montana looked even more beautiful in real life.

"Abigail?" Choy said, approaching her table.

The expression on her face was blank, as if she were pretending not to hear him. Perhaps she thought he was a celebrity stalker or an annoying fan.

"I'm Waylon Choy," he said. "I know I don't look like my name, but it's really me."

"Waylon?" she answered.

"Honest, it's me," he said, trying not to sound annoyed at her response, but his lack of sleep made that harder than normal. "It's a long story involving a Chinese multiple-great grandfather leaving China for the California gold rush and ending up in Canada then marrying a Metis woman, followed by their son marrying a white woman and then generations later, me, Waylon Choy, the White-looking guy with a Chinese name."

"I'm sorry," she said. "I didn't mean to … I had an image in my head and wasn't expecting someone looking like you. Sometimes I get fans, you know strangers who expect me to be like one of the characters I've played and it can get annoying, so my default is pretending I don't hear because I'm listening to music through earbuds or something. And now I'm babbling. I hate people who rely on stereotyping and here I've done it myself. I am so sorry. Sit down please."

Choy kept smiling even though it probably looked fake. That was how it felt.

"Do you get this a lot? People expecting you to look different because of your name?"

"All the time," he said. "And I feel very annoyed. But that's mostly because two co-workers and my girlfriend were all killed in the last 48 hours so I'm particularly grumpy right at the moment."

"Oh my God!" she responded.

"But I don't want to talk about it. I had to spend all day yesterday talking about it with the police and now all I want to do is focus on Julie. I want to talk about her, not the other stuff."

Her look had turned from embarrassment to pity.

"Can we start over? Right from the beginning?" he said.

She nodded. He stood up, took a few steps back towards the entrance and then turned back to Abigail. After closing his eyes for a moment, he looked at her and smiled.

"Abigail?"

"Yes."

"I'm Waylon Choy. Thank you so much for agreeing to meet me."

"Sit down."

"This looks like a wonderful restaurant."

"It is," she answered as he took a seat and she handed him a menu.

"I'm starved."

"If you're into sweet, I'd recommend the Tcho Chocolate Chip and Banana Pancakes or The Fancy French, made with brioche soaked in crème brulee batter but if you want something savoury and truly unique that you absolutely won't get anywhere else order the Chashu Hash Skillet, the key to which is a sauce that's been kept alive by the family that has owned this place for 70 years."

"Sound great."

"That's what I'm going to order."

"Make it two."

***

Abigail Munro met Julie Christie in a first year acting class at the University of Montana in Missoula and they became best friends quickly because each shared a love of acting that was deep and daring. Both would try anything a director suggested to illuminate their character. Both acted without fear, except when fear was required. Both were from working class mining backgrounds, Julie from Butte and Abigail from the Silver Valley in Idaho and then later from Missoula. A week into the school year, Julie had moved out of her university dorm and into Abigail's parent's basement. For three years they were like sisters, confiding in each other and keeping no secrets.

Julie was a brilliant actor and an excellent student, determined to succeed in a tough business, always serious about learning her craft. She constantly refined her technique, working on her voice when a teacher pointed out some flaw in her singing, spending hundreds of hours in the dance studio to be good enough to get the lead in a studio version of 42nd Street. Because of her natural skill, her willingness to work hard and her good looks everyone thought she would succeed, whether it was on Broadway or in Hollywood.

Abigail was certain that her best friend never did drugs; she even refused a toke at parties where pretty much everyone was smoking up. Most of the time Julie was also a teetotaller, although Abigail did witness her drunk once, after a successful opening, when a boy she really liked informed her he was in love with the male lead. Her abstinence in the face of widespread alcohol, marijuana, ecstasy and cocaine consumption amongst her peers was a result of growing up with a mother who consumed alcohol and painkillers in quantities that turned her from sweet and loving to mean or comatose. Julie talked a lot about her mother, who she loved very much and wanted above all else to please, but who also scared her. Despite her love Julie was determined not to become like her mother, who talked, especially when drunk, about the great actress she could have been, if she had not married and had children. Julie frequently said she hated weak people who spoke about what might have been, like Blanche in a Streetcar Named Desire. The truth was you either did or you didn't; either way there should be no regrets.

One time, not long before the accident Julie had explained her philosophy of life. It was like walking a tightrope, a skill she had mastered to become an even better performer in the travelling children's theatre troop her and Abigail worked for in the summer between junior and senior years. The key was to be confident, calm and focussed, while travelling in a straight line toward your destination. Technique was important but without confidence you'd fall and hurt yourself. It was critical to banish all self-doubt from your thoughts, because that was a cancer which eventually killed confidence. Abigail thought this statement of philosophy was critical to understanding what happened later.

At first, the car crash didn't change her at all, or at least that was Abigail's impression when Julie returned to Missoula after spending two months in hospital and rehabilitation for vertebrae damaged during the accident. At the beginning of her senior year Julie remained focussed and determined. She continued to be exuberant, outgoing and was sending resumes to New York and Los Angeles agents, some of whom actually contacted her, because of the rave reviews she received from her instructors and local newspapers. She was, however, taking medication to deal with the pain from her back injury, which at first didn't seem noteworthy, but as her agony grew worse, Abigail's perception was that the drugs grew stronger and the periods between taking them shorter. Because her best friend was withdrawing into herself and sharing less Abigail wasn't sure what medication Julie was taking. But it was definitely causing changes in her personality, making her very "up" and very "down" — sometimes in periods that lasted only a few hours. When she was "up" Julie was full of energy and fantastic stories that entertained, but when she was "down" her world was dark, dreary and dangerous. In these periods she spent most of her time in bed, hiding from people, including Abigail. Then she started having trouble learning her lines for a November play, something completely unlike her before the accident when she could memorize the entire lead dialogue of a three-hour play in less than a week. Finally, out of the blue, Julie announced she was quitting school and going to Los Angeles, where, she said, an agent was interested in representing her and thought her perfect for a recurring role in a TV series that would be casting in the next few months. And that was the last Abigail saw of her until the following summer, after graduation, when she too began chasing the Hollywood dream.

Not having heard anything from her former best friend for more than eight months, despite sending emails and writing letters via her parents' address in Butte, Abigail was surprised, but pleased, when two weeks after moving into a tiny North Hollywood apartment Julie showed up early on a Sunday morning. She claimed to have been at an important party in the neighbourhood and was too tired to go home and of course Abigail let her crash on the sofa. That was the beginning of an intense few months, during which the two women again became close, but never the way it had been before the accident. In Los Angeles a part of Julie's life was hidden, and when Abigail tried to get her friend to talk about it a fight would ensue. Julie insisted she was doing okay and had an agent who would soon get her a breakthrough part in a film or TV show, but she'd disappear for days and would never talk about where she'd been.

One Friday evening, when she showed up at the apartment after a week without calling or texting, they had a particularly bad fight and that night, after the yelling stopped, Julie confessed that her stories about the agent and roles she was up for were all lies. She hadn't been going to auditions for months. She had fallen off the tightrope and couldn't get back on. Her confidence had disappeared. While technically still capable of acting, unless she somehow found that lost confidence, there was no hope of ever being able to get back onto the tightrope. She admitted to experimenting with marijuana and acid, in an effort to get her poise and self-assurance back and said it worked sometimes, being stoned had allowed her to make a few auditions and each time did well, but never received a call back. When pressed further about the drugs she used, speed and cocaine were added to the list and, it turned out, selling acid was her means to pay for it.

Learning this, Abigail got angry and compared Julie to her mother. That's when the crying really started. "You're wasting your talent and all you'll ever have are stories about how good you could have been, just like your mother," were the words she used and remembered ten years later, because of how much they hurt her friend. Rather than respond with anger, Julie had simply said, "I know. My mother, that's who I am, weak, afraid and in pain. And I'll never be anything different."

Abigail felt terrible, took it all back, and tried for a while to say things that might motivate Julie to believe in herself again, but something inside had died. It was like she had lost the will to live, or at least the need to assert herself. While once she had been outgoing and sociable, she was now completely focused on her inner self where only demons dwelled; while once she felt able to audition for and win any part that interested her, from Jane Fonda's role in Barefoot in The Park to Miranda in the Tempest to Lady Macbeth, she now was unable to even submit a resume because the very idea of an audition filled her with dread.

They talked about her seeking medical help, counselling of some sort or even just joining a support group and Julie was interested but did nothing to make it happen. Even calling her parents and asking if their medical coverage might enable her to go see someone was beyond her; the thought of telling her mother about what her life in Los Angeles was really like was so scary that she began to shake when Abigail suggested that as a first step.

Instead Julie disappeared for even longer stretches, like she was embarrassed to face Abigail, and when she did show up at the apartment was usually stoned. This might have been when she started using heroin, or at least using needles to shoot up whatever she was using, because one notable change was that she always seemed to be wearing long-sleeved blouses. After a few months of one or two day visits, and increasingly frequent requests to borrow money, they had their biggest confrontation ever. Julie had showed up at the apartment on a Tuesday night, wanting to talk about a fantasy she had about getting the money together for a short film that would showcase the two of them, but Abigail had an audition the next morning and wanted to talk about that and get some help with the three different ways she thought the part could be played. Julie insisted upon going to a bar to see a guy who supposedly was interested in producing a short film that would feature both of them. She promised to spend a couple hours early in the morning helping Abigail prepare for the audition. Or course the guy didn't show and after an hour Abigail went home, but Julie stayed, claiming he would eventually arrive. The next morning, at the time she'd promised to help with the audition, Julie wasn't there, only showing up a few minutes before Abigail had to leave. Worse than the lack of help, her supposed friend was high and laughed at the very idea of attending auditions. "It's all bullshit," she said. "Audition for what? For the producer to get in your pants? A job that will make you happy? Give you self-esteem? Well it won't. Your entire life is based on pretending in order to obtain an illusion." Their fight and these words were all Abigail could think about while auditioning for a part she would have been perfect for. Of course she never heard back from the producer.

A few weeks later, the next time Julie showed up at the apartment. Abigail issued an ultimatum: Get help or go away and never come back.

Maybe it was cruel, maybe it was a mistake, maybe it was what caused Julie to spiral even further downward, leading directly to that street in Vancouver where she died, but to this day Abigail believed there was no viable alternative.

"It was bad enough she had lost all her self-confidence, that morning she was trying to destroy mine, trying to take me down with her," she said, staring at a barely touched plate. "How could I allow that? What choice did I have?"

"What was the comment about producers wanting to get in your pants at auditions all about?"

"I wondered about that myself. It was probably nothing specific. I mean, every actor has a story about some sleazy SOB offering them a job, if only they'd take off their clothes or give them a BJ or …"

Maybe that's all it was.

"She never said anything about a specific incident?"

"No, and I'd remember if she had. I told her about a few incidents that I experienced, but she never said anything to me."

"Did you know that she appeared in one porn video?" Choy wasn't certain if asking this question was a good idea, but it seemed relevant at that moment.

Abigail shook her head. Choy couldn't tell if it signified she didn't believe what he had told her or she was shocked.

"Did you see it?"

It was Choy's turn to shake his head. "No but I interviewed a couple of people who have. They said she said a good actor must be willing to experience everything, at least once."

"That sounds like Julie," Abigail said, as tears welled up. "You're sure she was a street walker in Vancouver? A prostitute? When I first met her she was more in control of her body than any woman I'd ever met. I mean she was willing to do nudity, if it made sense in the context of the story. We talked about that a lot. But she would never have allowed anyone to exploit her, never."

The memory caused even more tears to flow.

"She was tough, but a romantic at heart," she said, crying harder. "I can't imagine what must have happened for her to have sex on screen."

The sobbing continued until Abigail noticed people at other tables glancing at her.

"I'm sorry," she said, pulling herself together.

"That fight was the last time you saw her?" he asked after a painful silence, mostly to change the subject.

"No, it was at least a year later, at an audition. I was in the waiting room when she walked in. We were auditioning for the same part. She looked beautiful, like the old Julie. Said she had been going to rehab. We talked for maybe half an hour and it was great, exactly like after we first met. She was full of enthusiasm and looked really alive. But there was one change: She still didn't have that old look of self-confidence, which used to really set her apart from every other actor. There's something in an actor's eyes, in their demeanour, in the way they talk, that shouts out to everyone: 'Pick me, pick me, because I am perfect for this part.' She used to have that self-assurance, but it was no longer there. Still, it was good to see her looking as well as she did and when I was called in for the audition, I was happy and relaxed and I absolutely nailed it. Best audition I ever did. I knew I had the part. Just knew it. I was so elated. It's hard to explain to a non-actor about the high I was on because of how right I was for that part. All I could think about afterwards was going back to the room and telling Julie, or at least waiting for her to audition and then telling her how great I had done. But, she wasn't there when I came out. I don't know what happened. Something spooked her, probably me. Maybe I had that self-confident look that used to belong to her and she saw it, knew that meant there was no chance for her. Or maybe … I don't really know, but that was the last time I saw her."

"And did you get the part?"

"My first big break," she said nodding. "I've made a very good living since then."

"You never heard from Julie again?"

"Tried reaching out, sent emails to her and her parents, letters to her parents' place; a few years ago when I was in Montana I even drove down to Butte, but her parents weren't living there anymore."

"They moved to Boise," said Choy. "But they don't live there anymore either."

"I was so happy and so sad when that woman from the university contacted me. Like I told you before, what you're doing is a really, really good thing. She wasn't just some junkie hooker, she was a real person with potential; she had family, friends and a life."

"They all are and they all do," he quickly responded.

Abigail immediately blushed and even though she was a professional actor, Choy could tell she was genuinely embarrassed.

"I didn't mean …"

"Tens of thousands of people are dying every year from drug overdoses in North America," said Choy. "Some months as many people as died in the twin towers on 9/11, and I'm pretty sure they all had family, friends and a life. They all were real people with potential. I haven't been able to sleep much lately and I've been reading a lot of books and studies about drugs and overdoses and the so-called war on drugs. It's all so absolutely absurd."

"Absurd?"

"What else would you call treating sick people like criminals and providing opportunities for real criminals to make a whole hell of a lot of money while corrupting our governments, police and legal systems?"

"Absurd?" she repeated, as if she really wanted to understand.

"Everything about the 'war on drugs' is a lie. The more this war is waged, the more people use drugs, the more criminals there are, the more violent those criminals become and the more human potential is wasted. Wouldn't you call that absurd?"

She didn't look convinced.

"I'll send you a copy of my book when it's published, maybe I'll be able to explain it better in that," Choy said.

"It's difficult to think that Julie's death was absurd," she answered.

"Hers and hundreds of thousands of others. It is very difficult."

The two of them stared at each other for maybe a minute, only interrupted by the occasional sip of coffee.

"So you don't know how to contact Julie's parents?" Choy finally said, not able to think of any other questions he should ask.

"I almost forgot," Abigail answered, as she pulled a piece of paper from her large bag. "This is an email I got from her mother three years ago. I don't know if the email address on top is still current, but it might be."

***

The words in the email haunted Choy as he walked back to the hotel. Every few minutes he pulled the piece of paper from his pocket to read it again.

Dear Abigail,

I am very sorry that I have never responded to your many requests for information about Julie until now. Please understand that the reason for this has been my illness and certainly not a lack of affection for you or my daughter. I know you have always been Julie's good friend. But I was incapable of looking after myself, let alone my daughter, until a short time ago. I understand now the hurt I caused everyone close to me and am very, very sorry. My greatest fear is that the harm done to Julie has been so great that I will never see her again. Have you been in contact with her? Do you know where she is? If you can help me in any way to reconcile with my beautiful daughter, please let me know.

An errant parent,
Gwendolyn Henderson

The few words pressed onto the now brittle paper by an old dot matrix printer spoke of pain and regret and made Choy wonder if the news he had for Gwendolyn would be the spark that lit a crematorium fire, burning a frail, former alcoholic mother, to ashes.

Maybe she'd be better off not knowing. I certainly can't just send an email to this address saying, "I'm sorry, but your daughter has died, would you like the details?" I need to find where Gwendolyn is living, visit her and read her face before saying anything.

This was going to be harder than he thought. In fact, he had never thought through the part where he informs her parents about the details of her death. And then ask them, 'what happened that led her to this?' How could that not be the hardest thing he would ever do as a journalist?

What was the hardest thing I ever did before?

He remembered one of his first assignments as a night general assignment reporter at the *Vancouver Sun*. Police reports had a man and his four-year-old daughter killed when a car went up on the sidewalk at a bus stop across from a public health clinic and it was his job to find out where the family lived, interview them and if possible get a picture of the two victims of this random piece of bad luck. Eager to prove his worth he found the address of the surviving family members and immediately went to their house on one of south Vancouver's busiest and poorest streets. Turned out the family were recent refugees from El Salvador, who had been given asylum by Canada. After years of trying they had finally found a safe place to live, away from the civil war that engulfed their homeland and now, a month later, a 26-year-old mother no longer had a husband or a daughter and her two-year-old son would grow up without a father or a sister. Choy got the painful story, and the photograph of a loving papa with his daughter to illustrate it, through a cousin who spoke to him in English as a roomful of crying people interrupted their pain to accommodate the needs of a media outlet that would use their grief to sell tomorrow's newspaper.

That was definitely the hardest thing I've ever done as a reporter.

Telling Julie's mother what he knew about her daughter's death would be harder. Twenty-five years earlier he had been an intruder who was exploiting a family's tragedy, but at least he hadn't been the bearer of the bad beyond belief news. This time he would have a responsibility to both the dead and the living and he needed to sort out what that meant. No, he had a responsibility to the dead, the living and his story — that was the honest truth — and it made Choy feel uneasy, uncertain, unclean.

But maybe he was getting ahead of himself. Maybe the email address was no longer current. Maybe Gwen had died since she sent it. Or simply changed email providers. The chase might not be anywhere near its climax.

As he was reading the email for the fifth time, a car pulled up to the curb in front of him and three tall, muscular white men jumped out. Stopping to face them, Choy knew immediately these were Billy-Bob's guys and the image of a dead Joy, lying under the blood-soaked sheet flashed through his consciousness before he could even react.

They've come to finish the job. Good. How will they do it? Will it be painful? I probably deserve at least a little pain.

14.

"Have you read what your friend wrote about me?" said Billy-Bob Baker, sitting in the same chair in the same room where Choy had voluntarily visited him a few days earlier.

"I've been rather busy," said Choy, trying to avoid a straight answer. "What with the murder of my fiancé and your friends in the police department trying to pin it on me despite my lack of motive, my watertight alibi and all the evidence pointing in other directions."

"My friends?"

"The racist white nationalists that infect police departments throughout this country who, I am reliably informed, you and your kind make a special effort to recruit," said Choy.

"According to the *Los Angeles Times*, the police suspect this horrible crime was a robbery gone wrong and a story on one of my favourite websites informs me that the most likely perpetrator is an illegal immigrant who is well known but has long been coddled by the legal system in California."

"So that's what you're going to do? Blame immigrants for killing my girlfriend to deflect attention from your own botched attempt to shut me up."

Baker looked genuinely surprised.

"That's what you think? That I ordered you killed, but my paid assassin couldn't tell the difference between a sleeping man and a woman?" He shook his head. "I was hoping you trusted me or, at least respected me, more than that."

"When Prince Charming finds a foot that fits the slipper he's going to think it belongs to Cinderella," answered Choy.

"What would be my motive?" said Baker. "You've done what I asked. My sources tell me that *LA Times* reporter killed two days ago was working on a story about Emerson Lee and the Chinese government's involvement in the drug business. And I know you were the one who contacted him."

"So Lee had him killed and you had my former colleague in Vancouver killed for writing that story about you and maybe the former Aryan Brotherhood goons tried to have me killed just to prove they could knock off a journalist too."

"I never killed anyone," Baker quickly answered. "And I never ordered anyone to kill you or your friends."

It was pointless to debate a man he knew capable of having someone killed and then lying about it.

"Why did you bring me here?" he asked.

"To tell you the truth."

"About?"

"About these recent killings."

"Why would you do that?"

"Because I calculate it is to my advantage."

"So, tell me."

"There is no proof of what I am about to tell you and you have been searched for recording devices, but if you ever attempt to use this information against me, there will be consequences," he said. "Do you still want me to continue?"

Choy nodded.

"Where should I begin?"

"Who killed Jan James?"

"Who? There have been dozens of killings."

Dozens? A gang war, just like Lee said.

"In Vancouver, the *Sun* reporter who wrote the story about you, stabbed in a parkade?"

"Yes, her. The one who wrote the story where I come across as a powerful, mysterious, brave young white man up against the Chinese and Mexican drug dealing hordes."

"Who killed her?" repeated Choy, ignoring Baker's white nationalist fantasies.

"There's a team of Russian patriotic nationalists in Vancouver who are conducting certain operations ..."

"Russian mafia taking over supply networks that once belonged to Mr. Lee?"

"That would be one way of looking at it."

"They killed Jan James?"

"The nature of the work they do, considerable free rein must be given. They do not ask permission for every little job they do."

"A little job?"

"In the context, yes," he said, continuing to look Choy in the eyes. "Unfortunately one of them assumed it was best to eliminate any reporter who dared mention my name. It's the way business is conducted where he is from. He now knows that is not how we do business here."

"Killing a reporter is a 'little job'?"

"Would you expect a general who has planned the invasion of Iraq or Afghanistan to know or care about the killing of a journalist in Kandahar or Mosul? Wouldn't you expect him to leave such matters to people much further down the chain of command?"

"Is that how you see yourself? As a general?"

"There have been soldiers in my family since the Civil War and in Amanda Bennett's family for over 300 years. You may be unaware, because the media ignores it, but we are at war for control of the world and I am in charge of an important theatre of operation that could determine the ultimate winner."

"Which war?"

"The clash of civilizations."

"What does that mean?"

"You should expand your sources of information and analysis. For the last two centuries white Christian civilization has ruled the world …"

Here comes the racist bullshit.

"And more progress was made in those 200 years than in all the previous millennia combined. We have brought enlightenment, freedom, capitalism and the Word of God to every corner of the planet, but many of those who have benefited are not grateful."

"Maybe because those white Christians, in fact, stole the brown and black and yellow and red people's land, even their people and redirected their economies to benefit Europe and North America. Ever hear of colonialism, genocide, slavery, destruction of the Indian textile industry, the Opium Wars?"

"More advanced people have always taken over from the primitive. It's how human progress works."

Why am I arguing with him?

"But these inferior people are now taking the knowledge and wealth we gave them to create their own world order, one that benefits them and will ultimately make us subservient."

"The USA has tried its best to turn everyone into capitalists and you won, everyone is now a capitalist," said Choy. "But now that scares you?"

"Only because white Christian civilization is divided. We fight amongst ourselves. We need someone who can unite us and we will be invincible for at least another 200 years."

"And that's where you and Amanda Bennett come in? The Saladin of the Christian Empire? The biblical saviour?"

"Perhaps I will play the role of John the Baptist."

Like the Trotskyists who taught at his east Vancouver high school 30 years earlier who all wanted to be Lenin, young white nationalists also had messianic desires and wanted to grow up to become their favourite figure from the Bible.

"The history of the world is one of great civilizations rising and falling," said Choy. "Europeans had their centuries on top and now there's nowhere to go but down. Or maybe the world has moved past the age of empire, to a time with no more ruled and rulers."

"Exactly the dangerous beliefs of the international financiers, the multiculturalists and the one-worlders," said Baker. "Meanwhile, on the other side of the planet, the Chinese, Indians and Arabs are preparing for the day when they are stronger than us. Your sort always tells us that white nationalism is racist and dangerous, but you don't say anything at all about Islamic or Chinese or Indian nationalism and let me tell you, it is growing."

Choy thought about pointing out the truth that nationalism had long been used by the rich and powerful everywhere to divide and conquer the masses of ordinary people and about how every nationalist war had been fought to benefit tiny elites, but that would have been akin to discussing baseball strategy with someone who played right field from outside the stadium.

"The white European Christian world must prepare for the fight of our lives, but the elites have been blinded by the profits to be made financing the growth of our enemies."

"So I understand why you are working with Russian white nationalists, that makes sense, but why get into the drug business?" said Choy. "I'm having trouble getting the connection."

"Because, unlike Amanda Bennett, you were not brought up to think strategically, like a commanding general who must always see the big picture."

"Help me understand, or am I an inferior person too stupid to get it?"

"I would not waste my time talking to someone too stupid to understand," he answered, evidently resorting to a sort of flattery. "We must prepare ourselves for the war to come, to be able to endure in the shadows, to go underground and learn to survive despite the hostile forces arrayed against us. We must fight and become battle hardened. We must create alliances with white people willing to fight all across North America, Europe, Australia and wherever else they can be found. We must find the resources to grow, without being dependent on the few people with money who fund us today but will someday be too scared to continue. The drug business allows us to accomplish all that. And it enables us to take control of where drugs are sold, taking them out of white communities, leaving them where the harm done is to people who will never amount to anything anyway. We will look after our own much better than the pharmaceutical companies who created an opioid epidemic amongst us."

"You can justify getting into the drug business to good Christian folk?"

"Drugs may have a certain stigma attached to them today, but the business has a long and successful history," continued Baker. "The Opium Wars you mentioned? The British used the profits made from buying and selling opium to rule India and conquer China. Our goal is much the same."

If you start from the premise that the people of the world are divided into competing races, I guess he has an understandable internal logic. Not reality based, but understandable.

"Is it better that these drugs be controlled by Mexicans, Chinese and Indians and used to undermine our way of life? That's what our governments have allowed."

"Your governments have waged a war on drugs for the past 40 years," interjected Choy.

"A phony war," answered Baker.

The first thing he said I agree with.

"And many elements within our security agencies and police understand this. They see the phony war and ask themselves why. They are prepared to cooperate with us because we offer a vision of change, of an ordered society where everyone is in their proper place."

"You may offer them a vision but I'll bet you kick in a cut of the profits as well."

"In America we are not ashamed of profit and self-advancement."

"Certainly not," said Choy, adding a snort of derision. "You like your politics, business and religion with huge heaping helpings of profit and self-advancement, there's no doubt about that."

Baker looked at him carefully for a few seconds before speaking. "Despite your juvenile attempt at humour, I believe you understand my reasoning."

"You confirmed, more or less, what I figured out some time ago," he answered. "Like Trump you're willing to cooperate with the Russians because they're white and you want to go to war against the Chinese, because they're not white. The drug business is a good way of getting the money you need plus it allows you to play soldier. Meantime, you've started a real war and lots more people are going to die."

"The war was not started by us."

Choy was tired of this conversation and wanted to get away from this drug lord who considered himself a white philosopher.

"So, how many people have you killed so far? Not you personally, of course, but your side? Aside from Jan James?"

"As I said, generals do not necessarily know all the minor details. They are not relevant to the overall strategy."

"Who killed Max Parker? The *Los Angeles Times* reporter."

"Rivals to the gang members he was interviewing," said Baker. "You don't believe what the liberal media report? You think that is fake news?"

"Your turn at juvenile humour?"

"Much better than yours," was his riposte.

"Was it a rival gang associated with your or Lee's side?"

"Not mine."

"Do you know anything else about that killing?"

"I believe it and the botched attempt on you that resulted in the death of your girlfriend were directly ordered by Emerson Lee, your Chinese friend."

"He's not my friend."

"Your employer then."

"He's not my employer either. And the work I was doing for him is finished. I've told him that and I'll tell you right now my preference is to never see either of you again. I've lost my appetite for writing about drug dealers."

"Why do I find that difficult to believe?"

"Am I free to go?"

"It's not safe for you out there," said Baker. "Lee has hired a very skilled killer."

"But you're willing to protect me if I offer something in return? Been there, done that and now I want out."

"It's your life."

"Yes it is."

"Even if only for a short while longer."

"We all have to die sometime."

"My boys will help you find your way out."

The two guards on the other side of the door escorted him back through doors and hallways until he once again found himself on the sidewalk outside a dry cleaning establishment.

As he crossed the street, in the general direction of the downtown Los Angeles towers he could see in the distance, thinking about how to survive Lee's assassin, he was pushed flat on the pavement by an explosion that shook the building behind him and blew shards of glass, wood and roofing material onto the street around him. When he got to his feet Choy couldn't tell what had happened, just that dust and smoke were rising from the two-storey 1920s era commercial structure. But when he walked and turned the corner, the scene was one of devastation. The twisted skeleton of a vehicle, probably the remnants of a car bomb, was a few feet in front of the burning building, its facade partially blown away. Shattered glass and other material were spread across the road into a parking lot on the other side of the street. He couldn't see any bodies or injured people on the street, but the air was full of smoke and dust that greatly reduced visibility. Car alarms were wailing, but the noise seemed much too far away. This confused Choy until he realized the explosion must have damaged his hearing.

Someone planted a bomb to assassinate Billy-Bob Baker. I was in that room with him and could easily still have been.

Choy didn't consciously decide to walk away but realized later when he looked up and saw unfamiliar buildings and heard sirens coming from every direction that he had.

I'm walking. The sun is shining.

Emerson Lee and Svetlana Borovsky, both dressed in full military regalia, were playing chess, but it was at the beach, with those pieces that were life-sized and as the white knight took a black pawn, he suddenly came to life, pulled a knife from a sheath on his belt and slit the pawn's throat. When Choy looked closer at the chess piece it turned out to be Joy, blood flowing from her many stab wounds.

Joy had already shipped some of her belongings to Vancouver. What will I do with them?

Julie Christie's mother, who looked very much like the woman he had found dead near the sidewalk, was crying blood-red tears.

Jan James had her throat slit and was lying on top of his hotel bed beside Joy, as the two generals, Lee and Borovsky laughed like the crazy guy riding the bomb in Doctor Strangelove, which he had seen at the Simon Fraser University film club.

More sirens and it's dark. Is it night or has the light disappeared because of the cloud of dust?

The two detectives, Martinez and Carroll, were trying to question Joy, but she did not answer. How could she when her head sat on the table in front of the rest of her body? But still they persisted.

"What happened?" said Martinez.

"Did you see anything? Anyone?" said Carroll.

"Were you inside or outside when the bomb went off?"

"Are you okay?"

It seemed like a ridiculous question for someone with her head on the table, but then Choy realized it must be for him, not Joy. Carroll and Martinez were kneeling in front of him as he sat on a portable chair, the sort of thing people bring to concerts. But he wasn't on the field of a stadium or in a park, he was in the middle of a street with police cars and cops and paramedics. Everyone was talking but he couldn't hear because of an overwhelming buzz that filled his head.

"They found you propped up against the side of a building, like a drunk sleeping off his binge, a few blocks away," said Martinez, who was touching the back of his head when he began to hear again. "He's got some tiny pieces of glass stuck in his backside."

She was talking about him.

She's talking about me.

"Medic!" shouted Carroll. "We've got another injured person here."

He's talking about me.

"Medic!"

Am I injured?

15.

He had to stay in the hospital overnight for observation, said the doctor who kept shining bright lights into his eyes. Choy had suffered a concussion so they woke him up every hour to make sure he didn't fall into a coma or at least that's what he thought a nurse told him. Perhaps it was the concussion, or maybe the repeated awakenings, but whatever the cause, he felt as if his body was there but his mind was somewhere else when Martinez and Carroll showed up in his room at 9 a.m. to finish the questioning they had begun the day before. It wasn't until an hour later, when they dropped him off at his hotel, that he started to think half way straight again.

Someone had tried to kill Billy-Bob Baker, but apparently failed because investigators had only found the bodies of two much bigger men, who likely had been just inside the building from where the car packed with explosives had been parked. A couple of passers-by had also been hit by flying glass and other debris, but anyone else who had been inside the building was either unharmed or had fled injured before the police arrived.

Since it was unlikely Baker had blown up his own office, the most probable suspect was Emerson Lee, who Carroll and Martinez now acknowledged was not just some Chinese businessman with a fancy Beverly Hills mansion. Both cops seemed to have accepted Choy's theory of a gang war that was likely to grow in intensity and could have flare-ups in cities anywhere in the world. But the police did not know the whereabouts of either Lee or Baker so it was impossible to question them. Given the bombing, neither drug lord was likely to make a public appearance anytime soon.

Both of them in hiding and focused on each other suits me just fine.

He wanted to get out of Los Angeles and back to Vancouver as soon as possible. From the hotel room he sent a message to the address on Abigail's email that simply read, "I am a journalist from Canada and have information about your daughter Julie. Please contact me if this email address is still current." Then he went to the hotel gym and spent an hour using the elliptical trainer, driving his heart rate up to 145 for two minute bursts a half dozen times. He felt much better when he returned to the room, took a shower, then laid down on the king-sized bed with his iPad to check his email. There was a message back from Gwen that read, "Yes, this is Gwen, Julie's mother. What information do you have?" Choy sighed after reading it as he thought about how to respond. After writing various versions then erasing them, he settled on: "Where do you live? If possible, I'd like to speak with you in person." The wait for her response was not long and it was the best he could have hoped for. "I live in San Bernardino, California. Where are you?" Choy was pretty sure San Bernardino was part of the Los Angeles metropolitan area and that meant they could meet today! A Google search gave him the information he needed: from downtown Los Angeles to San Bernardino was less than sixty miles. If he rented a car he could drive there in just over an hour in reasonable traffic, so he emailed that he was nearby and could be at her home in two hours or so.

Less than 45 minutes later, after a quick stop at the car rental office off the hotel lobby, he was in a brand new Ford on the San Bernardino Freeway. Another hour and he was using the GPS in his vehicle to find the address she had directed him to. It was an old trailer court, a square block of tightly packed tiny structures built to last a few years many decades ago, in the middle of a run-down neighbourhood that spoke of poverty and broken dreams. The nearby wide freeway, speeding vehicles and the scenic mountain looming above it seemed ironic counterpoints to the people trapped in such a desperate place.

While Gwendolyn Henderson's trailer was among the smallest and oldest in the entire old and rundown so-called park it was freshly painted and clearly well cared for.

"Gwen," he said as he knocked on the screen door with hinges that had recently been replaced. "This is Waylon Choy. I emailed about your daughter."

"Come in," she said.

The living room/kitchen was tiny, sparsely furnished, but clean. Its inhabitant sat at a table for two with an ancient laptop in front of her, wearing a threadbare, but clean, pink housecoat.

"I'm watching Doctor Zhivago. Have you seen it?"

Choy nodded, then said: "You are Gwen, Julie's mother?"

"Yes," she answered, but didn't look up from the screen. "This is the 412th time I have watched this film. "

"It must be one of your favourites."

Or she only owns a few DVDs.

"The best of Julie's three greatest performances on film, although it is very difficult to choose."

Choy thought she was talking about the other Julie Christie, not her daughter, but was not completely certain.

There's definitely something off about this woman.

"Doctor Zhivago is by far the best from the young Julie. But McCabe and Mrs. Miller reveals a more complex, experienced actor, while Away From Her is a subtle, nuanced, richly layered performance that demonstrates what someone at the peak of her craft can achieve."

It's like she's speaking in blurbs from TV Digest.

"Every young actress can learn from watching Julie in these three great films. I told my daughter that and she promised to see them all, although I'm not certain she ever did. Has she said anything to you?"

How to break the news? Choy had thought of buying a bottle of wine, either to give Gwen or share with her, but then changed his mind, because she might not drink anymore and he didn't want to add any more awkwardness to what already promised to be a delicate conversation. Looking at her now though he wished he had bought a bottle. Downing a tumbler full of wine might make what he was about to do a little easier.

He guessed she was no older than 55, given when she had gone to the University of Montana and when Julie was born, but she looked at least 70. If he hadn't written a story a few years earlier about the disease called rosacea, Choy would have described her as having a drunkard's red nose. But because of the research done for that story he knew that while alcohol didn't cause it, red wine was a common trigger for a flare-up of the skin condition and that Gwen most likely had curly blonde or red hair in her youth and blushed easily. The curls were still there, but the colour was now a dirty gray. She looked extremely frail, weighing no more than a hundred pounds on a five foot eight or so frame.

Her frailty and inability to look away from the computer screen contrasted with the clean and neat condition of the room. Either someone was helping her keep the place tidy or she had extended periods of activity and alertness.

"Do you want to talk about your daughter Julie?" Choy said after listening to the part of the movie where Omar Sharif and Julie Christie are working together in a hospital near the World War 1 front.

"Julie Christie and Julie Christie," Gwen answered. "You know my Julie was named after this Julie?"

Choy nodded, but then realized she remained stuck staring at the screen, so he said, "Yes."

"They are both wonderful actresses. Have you seen her perform?"

"The Julie Christie in Doctor Zhivago or yours?" he asked.

"Mine."

"Yes, in Vancouver," he said, thinking of the recitation of the chorus from Lysistrata. "She was very good."

"She's every bit as good as this one. She hasn't had her big break yet, but it is only a matter of time and perseverance. Acting is a very tough business."

She thinks her daughter is still alive.

"Gwen, could you pause the movie so we can talk?" said Choy, weighing how best to proceed.

This woman is not well.

After looking up at him for a few moments, she pressed a key and the sound track stopped playing.

"My Julie played a better Helen Keller than Patty Duke, everyone said so. She was able to transmit so many emotions without speaking."

"When was the last time you heard from your Julie?" he asked, probing to determine how lucid his partner in conversation was.

"She emails me every day," Gwen said, suddenly smiling, as if the thought of her daughter's emails brought her great joy. "She tells me about the parts she is playing, the auditions she goes to; she prefers live theatre to film, like most great actresses. The connection between a live audience and an actor is essential to the process of emotional reality, which is at the heart of all great performances."

"When was the last time you saw her, in person?" said Choy, wondering if it was possible they were talking about different people.

"It's been some time. Much too long really, but we didn't have any contact at all for years — she, we had a very rough time after my youngest daughter died in a car accident — and it has only been in the past few months that we have begun to communicate again. We've been getting to know each other once more and I hope when the time is right she will come visit me. She's been mostly in New York and other cities back east, that's where all the serious actors must live because that's where the theatre is, but maybe one day she will decide to audition for a part in a Hollywood film and then she will take me to Musso and Frank Grill for drinks and dinner. She's promised me that, if she comes to Hollywood, she will take me to Musso and Frank Grill for drinks and dinner. Did you know that all the greatest stars have been going there since 1919? Right back to Charlie Chaplin and John Barrymore."

"I did not know that," said Choy, even more at a loss how to tell this mother that her remaining daughter was dead.

"I was invited to go once, a very long time ago, but the man who invited me ... he wasn't very nice, so I didn't accept his offer," she continued.

"You came to Hollywood when you were young?" he said, taking out his pad and writing a note. "You were an actress, as well?"

"Oh yes. Everyone said Julie followed in my footsteps."

"Did that please you? People saying that? And that she followed in your footsteps?"

Gwen looked away as if she had thought of something important. "If I had stayed in Hollywood, there would have been many more invitations to Musso and Frank Grill, from nicer men, but I didn't, I returned home."

She seemed to live her memories while speaking about them. *She's definitely not completely in the here and now.*

"To Montana?" Choy asked. "That was your home?"

"Yes. Montana is wonderful place for an actress to be from, all the casting agents said that. 'Fresh air creates fresh faces,' that's what I was told. I grew up on a ranch, riding horses and living a healthy, good life. They said that was a perfect story to tell when I became famous. Everyone wanted to live on a ranch, ride horses and breathe healthy air. Everyone would love me because of my growing up in Montana on a ranch."

"When you went to Hollywood, you had an agent?"

"Yes."

"Before Julie was born?"

"Yes," she said, as if an old home movie about the time was playing inside her head. "Everything was so glamorous and everyone so nice to me. It was a truly enchanting time."

He almost said, 'so what happened?' but thought better of it. He sensed the answer would cause Gwen to relive something unpleasant that had followed her enchantment. There had to be a safer way of asking the same question.

"Was this before or after you went to the University of Montana?" he asked.

"Before and after," she answered, the pleasant memory gone. "I sometimes think Julie left university because of my stories about doing the same and going off to Hollywood to seek fame and fortune. You know how children so much want to emulate their parents."

"She wanted to be an actor because of you?"

"Oh I think so, yes. From the age of two we would act together in little plays that I would write and direct. She loved to perform. She loved it when people would watch and then clap their hands. It made her feel so special!"

Clearly it also made her mother feel special.

"Acting is all Julie ever wanted to do," continued Gwen. "If we had lived in Los Angeles I'm certain she would have been a child star. She was so very good."

"I spoke with someone recently who told me he saw her in A Miracle Worker and still remembers the performance to this day."

"Julie toured across the entire state of Montana in that production. Would you like to see the reviews? All the newspapers raved about her."

"I would love to see them."

For the first time, Gwen stood up, took a few steps and opened a drawer below the tiny kitchen cupboard. She pulled out a very well kept scrapbook, turned and placed it on the table in front of Choy. Standing beside him, she opened the scrapbook to a spot a few pages in. There were newspaper clippings of pictures and reviews from the play. One had the headline, "Local girl wows audience in Miracle Worker."

"The director never knew, but I helped Julie get that part just right. I'd sneak in the back of the theatre to watch, listen and take notes during rehearsals then when we returned home, I'd go over everything with her. She trusted me then and listened to what I had to say. Do you have children?"

"Yes, two of them. A girl who just started high school and a boy two years younger."

"Then you'll know."

Choy looked up from the scrapbook because Gwen had stopped talking in mid-sentence.

"How one day they just stop listening to you," she continued after a few seconds, during which she again looked lost in a memory. "I'm not proud of many things I did as a parent, but I'm very proud of a few."

Once more she disappeared into her thoughts, sitting back down in her 1950s metal-framed kitchen chair with an upholstered vinyl seat. Choy looked away and back down at the scrapbook. The pages after the four concerning A Miracle Worker were filled with clippings from other local amateur performances then university productions. Clearly Julie had been a big star in a small world.

"What did you want to tell me about Julie?" Gwen said, suddenly remembering his email requesting the meeting, as she enjoyed watching him look at her daughter's successes.

"I'm writing a book about her," he said because it was true and because it helped avoid a less pleasant topic that might destroy a fragile soul.

"A book! How absolutely wonderful!"

"And I was wondering if you could tell me all about her as a child," he answered, the only non-lie he could come up with that would allow him to get the information he needed before finally telling her the sad truth about Julie.

"The first book about her! I knew she was going to be famous one day."

"I hope that dream does indeed come true," said Choy and felt even guiltier about further obfuscating his relationship with this woman's daughter.

"Are you from New York?"

"I'm a journalist from Canada."

"She's performed in Canada?"

"Yes." It wasn't exactly a lie, but close enough to one to grow his discomfort. "Many serious actors from the United States and Great Britain come to Canada to perform at the Stratford Festival and other of our regional theatres specializing in Shakespeare."

"When she was in university she talked of doing Shakespeare."

"I'm told she did a great Alabama King Lear and was very good at accents since she was a little girl," said Choy, trying to figure out a way of manoeuvring the conversation into a question and answer format where he would not be obfuscating on thin ice.

"Oh yes, she was excellent. She would hear someone on TV with a Cockney accent and she would speak just like that for the next half hour. She had an actor's ear, that's what everyone said."

Choy smiled, as Gwen enjoyed reliving a happy memory. He needed time to think about what he was doing. Was it ethical to interview a mother with issues about comprehending reality regarding her daughter's life and then at the end of the conversation tell her, 'oh by the way, your daughter is dead?' Maybe this woman's mental state was such that she could never be told the truth about her daughter. Or maybe she had a friend who he could talk to and find out what was really going on.

"Can I take you out to dinner somewhere? I mean it's the least I can do if you are willing to help me with information for the book. Dinner and drinks. Do you have someplace you'd like to go? I could come back in an hour, so that you'd have time to get dressed. It would make me feel better for all the trouble."

"Talking about my daughter is no trouble."

"Would you allow me to buy you dinner? "

"I'd like that, but …" again she broke off in the middle of a sentence. "What is your name again?"

"Waylon Choy."

"I knew a Bobby Choy once. His father owned a Chinese restaurant. He wanted to be an actor just like me, but his father disapproved. Wanted him to become a doctor. He was very good in school. Top marks in our high school. I'm not sure what happened to him. But he was Chinese and you're not."

"I am a little bit Chinese."

"Really?"

"Yes. A little bit Indian, a little bit Hawaiian, a little bit Russian, a little bit lots of other things and a little bit Chinese from a great-great-great-great-great grandfather who also left me his last name."

"How wonderful!"

"I think so," Choy said, not at all annoyed at having to once again explain his name because she seemed so genuinely naive.

"Gwen, do you have a friend who helps you with things? Cleans up and does errands or other stuff? If you do, she could come to dinner with us. I don't mind paying for the two of you. Would that make you feel more comfortable?"

She shook her head. "Most of the people who live here speak Spanish. They are nice people, but not my friends. I had friends in Butte and Boise, but not here. My husband made me come here."

"Your husband? Does he live here with you?"

She shook her head.

"Where is your husband?" Choy asked after it became clear she wasn't going to volunteer anything.

"Dead," she answered. "He brought me here so we could look for Julie, but we couldn't find her and our money ran out so all we could afford was this trailer."

"How did he die?"

"I killed him," she answered and then glanced ever so slightly up at the stranger sitting across the table from her. "I was never a good wife. I understand that now."

Does she mean a metaphorical murder? Can I trust anything she says?

"I'd like to go to Applebee's. They have a Long Island Ice Tea for only one dollar."

"I'll take you wherever you want to go. If Applebee's is where you feel like going then that's where I'll take you. But you really don't need to worry about how much it costs, because I'm paying."

"I like their Bourbon Street Steak," she said. "It comes with sautéed onions and mushrooms and crispy red potatoes."

It sounded like she was repeating a line from a commercial.

"Okay, if that's where you want to go, that's where we'll go."

"Should I get dressed now?" she said, half standing up.

"Yes," said Choy, also standing. "I'll leave so you can dress and come back in an hour."

"I'll be ready in half an hour," she said, heading into the bedroom.

"Okay, half an hour," said Choy. "I'll see you then."

***

Jorge, the man in the trailer court office spoke limited English but managed to get across that Gwendolyn Henderson was a nice old lady whose rent was always paid on time, but she was a little crazy. He also said she didn't have any friends as far as he knew, but since her pad was at the back end of the park he wasn't really familiar with the comings and goings at her place. When asked if someone cleaned her trailer and washed her clothes or if Gwen did these tasks herself, Jorge indicated his ignorance about the subject with a shrug.

Next Choy knocked on the doors of the four trailers nearest Gwen's but at the only one where someone answered, the young woman didn't speak much English and Choy's poor grasp of Spanish limited the conversation to a few sentences from which he understood that the neighbours didn't have much to do with the crazy old gringa, because she seldom came out of her trailer, but she did have some regular visitors.

When a half hour had elapsed and he knocked once again on Gwen's screen door, she wore a pretty green dress that fit her perfectly, a blond wig and was fully made up. While still appearing frail she looked much better and Choy could tell she had once been a glamorous young woman who carried herself with grace and confidence. She clearly enjoyed dressing up and going out, but while her demeanour was livelier, Gwen's participation in the conversation remained tentative. Her responses to questions about Julie's childhood were lucid and animated, but when the subject drifted to more recent times she shut down or repeated the same words used before to describe her daughter's supposed life as an actor back east. It was like she had a friend who was telling her stories, probably to protect her, about the imaginary life of the only daughter she had left and some part of Gwen knew they were only fairy tales but chose to believe them anyway. Repeating the exact phrases that someone said or emailed was Gwen's way of assuring herself that Julie was still alive and had reconciled with her mother.

Despite spending almost three hours in the restaurant listening to a proud mother describing her eldest daughter's life up to the point of the car accident, Choy learned nothing that helped answer the question of why Julie had become a drug user. Or at least nothing beyond the obvious fact that her mother suffered from some sort of mental illness and for some reason Julie felt responsible.

When he dropped Gwen back at her trailer Choy asked if he could return the next day to continue the interview and told her that he'd like to move on to the car accident and what happened after that. She agreed that 11 a.m. would be a good time for him to come but didn't acknowledge his statement about what they would talk about. The prospect of getting useful information directly from Gwen seemed dim, but he hoped to use the interview to discover who was sending her emails purporting to be from Julie and who her regular visitors might be. Choy was fairly certain that the emailer was also a visitor and she/he was the key to unravelling the rest of the story.

***

After nine hours of deep sleep Choy finally felt a clarity of thought that had been missing all week. The bomb wasn't aimed at Billy-Bob, or at least not just him.

Someone is trying to kill me. What can I do about it?

First he called Detective Carroll, who had no new information, but agreed that it was possible the bomb could have been aimed at both Baker and him, which might mean Lee was still actively trying to kill both of them. But, given the number of LAPD, DEA, ATF and FBI agents actively working on the case, Carroll thought it much more likely that the focus of the war between Lee and Baker would move to another city and therefore any assassins in the employ of either drug lord would also be moving on.

"Lee and Baker are probably half way around the world by now," said Carroll. "Some place where they own the cops."

He assumes that couldn't be here.

Choy didn't say anything, but Carroll clearly understood his silence.

"Maybe you should get out of LA, go someplace that nobody knows about," the cop said.

"I need to stay at least one more day," Choy answered, thinking about Julie's mother.

"I could ask about assigning some uniforms to protect you."

"Your superiors would probably say no and even if they agreed it might be like waving a big red flag over my head and shouting 'here he is, come and get him'."

Carroll's lack of response suggested a shared concern about the efficacy of the LAPD in keeping someone who so many cops hated safe.

"I can ask around, see if any of my contacts have heard anything," the cop said, perhaps feeling a little guilty.

"That would be great," Choy answered, even though he had his doubts that anyone, especially the police, could protect him if Lee wanted him dead.

***

As he drove to San Bernardino, Choy checked his mirror every now and then to see if someone was following him. When he arrived at the trailer court, before knocking on Gwen's door, he called the cell number he had for Emerson Lee. A woman answered.

"Is Emerson Lee there? It's Waylon Choy."

"He's not here."

"Can I leave a message?"

"He doesn't use this phone anymore."

"Tell him I need to speak with him."

"He doesn't use this phone anymore," she repeated.

"Tell him that Waylon Choy wants to talk. Tell him that he'll regret not talking to me." After saying these words Choy immediately ended the call.

While putting the phone into his shirt pocket he stared at Gwen's trailer while considering what to do next. Lee now had his new cell number, as did Baker after his goons had taken the phone out of his pocket when they searched him. He wondered how long it took from obtaining the telephone number before they could exploit the SS7 cellular network that Detective Martinez had told him about.

Will Lee call me back? Maybe I'm already dead as far as he is concerned.

It was the damned uncertainty that bothered him more than the prospect of actually being killed. Not that he would necessarily choose death over uncertainty, but anything one could do to reduce it, the better the quality of life remaining..

I have to change Lee's mind.

Why would he agree to talk? He wants me dead.

If Lee was going to kill him, better here, away from his children or friends, who could be caught in a crossfire or mistaken for him.

There's no point to worrying. Better to keep working on Julie's story.

16.

After spending three more hours in and around the trailer court, Choy had learned little more about Julie Christie. Gwen continued to enjoy talking about her daughter's first 21 years but shut down when the conversation was steered towards the car accident and what happened after that.

He worried about ever learning more as he drove back along a jammed freeway to his downtown hotel. After about 20 minutes during which the car moved less than a kilometre, he decided to get off the No. 10 at the next exit and find his way down to the No. 60, which the GPS showed would take him close to downtown. Other drivers had the same idea and the street that ran under the freeway was also jammed, so he turned right at the next major intersection and got into the left lane, planning to head south as soon as he could. A glance at the rear view mirror revealed at least one car and one van he was pretty sure had been on the freeway behind him, but he guessed his plan to get where he was going a little quicker was an obvious one, considered by most drivers heading towards downtown. It wasn't until after another turn and a half dozen blocks later that the presence of the same two vehicles behind him began to worry Choy. Then, when he finally made it onto the No. 60, the van was still following. But two hours later, finally back downtown he didn't recognize any vehicles behind or in front of him.

Pulling into the hotel underground parking garage, his worry about an assassin following him had been replaced by a generalized stress due to the ridiculous amount of time spent driving in the rented car.

Sam and her teacher are right.

While a private automobile offers an illusion of freedom, the reality, especially in a big city, is wasted time, energy, money and health. Urban areas designed for walking, cycling and mass transit offer a much better quality of life. There was absolutely no doubt that Vancouver was an easier, more pleasant city to get around in than Los Angeles. On the other hand, the winter weather sure was nicer in southern California.

Rather than go up to his room, or even into the hotel itself, Choy left his phone in the rental car and walked up the parking ramp, past the automated ticket gate into the bright sunshine. It was a perfect afternoon to take a stroll and if there was an assassin looking for him he didn't have to make it easy. He wanted to see the ocean so he headed for 7th Street to board a train to Santa Monica. A little more than an hour later he was comfortable in his short-sleeve shirt walking along the oceanfront of Santa Monica State Beach, with the pier towering above him, while thinking about the information gathered earlier.

There were a few tasty, albeit tiny, tidbits of information that had slipped out in today's conversation with Gwen, mostly from reactions to questions he posed: Something happened between Julie and her father after the accident that made Gwen extremely uncomfortable; Gwen admitted to being an alcoholic and blamed herself for Julie's 'bad times' although she didn't mention any substance abuse problem or sending her daughter to a treatment centre; An event occurred that caused a loving, hard-working husband to turn into an object of hatred. Had she really killed him? He was not sure, although the notion that this gentle, damaged soul could be a murderer seemed far-fetched. Even crazier was the idea that she could have done it and gotten away with it, at least on her own.

Choy convinced her to walk with him around the trailer park and a few blocks beyond, by insisting that he needed to stretch his legs and offering to buy her some groceries but found no signs of a friend who lived nearby. Perhaps she was able to look after herself.

She seemed a competent computer user and clearly knew her way around the area where she lived. Given limited needs and a meagre existence perhaps someone like her could survive on her own. Maybe the imagined success of a daughter doing what mother always wanted to do herself was giving her the will to live, to keep herself clean and decently fed. Perhaps that and watching old movies on an ancient laptop were enough to sustain a sort of happiness. How the hell could he destroy this life by revealing the truth about her daughter?

Riding back to downtown Los Angeles Choy noticed a guy in the back of his car who looked familiar. He had seen the balding 50-year-old wearing faded jeans, T-shirt and a tattered light jacket in the park and maybe somewhere else.

What did an assassin look like?

This guy looked more like a janitor or a handyman, coming back from the beach, where he had gone to get some fresh air after a hard day's work. Maybe he worked at the hotel. On the other hand, this would be the perfect look for a hit man, no one would ever suspect him of being a killer. If people noticed him at all, he would remind them of a favourite uncle who was poor but always willing to lend a helping hand.

Did I make a mistake by calling Lee? Maybe I should take Carroll's advice and just disappear.

But if he were hiding what would he do?

Write fiction.

You can do that from anywhere. But he'd never see his kids or his father again.

They'd be in danger if Lee couldn't find me.

On the walk back from the Metro station to the hotel Choy was pondering these questions, alternating with the dilemma he faced talking to Gwen, when, no more than a few metres from the hotel entrance, a black Mercedes pulled up at the curb just in front of him and two rather large Chinese looking men quickly got out. The guy from the passenger side was almost immediately grabbing his right arm, while the guy from the back driver side was holding on to his left.

"Mr. Lee will talk to you," said the man to his right.

"Quickly please," said the man to his left.

But Choy resisted, pulling his arms away, first from one and then the other. People on the street were watching as the two bigger men glared but didn't put their hands back on their target.

"I wanted to talk to him on the phone," said Choy, who understood what was really going on.

"You asked to speak with him," said the man on the right.

"Is he in the car?" asked Choy.

"It's dangerous for him to be out now," said the man on the left.

"So he's not in the car?"

The man on the right nodded to the man on the left as each of them stuck a hand under an arm and picked up Choy, carrying him to the open back door of the vehicle. He struggled just enough to make the point that he was not doing this willingly. A few passers-by looked concerned, but no one did or said anything. Maybe they thought someone was shooting a scene for a movie. Perhaps if he had made a bigger fuss, at least cried out, someone would have helped, but the goons were right, he was the one who called Lee and asked to talk. Might as well get this, whatever it was, over with. The two muscle-bound men pushed him into the car and the driver quickly sped away from the curb.

"Where is Lee?" said Choy.

"We'll be there in 10 minutes," answered the goon who had grabbed his left arm and was now seated beside him.

Choy stared but the guy avoided eye contact by looking straight ahead.

"Is Lee a good boss?" he asked, after a few minutes of silence, as the car was leaving downtown. "I mean does he pay well and offer good working conditions? Or do you need a union to negotiate a better deal for you?"

There was no answer, but the guy in the front seat turned to look at the guy in the back.

"I mean your job has got to be pretty dangerous what with all the shootings, stabbings and bombs. Have any of you guys ever been nearby when a bomb exploded? It's pretty intense; I still have some ringing in my ears three days after being 30 yards away from where that car bomb blew up at Baker's hideout."

There was no reaction from any of the three other men in the car.

"And it's not just the danger you guys should get paid extra for," continued Choy. "I mean there's the PTSD too when you see some terrible shit, like when I found my girlfriend Joy Lee, dead on the hotel bed, stabbed straight through the throat so it almost looked like her head was falling off. I mean there was blood soaked through all the sheets, right down into the base of the bed. Shit like that stays with you. I close my eyes, and there she is, a good Chinese girl from Oakland, who happened to be in the wrong place at the wrong time. I'm never getting over that; it's going to be with me for the rest of my life. You know what I mean?"

There was still no reaction from the hired hands.

"Of course you guys know what I'm talking about. You can't work security for someone like Mr. Lee without running into a lot of terrible stuff, especially during times like now with a war going on. Right? I sure hope you get paid enough to make it all worthwhile."

The silent staring straight ahead continued. The car was now in an old industrial neighbourhood.

He was only talking to keep his mind off thinking about Mr. Lee and what was about to happen. Unfortunately, thinking about not thinking about what was about to happen made him think about what was about to happen.

Better to get this over with now. Better to ask Lee if he has hired an assassin. Better to die now than live a few more days in fear and uncertainty.

As he was trying to focus on exactly what he would say to Lee, the car pulled into an empty parking lot and parked in the middle of it.

Is this where I'm going to die?

As various images of his kids, father and Joy flashed on the little LCD screen inside his brain, another black Mercedes entered the parking lot and slowly pulled up beside them, causing the replay of his life to end.

"Out," said the guy on the passenger side front seat.

As Choy climbed out of the car, the driver of the other car got out to open his passenger side back door, an obvious invitation to enter.

Emerson Lee was sitting inside, offering a smile and a hand to shake. "Waylon, I am so happy you asked to see me again. I felt sad that our last good-bye was rather unpleasant."

Rather than return, the driver of Lee's car got into the back seat of the first car, leaving the two men alone to discuss matters in private. When Choy saw this, his confidence grew that life would last at least a little longer. A drug lord was unlikely to do the dirty deed himself and probably preferred not to be present immediately before it occurred as well.

After shaking Lee's hand, Choy immediately began speaking as if he had called this meeting. "Thanks for getting back to me so soon, I appreciate it," he said. "Given your present situation with the police I understand this talk must be short."

"Which situation?"

"Well, see that's why it is so important we talk. I did not know if you understood the depth and breadth of information that the police have about you and, of course, my worry was you didn't."

"Your worry?"

"The Los Angeles police regard you as a primary suspect for ordering the car bomb at Billy-Bob Baker's Los Angeles office. Not to mention the stabbing death of my girlfriend Joy at the hotel. I had to tell them all I knew about you and thought it important to inform you about that in person."

Lee gave him that same faux inscrutable look he always employed.

"They think you may have ordered me killed as well," Choy said, as casually as commenting on the day's weather. "Detective Carroll even offered me police protection, but of course I declined. I told him that if you wanted me dead a few cops wouldn't protect me."

Choy maintained eye contact as he spoke. Lee remained expressionless.

"I also said that you wouldn't be so foolhardy as to have me killed when you would be the main suspect."

Still no change in his expression.

"I thought I better tell you all this and equally important, another meeting offers an opportunity to apologize for my previous rather emotional response to all the unfortunate recent events. I am so sorry for being cross with you. All things considered you were a decent client: you did me and my father the favour you promised. What more could I ask? I mean, other than you not being a drug lord at war with another drug lord. That's more than a little unfortunate."

Lee continued to look like a professional poker player who had just shoved all in.

"Do you accept my apology?"

Lee's stern visage softened slightly as if he was making some sort of mental calculation. "I too must apologize once more," he finally said. "For what, unfortunately, I must soon do."

The two men looked at each other carefully.

"Have me killed?" Choy asked, trying not to sound over dramatic.

"The business I am in and the position I hold, come with certain responsibilities and rules of conduct."

"I understand," answered Choy and he did. "Noam Chomsky explained it well in some article or other I read. 'The United States, like a Mafia don, cannot allow any challenge to its authority, especially the small ones, because the world is a dangerous place, with lesser criminals just waiting to prove themselves the toughest guys on the block,' or words to that effect."

"It pleases me that you understand my predicament and also that you have enough interest in understanding the world to read Noam Chomsky. I have found in my previous interactions with journalists that they are generally politically very naïve."

"Because you are a civilized man, you don't want to kill me, but the business you are in is uncivilized."

Choy's tone had turned to sarcasm.

"You don't want to do it, but you have to, or as my son said once when he was seven years old, 'the other kids made me do it.'"

Lee pursed his lips. "I understand your cynicism, and in many ways share it," he said, looking away, "but the sad reality of war is that turning one's cheek after being slapped only leads to more and harder slaps."

"I never hit you," said Choy.

"Oh but you did, more than once, even though you were unaware of it."

What does he mean?

Choy could not contain his curiosity; it leaked quickly from his brain to his face.

"You consorted with my enemy and helped him achieve an important goal," said Lee. "Unwittingly perhaps, but that hardly excuses your behaviour or enables me to ignore it."

"I don't know what you are talking about."

"Of course you don't, which makes your transgression worse, not better."

"Can you explain?" said Choy, unable to even guess at what he was being accused of.

Lee studied him for a few seconds. "Why do you suppose I did not want you to meet with Svetlana Borovsky?"

"Because you worried she could manipulate me."

"Which she did, but to what end?"

"I was a pawn in a public relations war between two drug lords fighting over supply routes."

"For someone who prides himself on seeing the big picture, you have been remarkably myopic."

Choy's look of curiosity had turned to one of bewilderment.

"Based upon your conversations with me and Billy-Bob Baker do you really think the point for either of us is control of supply routes for drugs?"

"He babbled on about using the experience of the drug trade to create an organization capable of surviving underground," said Choy, partly thinking out loud.

"He told you what they are doing, but you ignored him."

"I am failing to see the significance of this."

"Ignorant and insubordinate," said Lee, shaking his head.

"I never worked for you, so how could I be insubordinate?"

"But you admit to your ignorance?"

"I don't know what you're talking about."

"Exactly," said Lee, shaking his head. "Billy-Bob, Svetlana and Amanda Bennett are setting up their own private intelligence network and offering it to Trump as a way around the CIA, who are currently our allies. The drugs are a way to finance it, but more importantly to develop assets in Afghanistan, Pakistan, Iraq, Libya, Burma, Laos, Colombia, Cambodia and everywhere else government officials are bought off as part of the trade in illegal drugs."

"Blackmailing government officials for information? Of course," said Choy, who then realized something else. "Baker and Bennett? She's using her connections in the white nationalist world to convince Trump and his people to use her services. Trump doesn't trust the CIA and it doesn't trust him, so a private, alternative intelligence network is attractive. You only gave me part of the story and told me not to meet with Svetlana and Billy-Bob because you knew I would do exactly that if you told me not to. I was supposed to discover the private intelligence gathering and the links to Trump. That's it. 'Ignorant and insubordinate.' I failed so now ..."

"Disrespect cannot be tolerated."

"I disrespected you when I talked with Svetlana and Billy-Bob or when I failed to figure out they were doing?"

"If those men in the other car see you getting away with disregarding my orders, your sarcastic remarks, consorting with my enemies what do you think the effect would be? I have no choice."

"But you knew I would disregard your order because that's what a good journalist would do."

Lee's smirk was ever so slight, but still visible.

"So you knew all along that you would have 'no choice' but to kill me," said Choy. "You set me up."

"You chose your own course of action.

"I have free will, but not you? You just said you have no choice but to kill me."

"My actions are circumscribed by a particular reality regardless of whether or not you, or I, approve. Free will is an illusion marketed by promoters of certain religions and economic systems. The truth is we are all constrained by ties that bind us to particular behaviours."

Rather than being filled with fear of what was about to happen, Choy only felt disgust at this man's absolution of himself. "You, right now, are choosing to kill me. You."

"You chose to ignore my orders."

"As any decent journalist searching for the truth would do."

"Have it your way then," said Lee. "Journalism is killing you."

There's some truth to that.

"Your fate was sealed weeks ago," said Lee.

Is he admitting sending the guy who killed Joy and the car bomber as well?

"My fate was sealed when I agree to meet with you."

"Before that," Lee answered quickly.

"When?" asked Choy, curious to the end.

"When I realized you would be the perfect journalist to become involved."

"Why me?"

"Because if someday we must work with Bennett she will owe me a favour."

"For killing me."

Choy looked down at his feet as the reality of his situation sank in. "I could write about Bennett and Billy-Bob and Trump now. It would be a great story. The *Sun* would love it as a follow to what they've already reported and to one of their journalists being killed."

"A *New York Times* reporter is already working on it."

"So, there's no way around it?" Choy said, as fear and regret began to do battle with anger.

"Well, you could benefit from the baseball rule," Lee answered after a few seconds of silent contemplation.

"The baseball rule? What is that?"

"Three strikes and the assassin is called out," said Lee, rather playfully, considering the subject. "If you escape your fate a third time, perhaps that outcome was not meant to be."

Is he serious?

"But I would not get your hopes up," Lee continued. "You were lucky and benefited twice from my instructions to disguise the motive. The next time there will be no such concern. Instead, your body will not be found. Your disappearance will be a mystery never solved."

Never solved?

Choy almost blurted out, 'why so cruel?' but this cold-blooded bastard didn't need to know he was worried about his kids and father not knowing for certain if he was alive or dead.

"So that's it?" he said.

"You have an hour or two left, and I have an hour until boarding a private jet that will take me back to Vancouver and onto places I would have enjoyed showing you," said Lee.

"Okay then." Not that he wanted to hurry the outcome, but Choy didn't feel like spending any more time with the man who ordered his murder. "Time for me to go."

Another nod.

"Is he going to do it here?" asked Choy while opening the car door.

"You will be driven to a secure location."

As Choy stood up outside the car, the two goons once again appeared on either side of him. The one on his left held a pistol to his head. "Walk slowly back to the other car," he said. "No sudden moves."

This time both men sat in the back seat with Choy in the middle. This time he did not feel like talking. Instead he wallowed in self-pity because it seemed the thing to do. He could think of no better way to spend the last minutes he had left. He had embarrassed himself, been manipulated and used like a cub reporter by a cynical politician. He'd never see his kids again. That made him the saddest.

I'll never write the book about Reb/Orchid/Julie, explaining her life to the world. I'll never meet Joy's parents and tell them how sorry I am and how much I loved their daughter. I'll never have a chance to find another ballroom dancing partner. I'll never play in a poker tournament. I'll never find another duplicate bridge partner. I'll never become a goalie.

And what would happen to the car he had rebuilt from junk? His daughter hated the entire automobile industry.

Are these really my last thoughts? Awfully maudlin.

The lesson was it's hard to focus on the positive where your life is about to end.

Choy had no sense of how long they had been driving when the car pulled up to what looked like an abandoned factory with a large, empty parking lot surrounding it. The goon to the left grabbed his arm and half pulled him out of the vehicle, while the other came up from behind and pushed him with the barrel of a pistol against his back towards an entrance to the building.

As they entered a small door into an old open factory floor with only a couple of working lights, for some reason Choy's thoughts turned to Reb/Orchid/Julie saying, "go with the wings of Mercury," while searching for a vein to stick the needle into. She knew the danger of Fentanyl contamination in every packet of heroin she bought, that she might die, but the desire — or was it need? — for the drug was too strong. What were her last thoughts? Or were there none, only the blind bliss of satisfying a need? The rush, or whatever it was, once you had a decade-old addiction. Was she thinking of her mother Gwen, some image from her happy childhood? Playing Helen Keller in A Miracle Worker? The greatest time in her life, rehearsing a scene from King Lear with her best friend at university?

She was probably feeling good. Better than how I'm going to die.

Or maybe she was also worrying about the possibility that she was about to die, that she had just shot a grain of Fentanyl into her veins. There was certainly enough talk about the epidemic of overdoses to cause every drug user in Vancouver to stress about that possibility.

He was pushed into a smaller, better-lit room with the remnants of an old assembly line. There was an overheard wire, from which a few clamps still hung that passed over a large cement tank filled with a liquid, maybe dirty water, or maybe something else. It could have been a paint room, where parts of some sort were dipped into a solution and then continued along the line to the next process. A few feet from the vat stood a muscular short man, who looked sort of Chinese, but also sort of Mexican, wearing a rubberized apron, hip waders, rubber gloves that went all the way up his arms, and goggles.

Regardless of whether her last thoughts were positive or negative, Julie is dead. Whatever my last thoughts I will soon be dead.

The man in protective gear pointed to a chair where the two goons sat him down and tied his hands with a thick cord behind it. Choy watched as the man wearing goggles moved his head in the direction of the door and the two goons disappeared in that direction. Then the man who probably would be his executioner went back to work. He picked up a pail from a table along the side of the room, walked it to the cement vat, and emptied whatever was in it. He quickly backed away from the vat as a cloud of smoke or steam rose from it.

An acid bath.

Choy immediately regretted his active imagination.

This guy is going to shoot me or slit my throat and then put my body into a vat of acid, dissolving every bit of me except for my two gold crowns, or maybe the acid was strong enough to make them disappear as well.

He'd read about Mexican drug cartels disposing of bodies this way.

The executioner went back to the table and repeated the exercise with another pail, then a third. He put on a breathing hood like Choy had seen guys in the paint department of body shops wear, picked up what looked like a metal canoe paddle and then stirred the liquid in the vat. After a few minutes he walked back to the table, pulled the hood off his head and the rubber gloves off his hands then looked towards his victim.

Strangely, Choy's only thought was, 'knife or bullet?' Nothing else.

How is he going to do it?

Then a moment of pride that he was being so analytical, so calmly curious, paying attention to detail. He was being a journalist to the end.

The executioner turned back to the table, picked up a machete and ran his thumb along its edge to test the sharpness.

Knife. Cut not shoot.

Then Choy looked down at the floor and saw a large sheet of thick plastic covering it all around where he sat.

He's going to take a few steps towards me then using both hands swing that machete at my neck. That's how I'm going to die. And the plastic sheet will catch my head and blood. He'll put my body parts and the blood-covered plastic into the acid and there will be nothing left, except the memories people have of me. That and the stories I have written.

At that moment he regretted never having written a novel, or something more permanent than journalism. Newspaper stories were consumed today and thrown away, dissolved in an acid bath of indifference to anything that can be labelled old. Of course that wasn't exactly true, there were historians who might resurrect what you wrote decades, even centuries later.

That's a sort of immortality.

The executioner placed the machete back on the table, put on clear latex gloves, a plastic poncho with a hood that he drew tight around his head and then picked up the machete again. As he took a step towards Choy and raised the machete as if he were about to swing it. there was a loud bang and then another. Two small patches of blood appeared from exit wounds on the executioner's chest as he fell to the floor.

After a few seconds another man, holding a rifle that he kept aimed at the executed executioner, appeared from the entrance to the room. Choy thought he looked familiar but could not immediately place where he had seen the man before. He got close to the body, prodding it for signs of life with the barrel, before turning to Choy. The look on his face was one of concern and confusion.

It was the guy from the Metro train back from Santa Monica who he thought might have been following him. The guy he had taken for a janitor or a handyman working at the hotel.

"I sure as hell hope your life was worth shooting this guy for," he said.

17.

Choy barely remembered what happened after the police arrived, but some remnants of conversation in the few minutes after shots were fired was vividly imprinted on his brain, starting with: "My name is Tom Christie."

He stared, struggling to understand the meaning of these words. Christie? Could he be a relative? Or?

Julie's father? Gwen didn't kill him?

"Christie? Are you Julie's father?"

The man was startled by his question. "Do you know my daughter?"

Julie's father saved my life? Symmetry.

His search for information about what happened to her led him to this spot where he was about to die only to be saved by one of the people most responsible for creating her life.

"Do you know my daughter?" Tom repeated.

How to answer?

He must have been in a state of shock even before the arrival of dozens of cops and other investigators, because parts of the conversation with Tom were simply not in his memory bank. Other bits replayed as if they were recorded in Dolby stereo and high definition cameras.

"Gwen told you she killed me?" he said in one scene that stuck in Choy's damaged brain. "She doesn't want to see me anymore; maybe she wishes I were dead, but I'm very much alive."

He has a gentle, soothing voice.

"As I'm sure you figured out once you met her, Gwen is not well. She doesn't want to see me — I remind her of our daughter who has been missing for many years and that causes her great pain — so I have to hide when keeping an eye on her. I watched you go into her trailer and talk to her neighbours. To find out who you were and what you were up to I followed you. Saw you snatched off the street and luckily my van was parked only a few feet away. Watched you on my night vision binoculars in that car, talking or whatever was happening, then saw those two muscle men pull a gun on you and force you back into that other car. Didn't want to get involved, but I couldn't just let them … so I followed again and when the two guys in the car left I came in with my rifle and … he was about to cut your head off with that machete … I didn't really think about it … it was only a reaction … someone about to die … my adrenalin was pumping … all an instinct really … my finger pulling the trigger … What's his name?"

"I don't know."

"Why was he about to kill you?"

"He's a professional assassin. A drug lord hired him to kill me when I didn't write the story he wanted."

"A hit man hired by a drug lord?"

Choy nodded, then realizing Tom's concern, added: "Don't worry, the drug lord is out of the country and the assassin is dead."

Tom did not react as if he had heard reassuring words. "I shot a professional killer?"

"Not a very good one apparently. He tried to kill me twice before. Once with a bomb that killed a couple of other drug gang members and once with a knife in my hotel room that killed my girl-friend, Joy. He was a very bad man. By shooting him you probably saved a lot of lives, not just mine."

Tom must have been in a state of shock as well, because he stood there, eyes looking straight ahead, an absent stare. His body was present, but his thoughts were elsewhere.

"After he chopped off my head he was going to put my body in that vat of acid," Choy continued, because that was the thought bouncing back and forth in his consciousness. "And my kids would never have known if I was really dead or just missing. That uncertainty would have eaten away at them. That would have been worse than the actual dying. That's what I was thinking right before you shot him."

Tom was paying attention again, as if the words had awoken him from restless sleep. He nodded. "I understand."

"Thank you," said Choy. "For saving my life. For saving my kids from that pain."

"I understand," repeated Tom.

Of course he understands, because he's lived through it.

The arrival of the police added to the fog that enveloped his thought process. Bright lights, hours of questions, another trip to a Los Angeles hospital, followed by a ride back to the downtown police headquarters all melded into a sort of dissonant background noise, the foreground being reserved for going over and over the words he remembered Tom saying before the disorienting mayhem ended his ability to think in a linear fashion.

Did I tell Tom that Julie was dead? And about the way she died? Or that I'm going to write a book about how she was more than just another dead junkie? Did I arrange a time and place to meet so we can talk about his daughter? What else did I say about Gwen? I can't remember.

It wasn't until Carroll and Martinez began interviewing him that Choy's brain returned to somewhat normal functioning. Their familiar voices had a calming effect, slowing his thoughts down. They explained that the dead man was most likely an infamous hired killer known as 'El Chile Fantasma', the Ghost Chile, because like the hottest pepper in the world, he was very difficult to find and after one bite your head was on fire. He was rumoured to have killed hundreds over the past decade, mostly working for Mexican cartels. Carroll told him how lucky he was to have escaped three attempts on his life by one of North America's most ruthless killers. Then Choy remembered Lee's words about the baseball rule for hired killers and relayed them, along with the rest of the conversation in the car to the two detectives. Except for the part about how he had been used.

"Well the Ghost Chile definitely struck out," said Martinez.

"He actually told you it was nothing personal?" said Carroll. "And that he had no choice but to kill you?"

"He did," said Choy, "but I'll never testify against him if that's what you're asking. I've learned my lesson about drug dealers."

"We'll never stop them if the people they try to kill are too afraid to testify," said Martinez.

"The only way you'll stop drug dealers is by legalizing all drugs," Choy said quickly. "History suggests that if you take Lee or Baker off the street they will be replaced by someone even more violent. Why the hell would I risk my life and maybe my children's lives to accomplish that? I've got better things to die for."

"Maybe testifying against Lee is the only way to save your life," said Carroll. "You really want to rely on the baseball rule?"

"I've seen what drugs can do to a community," said Martinez. "It's isn't pretty. And you want to legalize that?"

"You've seen what illegal drugs do to a community and it is ugly as all hell," answered Choy. "When are you going to learn? Passing laws against stuff that people want and need doesn't work. It makes some bad people very powerful; it gives them a financial incentive to push drugs on people who have never used them before; it promotes violence and corruption; it ..."

He stopped mid-sentence and shook his head. He really didn't want to debate drug policy with two cops. That could only lead to saying something he would regret, like 'of course cops are in favour of the war on drugs because their jobs depend on it,' or even worse. These were nice people, police officers who had treated him well.

"Look, I'd love to debate this with you some other time, but I need to find the guy who saved my life. Do you know where he is?"

"He was released shortly after you were sent to the hospital," said Carroll.

"I don't suppose you guys could give me his address? I want to thank him properly and talk to him about his daughter. I have information he will want to hear."

"He told the investigating officers he had no fixed address," said Carroll.

Choy's disappointment was noticed by Martinez. "He lives in his van," she said giving a look of defiance to her partner. "Many people say a freeway should be the symbol of Los Angeles, but I think a bed in the back of a van captures this place one hell of a lot better. Real estate no one can afford, jobs that absolutely require a vehicle, lots and lots of parking lots, bathrooms in shopping malls, prepaid cellphones and nice enough weather you can spend most of the year comfortable in a metal box."

His first impression of this woman had been that she was a by-the-book, wound-too-tight authoritarian who was actually a victim of macho male cop culture, but he had been way off. After spending hours with her Choy realized inside she was a marshmallow with an empathetic heart.

"He parks the van most nights on the street behind the trailer court where his wife lives," said Carroll, exchanging a glance with his partner. "He said that's where he first saw you."

"Thank you."

Choy needed to get over there as soon as possible, but there was no way he could drive a rental car in Los Angeles traffic without some sleep. It was 3 p.m. and he'd been up for thirty-two hours.

"So you guys have my cell number here if you need anything else from me," he said. "And you got my number in Vancouver as well. If things go the way I hope, I'll be leaving the City of Angels in a day or two. Taking a couple of parents to claim their daughter's body in Vancouver. All three of them victims of your war on drugs."

***

When he woke up a light was flashing on the hotel phone, signifying someone had left him a message. It was from Dawn Roberts, the counsellor at the Malibu drug rehabilitation centre. He called her back immediately.

"Hello Dawn, it's Waylon Choy."

"I've been calling the number you gave me for three days, leaving messages, but you never returned them," she said. "Then this morning I got a 'this number is no longer in service' message."

"My girlfriend was stabbed to death by mistake by a hit man hired to kill me and the phone was in the room when it happened so the cops have kept it for forensic analysis."

"Oh my god!"

"I only remembered to cancel the number yesterday when I was being questioned by police regarding the third attempt on my life in the past week."

"The third? My word!"

"The second was a car bomb."

"The one on TV a few days ago?"

"I don't know. I was a little disoriented, and not watching the news. It's been a rough few days," said Choy. "So I didn't get your messages. I'm sorry."

"I understand of course. I just wanted to let you know what I found out about Julie. Her parents? They are both here in Los Angeles. Moved here about four or five years ago to search for their daughter."

"I found them in San Bernardino," said Choy. "Julie's father Tom saved my life by shooting the professional killer who was about to chop off my head and put my body into a vat of acid."

It sounds so fantastic. Why can the truth seem so unbelievable?

"Oh my!" she answered. "I am so sorry."

"Listening to myself everything that happened sounds unreal. Even to me."

After a short silence she said, "So they know how she died?"

"No. Or maybe. I don't really know because I can't remember what I said to him. I was in shock. We both were."

"That's understandable."

"I'm planning to go see them as soon as I get off the phone."

"Well I won't keep you then," she answered. "I just wanted to let you know that I dug around and found that Julie was definitely one of the patients who were recruited to sell drugs. She was supplied with whatever she wanted — painkillers, heroin, acid, speed — in return for claiming she was still in treatment. The insurance company was paying hundreds of dollars a day and she was out on the street selling what she was supposed to be getting off. It's all so horrible. The word is there will be arrests any day now, the owner and a half dozen other people. They'll be charged with fraud; apparently there were dozens of cases, kids young enough to be on their parent's insurance plans. They were kicked out onto the street once they got too old or the insurance company stopped paying."

As Choy was processing this new information about Julie, all he could think of was the pain it would cause Tom and Gwen. They had sent their daughter for what they thought was drug rehabilitation, but in fact was a deeper descent into the depths of addiction.

How can I tell them that? Am I nothing but a messenger who simply reports the news, whose sole responsibility is ensuring the veracity of the information? Or do I also have a responsibility to consider its effect?

Then another realization came: The "best" stories are the sad ones, the ones that make readers cry or get angry, the ones that appeal to emotions, not intellect, the ones that manipulate people. This was the business he was in: manipulating people's emotions to sell whatever product was being advertised that day.

I'm tired of this sort of journalism.

On the other hand he was not selling anything with the book he was researching, other than the book itself. And that was for a good cause: to humanize a statistic; to illustrate who was dying in the epidemic of overdoses; to convince people that a "war" on drugs was not working and society needed another approach. At least he was manipulating people for a good cause.

***

The call from Dawn Roberts made him realize that perhaps someone else had tried to contact him on his old cellphone so Choy phoned the contact number for TwoSpiritPhoenix. His hacker had indeed found some important information and sent him it almost 72 hours earlier. The text message had been: "I'm in. Be very careful. Lee has ordered you killed and hired a hitman to do it."

Would have been good to know.

***

Tom was sitting in the driver seat of his van directly across the street from the back of Gwen's trailer, staring straight ahead, deep in thoughts about his daughter or maybe meditating on the meaninglessness of existence. How do we ever really know what's going on in someone else's head?

"Hi," said Choy, after watching the van and its inhabitant for a few minutes while considering how best to inform this hero with no home that his daughter was dead and had suffered terribly over the years since he had last seen her. If he hadn't informed him already. "Can we talk?"

The movement of Tom's head suggested the visitor should sit on the passenger side front seat. After Choy got in the 20-year-old van the two men stared straight ahead for a time.

"Julie is dead, isn't she?" said Tom, still not looking at his conversation mate.

"Yes," said Choy, trying to make eye contact. That was the least a father deserved when being told about his daughter's demise.

"How did you know her?" Tom said, a quick glance toward him enough for Choy to see little lakes in his eyes.

"I didn't," he answered. "Not really. I'd seen her a few times on the street by my house in Vancouver, that's all."

"The one in Canada? Or the one across the river from Portland?"

"Canada."

"Good," said Tom. "I always talked when she was little about going to Canada. My favourite uncle was a draft dodger who moved up there. A town called Nelson. He wrote that it was very beautiful."

"I've been there and it is," said Choy. "Mountains, a lake and some of the prettiest 130-year-old houses you'll ever see."

"Never did make it up to Canada," Tom sighed,

"You should come with me to claim her body. She didn't have any identification and no one knew her real name."

"How did she die?" said Tom, his sobbing making it difficult for him to speak.

"Fentanyl most likely," Choy answered. "Contaminated heroin. I found her with a needle still in her arm. Death was very quick and painless."

"She was a junkie?" said a father, grieving his baby girl.

"I don't know what that means anymore," said Choy. "She was a person who fell in a hole and couldn't get out, exactly like happens to many of us. There are all kinds of holes. Hers was deeper than most and harder to get out of, but even the shallow ones trap people. I'm a journalist writing a book trying to explain who she was and how she got to where she died. I'm doing that to honour and remember your daughter. Too many people are dying of drug overdoses and not enough people care so …"

"Writing a book about Julie?"

Choy nodded. "I've interviewed people who knew her in Vancouver — they called her Reb, short for rebel, because she used this southern accent sometimes, like Scarlett O'Hara in *Gone With the Wind*."

"She loved to pretend to be different people. I played a game with her when she was very little, we called it Listen to the Accent. My mother had all these old records with people reading stories in different accents and I'd play them for Julie starting around when she was four. She got so good at mimicking whatever she heard and her mother would be so proud."

"She was very well liked by the women in the Downtown Eastside, skid row. She spoke up for others, would take no shit. I talked to three or four women who said that."

"Was she a … hook … prostitute?"

"Do you really want to hear this?"

"Yes, I used to hold her in my arms as she slept on top of me. I am responsible for her life. I need to know everything."

The vulnerability of a sleeping baby was something every parent understood.

"I think she performed sex acts to support her heroin addiction," said Choy trying to be as matter of fact about it as he could. "I saw her sometimes on the street and some of the people who knew her said she was a sex trade worker."

"You haven't told Gwen any of this?" he said, concern rising in his voice.

"No. She thinks Julie is back east working in live theatre. She seemed so pleased about it that I couldn't ..."

"I made up a Hotmail account in Julie's name and send Gwen emails from the computers at the library. It's the only pleasure she gets out of life anymore and no one knew for sure if Julie was alive or dead so ... How am I going to tell her the truth now?"

"Will you both come with me to Vancouver? I will buy the plane tickets and you can stay at my place."

"Neither of us have passports," said Tom.

"You can apply for an emergency one. I checked on the State Department website and you can get one within two days. I'll help you."

"I don't know that Gwen could do it. She doesn't ... You'd have to tell her about Julie and ... She wouldn't go with me in any event."

"Why is she so mad at you?" Choy blurted out, then realized this might be too intimate of a question. "I mean don't answer if it's none of my business."

"You're going to write a book about how my daughter came to be a drug addict?"

"That's an important part of what I think the book will be about, but it won't be just that. It will also be about the rest of her life. I don't think people should be defined by any one thing they do. All of us, including drug addicts, are multifaceted. I've interviewed people at the university, people who saw her in plays, a TV star who knew her, they all say Julie was a brilliant actor. Many people say she was a good friend. All of us, we have our good and bad parts. I'm hoping that's the central lesson readers will learn from the book: The people who are dying of drug overdoses are not just junkies, they are people with rich lives and families and friends. You know ... what do they say? There but for the grace of God go you or I."

Tom's eyes were red, but he had stopped crying as he listened. "Gwen hates me because I kicked Julie out of our house and she never came back. I thought I was being a good parent. Being firm, drawing an important line, but ... Do you know how Julie became addicted?"

"I'm guessing it had something to do with the car accident. She lived and the others died."

"It wasn't Julie's fault at all, it was the others, joking around, stoned; they dropped the burning joint onto Julie's lap and ... But none of that was the cause. It was the pain she felt afterwards, from her back. The doctor gave her Oxycontin and it took a lot of it to make her feel better, but he said not to worry, studies showed it wasn't addictive. Then, when she was taking too much, the doctor learned, in fact, it could be addictive, and cut back on her prescriptions. She tried to cope, but the pain was unbearable, she couldn't act, couldn't concentrate on learning her lines and that was the most important thing in her life. So one day, someone offered her heroin and it worked. Took away the pain and I guess, for a while anyway, was easier to get than Oxycontin. And she was hooked. I had a good job at the time with good insurance and it covered her until she was 25, going to school, and when she started stealing money from us to buy her drugs, I confronted her and she admitted her addiction so I made her go to rehab. Julie didn't want to, said she could kick the bad habit by herself, said it was just another part to play— she desperately wanted to quit, I really believe that — but I found this rehab centre in Malibu that the insurance plan would cover and it was close to Hollywood, so finally she agreed. Her dream had always been to live in Los Angeles, just like her mother."

Does he know about what happened there?

"But Gwen didn't want Julie to leave; she screamed and yelled and tried to stop me; she had already lost one daughter and didn't want to lose the other, or at least that's what I thought at first. Gwen has always been very fragile. She tried to be an actor herself and even had a Hollywood agent before she came back home. She's always had trouble sleeping and for a while took pills that only made her problem worse in the long run. So she began self-medicating with alcohol. Gwen understood how difficult it was to battle an addiction and I thought she wanted Julie nearby to offer support. But that wasn't it at all."

Tom stopped telling his story for a few moments as he relived some painful memories.

"I had it all wrong. Turns out Gwen didn't want Julie to go to Hollywood because she was afraid what happened to her would happen to her daughter."

Tom was crying again. As he tried to stop, Choy looked down as if offering some semblance of privacy.

"Gwen was raped by a producer on the proverbial casting couch, but she never told me, not until a few days after I sent Julie away. When we got married, back in university after Gwen returned from Los Angeles, she was pregnant. I always thought Julie was mine ... and of course she was, in every meaningful way, I know that now, but ... When Gwen told me I reacted very badly. I can't explain it, but I felt betrayed. I felt like everything in my life was a lie and I was the biggest victim of the whole story. I took it out on Gwen and didn't speak to her for almost a year. Then when Julie came back from Los Angeles and was still using drugs, I sent her back, kicked her out of our house even though she begged me to allow her to stay. I made her go back to the rehab centre, told her she couldn't ever stay with us until she kicked her addiction. And we never saw her again. Ever. She went back to the rehab centre off and on for another year but then just disappeared. It wasn't until after Julie was gone that I realized how badly I was treating Gwen and my daughter. I tried to make amends. I quit my job and we came down here to Los Angeles to look for our baby girl, but we never found her. Gwen has hated me ever since."

"Tom," Choy said, putting a hand on his shoulder, in an attempt to soothe some of the inevitable pain that would come from what he was about to say. "I learned some stuff about that rehab centre today … you need to know but it's going to hurt."

"I can't possibly feel more pain than right now," he said, looking like the dying grizzly bear that Choy saw while doing a story on big game hunters. The look in the animal's eyes had stayed with him for over a decade.

"Should I tell you later?" said Choy.

"Now."

"The police are investigating the rehab centre that Julie went to," he said, trying to take all drama out of his voice. "There's likely to be charges of fraud laid against the owner and a few managers. Some of the patients, it appears Julie was one of them, were given drugs to use and to sell. They never really attended rehab. The centre billed the insurance companies as if they were being treated, but it was all a scam."

"The centre in Malibu that I sent her to?"

"There was no way you could have known. The place had an excellent reputation. I've been there; it's a beautiful spot. It fooled everybody, including the insurance companies and most of the counsellors who worked there. I had dinner with one of them and she swears most of the staff didn't know. She told me this morning that charges are expected soon."

"The rehab centre I sent Julie to was giving her drugs and having her sell them?"

Choy nodded.

"I can't tell Gwen about this. I can't tell her any of it. She won't survive. We can't go to Vancouver to identify her body."

"Would you prefer that I look after all the details? Maybe have her cremated and send the ashes back here?"

"What did I do? How can I tell Gwen?" He was sobbing uncontrollably.

"I'm not sure how the process works, but I'll find out," said Choy, trying to focus on the practicalities to avoid thinking about the pain of a grieving father. "Maybe you'll have to give a DNA sample or maybe you can identify her through photographs, I don't know, but I'll look after everything. Don't worry about it."

What a ridiculous thing to say.

"Everything is gone," said Tom, his sobbing diminished. "My daughters, job, house, wife, dignity, self-assurance, self-respect. I sleep in a van and spend my days watching a woman who hates me so I can slip into her trailer and clean up when she isn't there. I made the woman I love hate me and want me dead because I blamed her for being raped and I killed our only remaining daughter, after turning her into a prostitute and a junkie."

He stared straight ahead, the tears exhausted. Choy couldn't think of anything to say. The silence lasted minutes that seemed like centuries.

"My punishment is to be alive," Tom finally said, calmly, as if he was stating an obvious fact.

After another, shorter silence, Tom turned to Choy. "Could you leave me, please? I need to be alone."

Choy nodded, opened the van door and climbed out. Standing on the sidewalk he forced himself to make eye contact, hoping Tom would see that he understood his pain. He desperately wanted to help.

There's nothing I can say or do.

18.

Choy needed to go home. The City of Angels smelled of automobile exhaust, death and people who suffered from the illusion that fame, money or power would make them happy. He was tired of seeing people living on the street. He couldn't avert his eyes like most people who lived here did. He saw them sleeping on well-manicured grass in Santa Monica and wondered what had brought them there. He saw them in makeshift shelters lining the sidewalks near freeways and couldn't help but think they were human beings just like him. He saw them under overpasses, on transit benches, in parks and knew each of them had a story just like Reb.

After leaving Tom, he drove back to the hotel, signed the car back to the rental agency and started walking to clear his mind and focus on what was important. He had come to Los Angeles to discover what had happened to Reb/Orchid/Julie that led to her dying on a Vancouver street. He wanted information to write a story and had now gotten the four most basic of the five "Ws" — who, what, where and when — but was still missing the essential glue that binds them together: Why?

Sure, he had what passed for 'why' in most journalism. The car accident, out-of-control painkiller prescriptions, scamming rehab centre owners, a father trying to do his best for a sick child.

But how can I explain all this pain and suffering? Bad luck? God's will? Fate? One of an infinite number of possible outcomes as a result of a big bang that occurred billions of years earlier? What is the lesson learned? Bad things sometimes happen to good people? Stay away from drugs? Avoid smoking joints in cars? Trauma suffered decades ago can remain with us, even through generations? The war on drugs is a war on people who suffer just like you and me? Evil exists?

The pain he had witnessed and suffered cast such a giant shadow over any satisfaction from a story well researched that it was no longer visible. There were no words or deeds that could comfort Tom or Gwen. There was no way to comprehend why he had escaped death at the hands of drug dealers, but others died.

When he last spoke with Detective Martinez it was clear that the police in the USA and Canada still believed Joy had probably been killed during a break-in, that *LA Times* reporter Max Parker happened to be in the wrong place at the wrong time and the stabbing death of *Sun* reporter Jan James was a random piece of bad luck. Even more incredible, the LAPD had received a statement from Emerson Lee's lawyer that six prominent international businessman were willing to provide affidavits that they were dining with Lee at the time Waylon Choy claimed to have talked to him an hour before a paid assassin tried to chop off his head. It was clear that neither Lee or Baker would suffer legal consequences for ordering the deaths of three people and the attempted murder of another.

What really happened doesn't matter. Powerful people are allowed to define their own 'reality'. If they can get away with murder what is the point of confronting these people and risking my life for the truth?

A journalist was like a pesky mosquito that can be swatted away or easily squished.

On the other hand, someone had to speak truth to power, someone had to try holding the rich and powerful to account for their actions. There was no meaningful democracy without a feisty free press. Voting every few years was meaningless if you didn't have access to the truth about the people you were voting for and those who were funding their campaigns.

Sometimes a journalist's story changes the world. But not often. Mostly we just distract people.

Across the street a cameraman was recording a reporter speaking into a microphone in front of a sign that read: "Skid Row City Limit, Population Too Many" and Choy realized where he was, at the gate to Hell. Many years earlier he had been paid by the *Vancouver Sun* to go to Los Angeles for a feature on the largest single concentration of mentally ill, drug addicted, homeless people in the new, more competitive economy that was North America. "Hell" was the 144-point hammer headline that a brilliant graphic artist had woven into the collage of photos that took up the top two-thirds of a broadsheet page.

But this particular hell was no divine creation. This was constructed by human beings, by people doing business, by ideologues, by politicians making decisions, by most of us averting our gaze. This place was the inevitable result of a society obsessed by competition; there can be no winners without losers and this was the place they gathered. That had been the point of his story back then, or at least he hoped that was what most readers would understand.

Choy continued to walk deeper into Hell. He knew the 50-square block area of downtown Los Angeles wasn't the safest place to stroll but it seemed a fitting location to contemplate the reason for his existence and other matters only significant to a journalist.

Skid row certainly seems no smaller now, despite all the talk about solutions to a crisis.

How do I write the story of Reb?

He had a choice between a telephoto and wide-angle lens, between the straight-up, unabashed emotional pornography of simply describing what happened to Julie and her family or that plus a bigger picture look at the context in which the smaller story unfolded. It could be a story about Julie, her father and mother, or a story about the war on drugs and one of its victims?

Which route is more manipulative?

One played with the reader's emotions for no reason beyond selling a book. The other used those emotions to make political points. Emotion without social and economic context or using emotion to effect social and political change?

A skinny Black woman was screaming at no one in particular in front of him. Choy looked away and hurried past.

If a journalist's job is to report on what happened, how could one ignore context and the bigger picture? Inevitably this meant challenging the status quo and sometimes noisily scraping a piece of chalk across the blackboards of entrenched interests. If a journalist's job is simply to sell newspapers or books then whatever grabs and holds the reader's attention is all that needs to be considered. In fact, one might argue that it is disrespectful to even attempt to challenge a reader's current opinions. Let them decide for themselves what 'what happened' means.

But the truth is, it is impossible for a writer to avoid making choices that impose her or his will on a story. Writing is more metaphysics than physics, most often a story is constructed like a house that is designed, built, lived in and then renovated again and again. You must always be prepared to go where the story takes you, but it is an adult-child relationship, the author being a parent who is ultimately responsible for ensuring the child grows up to be the best she can be.

He turned a corner and makeshift shelters, garbage and broken human beings lined the sidewalks for as far as he could see. He turned around. He had to escape this Hell.

I need to decide. Am I a journalist simply reporting what happened or a writer, playing god, creating new worlds? Am I a guileless chronicler or a usurper of the Almighty's power?

The truth is the truth is more complicated than binary choices will allow. All journalists are also writers; all writers are also journalists. The best journalism is always a good story; a good story must always feel real, as if it were journalism.

Don't think about it. Just write. Only that will make me feel better.

Writing as catharsis. As a professional journalist he had always looked down on the very notion that his craft could be considered a form of therapy, but here he was, he needed it.

***

When Choy returned home, he gave both his kids a big, long hug and a hundred dollars each, for coming closest to the true story about how Reb got to be the person she had become on the streets of the Downtown Eastside. He explained that neither had truly come close, so that made it a tie. Then he insisted that his father join the three of them in a game of four-handed cribbage. As they were playing he felt content, but when his thoughts turned to the story he had promised to write, a solitary tear made its way slowly down his cheek.

"Are you okay Dad?" Samantha asked.

"No," he answered. "But I'll be better soon, especially if you and me ever beat these two."

Everyone smiled.

The End

Also in the FAKE NEWS series
(Available on Amazon)
American Spin
Misogyny

Other novels by Gary Engler
(Available on Amazon)
The Year We Became US

About the Author

Gary Engler is a former journalist, local union official, marine engineer, apprentice millwright, postal worker, truck driver, playwright, audio-visual technician, and assembly-line worker. Earning money from writing while attending St. Francis High School in Calgary in the late 1960s got him hooked on literary endeavours even while he worked at various real jobs. His first professional theatrical production was Sudden Death Overtime at Factory Theatre Lab in Toronto in 1974. His first published novel was The Year We Became Us (Fernwood 2012 and Spanish language translation, Cuba 2016). He also spent 20 years as a reporter, feature writer and editor at the Vancouver Sun.

Made in the USA
Columbia, SC
22 July 2020